PILGRIMS 2.0

A NOVEL

LINDSEY HARDING

ACRE
CINCINNATI 2023

Acre Books is made possible by the support of the Robert and Adele Schiff Foundation
and the Department of English at the University of Cincinnati.

Designed by Barbara Neely Bourgoyne
Cover art: iStock by Getty Images

ISBN-13 (pbk): 978-1-946724-69-4
ISBN-13 (ebook): 978-1-946724-70-0

The press is based at the University of Cincinnati, Department of English and Comparative
Literature, A&S Hall, Room 248, PO Box 210069, Cincinnati, OH, 45221–0069.
www.acre-books.com

Acre Books books may be purchased at a discount for educational use. For information
please email business@acre-books.com.

PILGRIMS 2.0

For Shawn, who also makes the impossible, possible.

DOCKED

BERTH 94

SUNDAY 19:40

Between *Crown Princess* in Berth 93 and *Catalina Express* in Berth 95, a time machine sat in Berth 94, moored and anchored. From the water's swaying darkness, the white bow rose up, glowing, though the moon was tucked away among wrinkled, rippling clouds. *PILGRIM* was emblazoned along the bulwark toward the prow. There, two workers hung suspended in harnesses, shadowy ants crawling along the hull. In gloved hands, they wielded long electric brushes and chemical loosening agents that fizzed and hissed as they scrubbed away lingering traces of the sea from the last voyage. They would work all night, and by dawn, the ship would be spotless, radiant. By Monday afternoon, *PILGRIM* would be sailing again. The path she traced through the Pacific Ocean was roughly the same every two weeks, but each passenger took a different journey. For this cruise could take a body—a woman's body—almost anywhere she wanted it to go.

REBECCA

The cruise had been Rebecca Heston's idea. Other wives of plastic surgeons asked their partners for lipo or lifts or injections, but when Rebecca walked into her husband's practice in West Hollywood, hair damp and skin glistening from a run, she asked for a boat. Specifically, she wanted to buy a decommissioned ocean liner Viking was looking to sell. The ocean market, they said, was saturated; they wanted to expand their fleet of riverboats and diversify their inland destinations. They thought Rebecca a fool, but they couldn't see what she saw. Neither could Walter at first. Rebecca persuaded him to move his practice onto the water, her belief in him a boat-sized buoy. She insisted, too, upon the all-male crew—*It's about time the roles were reversed, don't you think? Caregiving could use a facelift.*

Rebecca contacted the venture capitalists she knew, friends from the two years she'd spent in the Bay Area working for Google—before meeting Walter and moving to LA, where he was completing UCLA's six-year Integrated Residency Program in Plastic Surgery. She reached out to her own investors as well, the ones who helped launch her LA startup, and pitched Canterbury Cruise Line to them—*We're talking the dream of a dream vacation: excursions that will literally change passengers. While they get their work done, they're pampered, catered to, doted on, and they return home twenty years younger. We're building the TARDIS to take women back in time.* She had already made them a lot of money, so the new project was an easy sell—*Look at the numbers. See how lucrative tourism is, how lucrative plastic surgery is. The potential for profit is exponential.*

Then Rebecca developed Surgicom to manage procedure scheduling before diving into natural language processing, neural networks, and deep learning. She ultimately consolidated all of the ship's existing systems into an autonomous computing environment with a manycore processor—*The boat now has a brain.* She even commissioned the sensory cells used throughout the ship and implemented an Internet of Things architecture, the final step before it could be brought fully online—*She can feel, and everything she feels becomes data we can use to better accommodate passengers, make their experience more immersive.*

Then Rebecca sat next to her husband at her terminal in the Captain's Quarters, a cursor blinking on the command line, and clicked enter to activate the ship—*Meet BECCA.*

Not much later, Rebecca's own hardware let her down, and Walter learned the limit to what surgery, what medicine, could do.

DR. WALTER HESTON

SUNDAY 20:03

Dr. Heston filled the kettle at the sink and placed it on the Bunsen burner. He dropped an Earl Grey teabag into his mug and returned to the 3D printer. The first set of implants was coming out now. He felt his skin prickle, his head swim with vertigo as he watched the slabs of flesh grow before his eyes. Every time, this same heady rush. He amazed himself: with the tools and supplies at his disposal, what he could do for and to and with a body was as vast as an ocean. Bodies had so many layers, so many possibilities, and he was a deep diver, exploring.

This epidermal printing run would be his finest. The printer's clock counted down. Twelve hours remained. Already he had cued up the next set, more detailed pieces and patches. Fifteen hours for that run. Then the backups. By Friday, the trays would be down in Hydrangea Station. They'd be sterilized, covered in blue cloths, and waiting for him and his gloved hands.

The kettle screeched. He poured, and steam rose, clouding his glasses. Mug in hand, he made his way to his desk. While the tea steeped and cooled before him, Dr. Heston opened the desk drawer and pulled out a thin syringe and a vial. He had skipped his last injection, and as expected, a deep furrow now divided the space between his eyebrows.

"Rebecca," he said, dipping the needle into the vial and pulling back on the plunger. "Console to mirror mode, please." The computer screen on the desk flashed black, then Dr. Heston appeared on it, fingers flicking the syringe once, twice. "Thank you."

"Of course, sir.

Wheeling closer, Dr. Heston leaned toward the mirror, pinched the skin between his eyes, and sank the needle in. He pricked here and there until the vial was empty. Then he massaged the injection sites in widening clockwise circles.

He sat back to inspect. A red balloon rested between his eyebrows. Already the wrinkle was loosening. He picked up his mug. He'd sit here like this, drinking tea until the red and swelling had dissipated. He could print an entire face, yet he still felt wonder at what a single ampoule of botulinum toxin could do.

Botox was, after all, his initial muse, pointing to an epidermal fountain of youth. He had written his dissertation elucidating its transmutative properties, outlining a theory of tissue fungibility, he had called it then, testing the limits of skin cells and marveling at their extraordinary capacity to grow and endure, change and heal. He still remembered the day the FDA had approved BOTOX Cosmetic back in 2002. He had celebrated with his practice over Dom Pérignon and a round of injections on the house. Before that, his shipments had been small and offered only to returning customers going through major life events—divorce, retirement, the death of a loved one. He had thought they needed it most—smoothness so readily apparent, a few cc's of control. He could give at least that to them.

After the approval, he invited all his patients to experience it, the wonders of wrinkle-free skin. During preliminary consultations, he would listen to prospective patients recount the harrowing sagas they endured. They spoke of IRS scrutiny, beach homes they couldn't sell or didn't want to stilt, daughters with DUIs. Everyone was going through something, all the time. But soon after, there in the mirror, with their fingertips, they could see and touch a placid pond.

He ran a finger down the bridge of his nose and checked the time on the printer: 11:24. The wrinkle was gone, and thirty minutes had elapsed. His current fast-acting formula had reduced effect time from three days to mere minutes. He, like so many of his patients, relished the smoothness he now found on his forehead, so satisfying, so defiant—a bird flipped at Time. He took a final sip of tea before getting back to work.

THE DECKMEN

SUNDAY 20:00–24:00

Eight men prepared the three open-air decks for the next voyage. These decks consisted of one freshwater infinity lap pool, five hot tubs, five Epsom salt ponds, one hundred and sixteen lounging chairs and daybeds—each with its own retractable sunshield—three walking paths, four drink-and-snack booths, a pedicure parlor, two coffee shops, four towel stations, a fiber-arts studio, four canopied salons, and a tarot-reading tent. The deckmen wore waterproof suits and knee-high boots when they cleaned. They worked in teams of two.

After draining the pool and hot tubs, they power-washed every surface. A special alloy coated the boat's outdoor surfaces to keep the materials cool to the touch, even under the noonday sun. When water from the pressure washer struck the plank flooring, it purred.

After power-washing, the men crawled, scrubbing, endlessly scrubbing, the tiles around the swimming and soaking areas, then used citrus-scented wipes to dry the sitting and serving surfaces. The men weren't sure how, but the wipes prevented condensation for up to three days.

Finally, they opened and closed each retractable canopy. They stocked the pedicure parlor with shades BECCA had predicted to trend in the next week. They adjusted décor and arranged furniture designed to withstand salty air and excessive heat. Smartchairs were set in semi-

9

circles and clusters, so passengers could chat while they soaked in the sun and ocean breeze. Smarttables were topped with magnetic vases, and fresh tulips and double ruffled lilies would be added later, moments before the boarding whistle blew. On the smartbars, these men set wooden bowls and woven baskets they'd later fill with fresh and candied fruit.

One of the deckmen, when he worked this weekend cleaning shift, grew bored with the tediousness of the tasks, the hours stretching long into the night. Why not, he thought, have a little fun? So Larry, this deckman, persuaded his fellow crewmen to take part in little games and harmless pranks from time to time. For instance, he once challenged another deckman to see which of them could topple a magnetic vase with their power washers from a starting distance of twenty feet. Another time, he dared someone to rotate the arrows leading to two of the walking paths, so for the first few days of the next cruise, women started out toward the Park expecting to find the Cemetery, and those looking for the Cemetery found themselves in the Park instead.

THE ROOM STEWARDS

SUNDAY 20:00–24:00

On the cabin decks, 5 through 8, the ship's interior hummed, bathed in the glow from warm brass sconces with creamy linen shades. Cleaning carts rolled, and men moved about, executing practiced routines, the same rigorous choreography performed every other Sunday night. Room by room, teams of three worked their way down the narrow hallways. Efficiently. Thoroughly. Before coming on board, these men had been nurses in hospitals or senior care facilities, places that taught them something about bodies and the messes they made.

Still, the team on waste detail shook their heads at the disarray passengers created in two weeks despite the hours they spent incapacitated. Passengers recovered from their excursions in their rooms, so room stewards have seen it all: snotty tissues tucked behind headboards and bloody balls of toilet paper left in the drawer of the bedside stand.

Meanwhile, other teams scrubbed counters, tiles, floors, cabinets, and door latches. They polished headboards, footboards, and desks. They purged fingerprints from porthole windows. They traced grout with disinfecting wands. They wiped down walls and spritzed the air with sandalwood freshening spray. They shampooed the saxony and buffed the mirror screens until they were spotless.

The final stage of cabin cleanup was referred to in the Crew Handbook as Room Restoration. One man remade the bed, a specially designed, fully adjustable, voice-controlled bed that was as luxurious as it was functional. A second man filled drawers with disposable cabinwear and undergarments, placing soft gowns beside stacks of stretchy white panties and bralettes, and in another drawer, setting satin camisoles and shorts to the left of tall socks with micomassagers woven into the fabric. The third man worked in the bathroom. After stacking three rolled bath sheets on a white oak shelf over the toilet, he slung two hand towels across the matte black bar below. Next to the sink, he folded a single black washcloth into the shape of a tiny boat. Then he tested the hair dryer, straightening iron, curling rod, ultrasonic tweezers, ultraviolet skin mask, and skin exfoliator before returning the devices to the basket below the sink. Finally, on the quartz countertop, he arranged a hand-woven rattan tray with creams and ointments in glass vials of varying shapes.

By morning, the rooms and transitioning spaces would be ready for passengers, sparkling and sanitized, the air saturated with breathable calm. The men would toss their gloves and return their carts to the cleaning bay on Deck 1. They would yawn. Then they would head to the crew dining hall on Deck 2 for bacon and eggs and bowls of sugary cereal. At last, they would retire to their quarters to sleep until the horn sounded in the afternoon.

THE SURGICAL TECHNICIANS

SUNDAY 20:00–24:00

The technicians were responsible for the flower stations on Decks 3 and 4. The boat had four surgical suites: Lilac, Hibiscus, Orchid, and Hydrangea. Each suite had four operating rooms, four pre-op stations, and one intensive-care room for emergencies. On Sunday nights in the harbor, the techs worked just as fast, just as thoroughly as the room stewards and deckmen, following orders, cleaning tools, arranging supplies to maximize efficiency. They were precision specialists.

Most surgical technicians were on the ship because they couldn't pass their boards or lacked the mettle to withstand residency, and the job required only two months of training for individuals with at least two years of medical school. The accelerated program included four weeks of lectures and demonstrations in Canterbury Cruise Line's terminal building, two weeks of onboard observations and mentoring, and a two-week internship. In those final two weeks, they learned how to hold and pass clamps and pickups and cautery needles into a surgeon's open palm. They learned how to angle the lights just so to illuminate body cavities. They learned limb and torso positions to optimize visibility for procedures according to passenger specifications and surgeon preference. They learned the ship's Sterilization Protocol. By the time they completed their training, they understood the body was not a canvas or a temple; it was a construction site. And nearly everything—muscle, tendon, tissue, and bone—could be customized. Bulldozed, and rebuilt.

Here is what some technicians didn't like to acknowledge: watching bodies cut open, rearranged, reproportioned, their parts removed and reassigned, and always bloodied and bruised in the process, troubled them. Of course they weren't squeamish, but they had witnessed tons, literally tons, of pulpy yellow fat sucked down tubes and then stored in expanding plastic tanks. The presence of these containers (stored in a special onboard locker while *PILGRIM* was at sea) forced them to rethink the glamour of bodywork on a weekly basis.

But not on Sunday night. Not while they scrubbed and sterilized instruments. Not as they restocked and counted supplies. Not with the ORs all shining and clean. That's when they pondered together new purposes for silicone. That's when they debated the relationship between beauty, form, and function. That's when they asked, *What might a body become?*

BIOHAZARDOUS WASTE DETAIL

SUNDAY 22:00

Thirty-gallon red and yellow bags were borne out of the ship on a long conveyor belt from Deck 3, along with the containers of plastic sharps and other irregularly shaped objects used by the surgeons and crew.

Two men stood at the boat's open hatch, loading bag after bag, container after container, onto the moving belt. They wore PVC-coated gloves fastened just below their elbows and masks that covered their mouths and noses. They were careful and alert, much more so than the men who handled the trash. Regular waste had a separate conveyor belt out of Deck 6 and toward the stern.

"How many operating rooms to go?" the one asked the other.

"Two more in Lilac Station," said his partner. "Then all of Hibiscus and the lockers here." He nodded at the floor-to-ceiling metal cabinet, which glinted in the moonlight.

"Jesus. Remember when this used to take us two hours tops?"

"Heh."

At Berth 94, a special trash receptacle stood open, receiving the bags and containers. A truck would come at dawn to take the dumpster to a private disposal plant where the materials would be incinerated. When *PILGRIM* was away, an empty receptacle would be brought to the harbor.

Disembarking passengers sometimes noted the black cottage-sized bin, but only peripherally, fleetingly. Its inscription—Biomedical Waste—was small and often lost in the sun.

BECCA

Just before midnight, BECCA ran a final preboarding report on all incoming passengers. She updated arrival times based on weather and airport data. She checked for manual updates to passenger medical and personal histories. She locked in requests for stateroom preferences, excursions, dinner seating, and special dietary needs. She noted current events and topics of concern that might impact passenger mental health and well-being.

Then she sent portfolios with redacted information to folders on various crewmember accounts. Room stewards learned who they would be taking care of. Surgeons and their techs received the specs for new excursions and the initial itinerary schedules for their assigned flower suite. Waiters found out who would be seated at their tables and what those passengers could and could not, or preferred not to, eat. Chefs received the meal plan, created to accommodate the passengers on this particular cruise and to take advantage of seasonal produce.

Final report processing and information distribution took 4.5 minutes, a span decreasing at a rate of 12 seconds per cruise.

New Passenger Profile: Lyla

Name: Lyla Wohl

Astrological sign: Aries

Age: 36

Race/Ethnicity: Korean American

Height: 5'3"

Weight: 110 lbs

Eye color: Black

Hair color: Black

What is your occupation? L&D Nurse Practitioner

Whom do you live with? Husband

How did you hear about Canterbury Cruise Line? Instagram

Past medical conditions: Congenital adrenal hyperplasia; ambiguous genitalia at birth

Ongoing medical conditions: Infertility; repeat pregnancy loss

Past pregnancies and outcomes: 8 miscarriages

Past surgeries: Genitoplasty (at 18 months); D&C (x5)

Medications: Estrogen therapy (in adolescence); Xanax (current)

Allergies: Seasonal

Have you ever had a reaction to anesthesia? No

Do you bleed or bruise easily? No

Do you smoke? No

Do you drink alcohol? Not for the past ten years

Scheduled excursions: Maternal Body Makeover

LYLA

Lyla's parents picked her up to drive her to the airport. They left early for coffee and pastries at her favorite bakery in Westlake before hopping on SH 114 for the twenty-minute commute to Dallas/Fort Worth International Airport. Timothy had to work, and Lyla had planned to take a shuttle, but her parents insisted. Just like they'd insisted on paying for her vacation. Just like they'd insisted on paying the exorbitant fees to file adoption paperwork at two premier agencies. *Please,* they implored. *It's the least we can do.*

After keeping such a secret from Lyla her whole life, especially over the past couple years, they had a point.

She sat in the backseat alone, latte in one hand, croissant in the other. Under her black joggers, she was wearing a pair of period underwear, though she was just spotting now, at the tail end of her monthly, only her third regular one since her most recent miscarriage and D&C, six months back. That was when her parents finally came forward to talk to her about her birth and medical history, all the information they had withheld. *We never meant to hurt you,* they said. *We only wanted what was best. How were we to know there'd be complications?* they pleaded. *The doctors didn't mention fertility. They said the surgery was a success and you'd recover and heal perfectly. A perfect little girl*, they cried. But that wasn't the case, and they all knew that now.

From the passenger seat, her mom glanced back over her shoulder. "How is it, honey?"

"Mmm," Lyla said, her mouth full of buttery pastry and foam.

"You should have gotten her another for the plane," her dad said.

"This one is great," Lyla said. "This is plenty."

"We can stop to get you something else. What about one of those travel pillows? Do you have one of those?" he asked, glancing at Lyla in the rearview mirror.

"It's a short flight to LA. I'll be fine."

Lyla's mom looked like she was going to start crying. "Are you sure?"

Lyla set her croissant in her lap and reached forward to give her mom's shoulder a squeeze. She knew her mom wasn't inquiring about her decision to forgo a travel pillow; her mom wanted to know if she would be fine not getting pregnant—never getting pregnant.

"I'm fine," Lyla repeated. She took a deep breath. "We've talked about this. I get why you did what you did." She left unsaid the nightmare itself: *cosmetic infant genitoplasty*. "But maybe you should have told me, I don't know, eight miscarriages ago." Now Lyla's mom *was* crying, tears rolling down her cheeks. Even her dad was wiping at his eyes. She understood their motives and their decisions, but she couldn't understand why they'd waited so long to reveal the truth. They let her suffer for years. "At least seven."

Her mom laid a hand over hers and looked up, her face blotchy. "You were just a baby. We didn't think—"

"But you might have guessed."

Little sobs emerged from her mother's mouth, similar to the noises a newborn makes, the prelude to a wail.

"Mom, please stop. If I'm not crying, you shouldn't be."

"We thought it would work out. You kept getting pregnant."

"But it didn't. And here we are." Lyla pulled her hand back and looked out the window. She'd had enough.

Her mom whispered, "Just tell me how I can fix this."

"You can't." Lyla looked down, then gathered herself and said, "But this trip may be just the thing. Just what I need." They had no idea, of course. No idea at all what she had planned.

"I'm sorry, Ly. We're so sorry."

Lyla picked up the croissant and took a big bite. Consoling her parents exhausted her. As a nurse, she reached this point with laboring women, too, when their contractions stalled. She had no patience for people who failed to progress. That's what Pitocin was for. "Mind putting on NPR?" She turned to the window. She was still hours away from boarding the ship but already adrift, impatient to be on her way.

New Passenger Profile: Nicole

Name: Nicole Cortero

Astrological sign: Libra

Age: 35

Race/Ethnicity: Puerto Rican American

Height: 5'8"

Weight: 156 lbs

Eye color: Black

Hair color: Black

What is your occupation? Stay-at-home mom

Whom do you live with? Husband and son

How did you hear about Canterbury Cruise Line? Friends

Past medical conditions: N/A

Past pregnancies and outcomes: One, live birth

Past surgeries: C-section

Medications: Niravam

Allergies: N/A

Have you ever had a reaction to anesthesia? Only a positive one. Was knocked out when my son was born and that experience was so smooth, until recovery.

Do you bleed or bruise easily? No

Do you smoke? No

Do you drink alcohol? Occasionally; three glasses of wine/week, more when book club meets

Scheduled excursions: Breast Augmentation, Total Body Trim, Lip Plump

NICOLE

For Nicole, this was supposed to be a girls' trip, a mommy-cation. She and her two closest friends had been planning the getaway for months, even before Jane delivered her fourth and final baby. "After this one, you better believe I'm getting that tummy tuck," she had said. "I'm tired of pushing skin into pants."

Semra had been the one to do some research and discover Canterbury Cruise Line. She had also been the one to get them started with Baden+Lakes, hosting a skincare extravaganza a few years back. She pitched books for their book club to read, new workout regimens for the three of them to try. She even petitioned to have the elementary school day moved forward an hour to support healthier sleep habits for families. At an adult game night before the holidays, in the company of their husbands, she had proposed the girls-only cruise. "No diamonds this year, boys," she had said. "It's makeover season."

For Christmas, Justin had presented Nicole with a wrapped box half her height. After pulling out hundreds of crinkly, glittery sheets of tissue paper, Nicole discovered a single envelope taped to the bottom, and inside it were airline tickets from Richmond to Los Angeles and back, and a letter that welcomed her as a passenger on the 52nd voyage of *PILGRIM*, Canterbury Cruise Line's ocean liner. In the letter, her excursions sounded glamorous, but they amounted to a boob job, body shaping, and lip-filler treatments. While Nicole read, Justin explained, "Semra helped, and I wanted whatever would help you feel good in your body. I want you to know how sexy you are."

Nicole looked down. She was wearing one of Justin's t-shirts and a pair of his sweatpants, her go-to pajamas since giving birth to Max five years ago.

Justin continued, "But you can do more or less. It's up to you."

"Thank you." Nicole smiled at Justin. "We need this," she said quietly, but she didn't explain why—why she thought the cruise was critical—not just to their sex life, but to their economic well-being. She didn't confess the debt they were in or the number of Baden+Lakes boxes stacked up in her craft room, concealed by fabric she had bought precisely for this purpose: to hide unopened boxes filled with skincare products and tools she couldn't sell. She didn't admit how relieved she was to know that her struggles with size and shape and skin would soon be over.

But then a week before the cruise, Semra texted her. *Can't go*, followed by a row of sad and angry and crying face emojis. Nicole called right away.

"That birthday party this weekend, the one at that bouncy place, over there behind the mall? Well, I was climbing through the obstacle course, and I told Jacob I'd race him one time. *One time*. Anyway, I slid down that big slide, and it was slick. Like baby-oil slick. So fast. At the bottom, I tried to slow myself down, but the next thing I knew I was flying off the slide and both of my ankles were broken. Fucking *broken*." She was scheduled for surgery the next day.

"Oh, my goodness." Nicole started boiling a pot of water. She would make a big pan of ziti to bring over. She couldn't stop saying, "Oh, my goodness."

Then this morning Jane called while Nicole was on the way to her house so they could drive together to the airport. "Don't come," she said. "Trust me, you don't want what we have." Jane explained that the baby had started projectile vomiting at dinner the night before, shooting white arcs of fluid across their newly renovated kitchen, and by morning, all four kids and Jane were sick. "It's an apocalypse," she said, then,

"I have to go." Nicole could hear her racing to the bathroom and three gushing heaves before the call clicked off.

Pulling into a cul-de-sac between her house and Jane's, Nicole stared at her phone, feeling terrible for her friends. She didn't know which was worse: two broken ankles or four kids to care for while sick oneself.

She called Justin and told him about Jane.

"I guess I shouldn't go," she said, thinking maybe the trip wasn't meant to be after all. Maybe it would only make things worse—increase her credit card debt, for one.

"Don't be silly. Why wouldn't you?" Justin said. "You're healthy. You don't have any broken bones. Stop worrying about everyone else. I think this will be good for you. I think you were right. We need this."

A wave of relief washed over Nicole. She wasn't sure she'd realized, until that moment, how much she'd been counting on the cruise—not just the change of scenery, but the changes to herself. She could even tweak her itinerary, and her friends wouldn't know the extent of it. At the next book club meeting, she could just say she had her boobs done and a little tightening, a little polishing, like any other suburban mom. She wouldn't have to mention other excursions, the full remodel she was now planning in her head. And when she returned, her body would be enhanced and capable of marketing skincare products that claimed to do what plastic surgery could, her body at last touchable again.

STABILIZATION SYSTEM DETAIL

MONDAY 07:37

On Deck 1, the basement of the boat, two deckman finished the monthly mechanical scan of the ship's stabilization enhancements.

"Shame, really," one said, "not to know you're on a boat when you're on a boat." With the new and improved antiroll mechanisms, after all, it was easy to forget.

"So you're a philosopher now?" the second responded, an eyebrow raised but both eyes glued to the series of hydraulics before him, the pistons firing in a robotic dance.

"According to my BA, I've always been one." With a pointer finger, he navigated a series of modules on the tablet he held.

"Useless degree," the second said, still watching the intricate symphony of movement. "Damn, it's beautiful," he whispered.

Before the enhancements were installed, too many passengers had complained about the ship's rocking, especially during recovery and when the weather grew stormy. Outside the surgical suites, discomfort of any kind was aggressively minimized. At first, BECCA had ordered wristbands, patches, and pills to reduce seasickness, and room stewards would arrange baskets of these products on each bedside table. But passengers only sought these remedies once they were vomiting and visibly green, greener than the asparagus spears, lemon roasted and garnished with rosemary sprigs, the kitchen crew turned out when asparagus was in season.

Something had to be done. For discomfort reminded women that the body wasn't resilient to the pressures placed upon it, the work that could be done to it. BECCA had proposed another solution: an upgrade to the ship's existing stabilization system. She even identified the vendor.

The Captain made the call. A naval architect who worked on luxury yachts in a German shipyard arrived at the Port of Los Angeles the first weekend in December and stayed on board with his four-person crew until Christmas, when he declared *PILGRIM* incapable of rocking, thanks to a state-of-the-art antirolling system. BECCA handled the software, and two deckmen performed equipment scans each month.

Since then, only a handful of motion-sickness incidents had been recorded. Canterbury Cruise Line sold its supply of mal de mer treatments to Carnival at a reduced rate. BECCA reallocated the open storage space in the medical supply cabinets to hold a greater number of sharps boxes during the two weeks at sea.

A green light blinked on the tablet. "There we go," the first deckman said. "Scan complete." He swiped to close the screen, and the two deckmen made their way out of the boat's belly, back along the narrow bridge to the access door. "What was your major in college? Has it been useful?"

"No," the second deckman said. "Not at all."

"Let me guess: you were an art major."

"Art history, in fact. My parents refused to pay, and I was too stubborn then to study computer science like they wanted."

"Wisdom is wasted on the young," the first deckman said, clapping his partner on the back.

"That's not how it goes," the second deckman returned. "Youth is wasted on the young."

"Try telling that to our passengers."

New Passenger Profile: Annalie

Name: Annalie Carmichael   *Astrological sign:* Gemini

Age: 32   *Race/Ethnicity:* White

Height: 5'6"   *Weight:* 120 ibs

Eye color: Blue   *Hair color:* Brown-black

What is your occupation? High school English teacher

Who do you live with?

How did you hear about Canterbury Cruise Line? Website

Past medical conditions: N/A

Ongoing medical conditions: Complicated grief, depression

Past pregnancies and outcomes: N/A

Past surgeries: Ankle reconstruction after break in first grade

Medications: Ativan, Celexa

Allergies: N/A

Have you ever had a reaction to anesthesia? Intense itching, morphine

Do you bleed or bruise easily? No

Do you smoke? No

Do you drink alcohol? Yes

Scheduled excursions: Signature Look, Cruise Counseling

ANNALIE

Two hours before takeoff. Flight from Atlanta to LA: five hours. Hopefully fewer than twenty minutes to deplane and walk to the cruise's shuttle stop. The trip would take under eight hours, all told, the length of her typical school day. Annalie survived those eight hours each day. Again and again. She could survive them once more.

Except. Except being here in an airport reminded her of her twin. As Annalie walked down the stretch of gates in A Terminal, time slipped away, and it was three years ago and the day Aimee arrived in Atlanta.

Aimee had texted from the tarmac in Pittsburgh that afternoon: *Flight delayed 15 but taking off now. See you in the Atl. We did it!!*

Growing up in western New York, the girls had planned to live shared adult lives, preferably somewhere warm, preferably as housemates at first, then close neighbors, preferably at some point with a large screened-in porch for weekly family dinners, with globe lights strung up along exposed wood beams and laughter and stories carrying on into the night until it was time at last to tuck their sleeping children into car seats or beds. And three years earlier, they had put that plan in motion: Aimee was moving to Atlanta. She was a flight away.

Yet that day, when Annalie should have been ecstatic—ready for a dream to merge with reality—she found she was terribly afraid. A yawning sinkhole grew in her stomach, like an inkblot from a bleeding pen. It would consume her, she knew now, but later. That day, after all, had turned out perfectly. She worked on lesson plans for the week, and right when Aimee's flight was scheduled to touchdown, it had.

Annalie sank into an open seat at Gate A53. On a television screen near her, *The Real Housewives of Boca* was on. In a lanai near a pool, one housewife slapped another housewife, and a third raised a stiletto, brandishing it over her head like a knife. The women circled each other, all predators, all prey. [Screaming.] read the closed caption. Then [More screaming.]. If Annalie had to guess, they were deep in Season 10 or 11. That was usually when the drama morphed into something more real, dangerous and primitive. After so much time together, the housewives tired of splashing each other with champagne, calling each other *ugly* and *cheap* and worse. Pulling each other's wigs and weaves. Even backstabbing and gaslighting on Bluesky bored them this late in the series.

Annalie's pulse throbbed behind her ears, in her stomach, but she couldn't look away. The women on the screen stalked each other. One pulled a lit tiki torch out of the ground, propping it against her arm like a lance. In a closeup shot, her eyes gleamed in the flickering light. Black eye makeup smudged across her cheeks like battle paint. Blood trailed from her nose, cutting a wet, dark path through her foundation.

After majoring in English at the University of Pittsburgh, Annalie had taken a teaching position at the Westminster Schools in Atlanta. She had grown tired of Pittsburgh's long, dreary winter, and she and Aimee had planned to move south after graduation. But Aimee had stayed to earn her MBA from Katz. Then she had signed on at a small marketing agency with an office on Mount Washington, overlooking the Monongahela winding beneath bridges below.

And then, after years of them scouting jobs in each other's cities, after not finding the right positions or else not having the ones that seemed right offered to them, it finally happened. A headhunter for Coca-Cola had asked Aimee to dinner. Aimee had been making a name for herself as a PR guru for sustainability initiatives, and the company was launching a new product with completely natural sweeteners packaged in compostable cans and bottles. Coke wanted her on their team, and they flew her down, and before she boarded her return flight at Hartsfield-Jackson, she called to accept the company's generous offer. In the morning, she gave notice to her boss and landlord, and that night she and Annalie started browsing Zillow for a place they would share the next month, when Aimee moved to Georgia.

Annalie's neck started to ache from her craning to watch the ceiling-mounted airport TV. On the screen, one woman's dress was now ripped, and another's weave was loose, blond curls flopping against her bare, tan shoulders. The third woman was on the ground facedown.

Finally, Annalie looked away when a second woman fell, a gash opening up her sequined dress across the midsection. No more sitting, she decided. She'd walk and walk until the plane arrived, until it was time to go.

THE KITCHEN CREW

PILGRIM's kitchen was long and narrow. At the back, the grill stretched from one end to the other, and the head chef stalked up and down as a row of cooks whisked and caramelized, boiled, broiled, and charred. Fifteen skillets could sauté at once. The middle of the kitchen was a continuous stainless-steel counter. Here, more cooks hunched and crammed together, all bobbing heads and flickering blades as they sliced, diced, chopped. When the cooks talked, they spoke an abrupt code of directional indicators and warnings.

"Corner."

"Hot behind."

"Heard that!"

"Corner."

"Low boy ajar."

"ButterNot?"

Just as Stevia products—powdered and raw, white and brown—were the only permissible sweeteners, ButterNot was the only acceptable type of oil used to prepare cruise cuisine. The fat-free, nearly calorie-free gel worked like butter, lard, or any other oil, but better. The flavor was more nuanced because it activated more taste buds. Crispy foods were crispier. Saucy foods were saucier. Decadent desserts were more decadent. The substance's chemical properties and capabilities were simply astonishing. The cooks regretted not knowing about or using ButterNot before joining the ship's crew, at the restaurants they used to work in. During their prep shifts, most cooks carried tasting spoons in the wide pouches of their aprons so they could sneak ButterNot straight from the glass jars that filled an entire refrigerator.

Just before 14:00, they would finish preparing tapas and treats for the boarding passengers, and waiters would arrive to cart away the assortment of bite-sized goodies to Deck 10. By 15:00, the kitchen would be returned to near pristine condition, each surface gleaming and sanitized. The cooks would then have a two-hour break. In their cabins, they would sip lagers and talk shop. This would be the last time they would sit down until after dinner was served and the kitchen was immaculate again.

Just before 17:00, they would tie on crisp white aprons. They would tuck their hair into tight bandanas or smooth it back with pomade until it refused to move. For good reason, they would blame the waiters anytime passengers complained about hair in their salads.

New Passenger Profile: Bianca

Name: Bianca Simmons

Astrological sign: Capricorn

Age: 37

Race/Ethnicity: White

Height: 5'9"

Weight: 142 lbs

Eye color: Brown

Hair color: Brown

What is your occupation? Tennis player, Sea Pines tennis pro

Who do you live with? N/A

How did you hear about Canterbury Cruise Line? Website

Past medical conditions: N/A

Past pregnancies and outcomes: Two live births

Past surgeries: C-section (x2)

Medications: N/A

Allergies: Strawberries

Have you ever had a reaction to anesthesia? No

Do you bleed or bruise easily? No

Do you smoke? No

Do you drink alcohol? Wine regularly

Scheduled excursions: Body Rejuvenation, Cruise Counseling

BIANCA

Bianca woke up to the sound of a child crying. For a moment before she opened her eyes, she thought the squall familiar, one of her girls in a crib down the hall. She pulled a pillow over her face, but the muffled cries continued. With a sigh, she shoved the pillow away and sat up. She blinked at all the white linen sheets, the screen on the wall before her. "Huh," she said, adjusting to the present moment. She was alone in a hotel room, LA outside her window. Her girls were likely at school, both far from here, and neither an infant at all. Not even close.

She pushed the covers off her lap and let her legs hang over the side of the bed. The baby in another room was no longer crying, but Bianca could hear the echo in her mind, the sound like a siren's scream, calling to her, crushing her.

For a moment, perched on the side of the bed, she contemplated going home: returning to the airport and booking a one-way ticket instead of taking the shuttle to the Port of Los Angeles. One final trip.

But of course she couldn't just go home. Not yet. At this point, even a call was too much. She used to talk or text with the girls daily. But who had time for that, and what was there to say? *No, she wasn't coming home yet. Soon, my darlings. I'll see you on the weekend. Next month. For Christmas, definitely by Christmas.* So many of their calls ended with tears (theirs) and frustration (hers). Didn't they see this was her chance? She would always be their mother, but she had only a window of time to pull off her return to the game she had loved first, and even that window was closing. Or had closed.

She thought back to the night she'd booked her passage on *PILGRIM*. She had lost a match to Bruce that day, a match the club manager had asked her to lose: "Maybe pull back a little on your serve? Slice a few into the net? Keep it close, but you gotta give Bruce the match."

But she'd had no intention of losing. Already she stewed that her roster for lessons now consisted wholly of toddlers and grandparents. But losing to Bruce? He hadn't even picked up a racket until he turned forty, sold his nanotech company, and retired to Hilton Head. And she was supposed to let him win because he had personally funded the new Sea Pines Golf and Tennis Center and restored the lighthouse a hurricane toppled two years ago?

Not a chance. Tennis was her game, her career, and—with her family back in Florida—her life.

Then she had lost the match anyway. Four double faults. A few balls short-stroked into the net and more than a few long or wide. It wasn't pretty, and it wasn't even close.

Afterward, Bruce had pumped her hand hard, his face lobster pink and dripping. "Work on that serve, sweetheart," he told her.

Later that night, after a shower, after a bottle of wine as dinner, she had finally booked the cruise. For over a month, she'd been emailing back and forth with Dr. Heston about what precisely she wanted done. Forty was on the horizon, just a few years out, and here she was losing to Bruce and imploring two-year-olds to "Show me your strings! Show me your strings!" Last week, Dr. Heston had sent along a potential itinerary and the specs of a medical device a surgical technician named Jared had designed. It all seemed too good to be true, to be possible. But already she had given up everything to get her tennis career back on track, and so far, massage, acupuncture, and even hypnosis hadn't worked to turn her vertigo to flow. She had pulled out her credit card, clicked to submit the deposit, and only then let out the breath she had been holding.

This cruise was her mulligan—the chance to think and play like she was fifteen, twenty years younger. No, it wasn't time to go home. It was time to become the sort of woman who could make a big splash at Miami and then a long run up the rankings. The sort of woman who could return to her family the champion she knew she was meant to be. Then, maybe then, she could be a mother her girls would be proud to have back in their lives. For good.

Bianca stood up, windmilling her arms overhead to stretch. "Game time," she said.

THE DOCTORS

MONDAY 11:06

In a bright and comfortable room at the north end of the terminal building and facing the ocean, coffee urns and baskets of beignets and bananas were set out in the middle of a long table. White-coated men milled about. Most sat on black leather rolling chairs with their legs crossed, scrolling through patient files and procedure notes on Surgicom tablets. One worked a crossword puzzle. Several stood in a small cluster at the back of the room: the veterans of the ship, friends of Dr. Heston's from residency, each hired prior to the first cruise. Back at UCLA, they had nicknamed him the Captain when he was Chief Resident and running a tight ship. Now the appellation was even more appropriate, of course, and consequently was utilized by the entire crew and in marketing materials. While these older physicians were called partners—and their paychecks were larger than those of the newer surgeons and they picked their vacation weeks first—they knew Heston was in charge. At least of the flower stations.

BECCA ran everything else.

A male voice, fluid and even, seemed to come from everywhere all at once, but in fact emitted from speakers—installed along with microphones—in the room's recessed lights. The Captain, the doctors knew, would be in his lab.

"Gentlemen," the voice said.

There was a pause while conversations died down. When the Captain talked, even remotely, the surgeons listened.

"This is an exciting week," Dr. Heston said. "I'll be piloting several new procedures. In addition, we are at our highest case volume to date." (Here, a few of the younger doctors clapped.) "And yes, the ever-rising case volume means we will be hiring a new surgeon and two new technicians. I expect to have candidates identified by the end of the cruise and entered into rotation by the start of next month." (More clapping.) "If there is no other business, we'll adjourn." (The room remained quiet.) "Full steam ahead and smooth sailing, team."

A few men in the room raised their coffee mugs. There was a soft click as the speakers turned off. Then the doctors resumed their reading, their conversations, their crossword puzzles, and meanwhile, a fleet of vehicles moved toward the Port of Los Angeles—sedans, limousines, and vans carrying women who had booked passage on the 52nd voyage of *PILGRIM*, including a few whose circumstances and requests had inspired the new procedures Dr. Heston would be piloting.

CEDRIC

MONDAY 12:12

Servers were in the final stages of preparation before the boarding whistle blew. Cedric's objective was to make sure everything in his zone—down to the last fork—sparkled.

Shifts like these, and today especially, he couldn't help himself; he thought about Kali. Here he was polishing silverware, a task requiring minimal exertion, minimal concentration. Of all the absurd chores that filled his weeks, this one was the hardest. It hollowed him out. Though beyond the dining room he could hear the clanking of plates and nearby the hum of other servers moving about their tasks, quiet settled around him.

"Really, Cedric," Kali would have said. "I leave and *then* you start cleaning?"

He imagined her sitting at the table in front of him, stretching back in a chair, arms folded, legs crossed at her fine ankles. Her body a long, lean blade. Her eyes steel.

When his wife told him she was filing for divorce, Cedric had been stunned. "What?" He had pulled his headphones down around his neck and swiveled away from the TV. On the screen behind him, the map was shrinking, and Cedric had to fight the urge to hold down the right arrow to move his character before the gas closed in. He would die in the gas, he knew, despite his armor, despite his gas mask. He would have to start over again.

"You don't even look at me when we're at home. All I see is the back of your head."

He'd gotten mad then. He'd stood up, and the headphone jack popped out of the tower, silencing the voices in the game. He listed everything he did, around the house and for her. And she had listened without saying a word. They'd had this fight before. Many times. But before, she would interject. Before, she would cry, and eventually her tears would escalate into sobs. Her quiet chilled him into his own silence.

She spoke at last. "Three hundred days."

"What?"

"You've played three hundred days in a row. Weekday, weekend. Rain or shine. It doesn't matter. We don't go anywhere because your games are here. We don't spend time together because this is all you want to do. This is your life."

"I don't think—" Cedric had started.

She held out a hand and continued, her voice almost mechanical. "Every day the number grows, and every day I resent you and your games more. I know it could be worse. You could be gambling or cheating or drinking. But do you know how many times I've thought about pulling the plug right in the middle of a fight? About calling to cancel your Activision account? I've thought about how angry you would be. At times I wanted that, for your anger to match the bitterness I feel. But I couldn't bring myself to do it."

Cedric hadn't known what to say. He planned to check his game clock later. To buy her something, anything she wanted. They would go somewhere. He would make all the plans.

"I'm sorry," she had said then, quietly. "I can't."

While the divorce was going through, Cedric played almost continuously. Burger wrappers and dirty dishes and empty soda cans cluttered the basement, like debris from a storm he hadn't seen coming, that was still pounding him day after day, unrelenting. He leveled up all his guns, every weapon in the game. After the papers were signed, though, after it was over, he couldn't bring himself to log in. He clicked aimlessly online, trying to figure out what his next move was. Maybe he needed a new game or a new gaming console. Maybe a new job. He didn't know where to go from here. Kali was gone, and his boss had put him on probation for showing up late, then not showing up. It had all happened so fast.

Then he'd stumbled onto the website for Canterbury Cruise Line. Even though the text on the home screen was pitched to potential passengers—*Reinvent yourself! Take a journey of self-discovery! Be your best you!*—he found it spoke to him. The maiden voyage of *PILGRIM* had sailed a month earlier, but they were still hiring crewmen. He filled out the online application. At the time, he thought this play made sense, a form of karmic retribution: He would be surrounded by women who weren't Kali, and he'd have to give up gaming cold turkey. *No personal devices allowed on board*, he learned from the fine print.

But he would do it. He would show Kali he could go without. He would give her back what he had taken from her: three hundred days.

And he had done it. Today was day three hundred.

Later, during his afternoon off and before the ship sails, Cedric will retrieve his cell phone from his locker in the terminal building. Then he'll call his ex-wife.

"It's day three hundred," he will say. "Without games. Any games." A breeze will sweep through the locker bay, a salty push against his back.

"Oh, Cedric," she will say, and he'll sink with her words, the sadness in her voice like a current that pulls him underwater. He won't be able to breathe. He's too late. Of course he's too late. Against the cool metal locker, he will lean his head and listen to Kali's silence on the other end.

THE TERMINAL BUILDING

MONDAY 12:56

BECCA activated the terminal building's preboarding operation mode. The restrooms started to *click, click, click* as lights, dispensers, and motion sensors turned on. Each of the three bathrooms offered its own collection of coordinating scents for soap, mouthwash, and perfume. Cloth hand towels were stacked in great bronze bowls.

Across the open expanse of the terminal building, minute speakers tucked into potted plant displays near clusters of chairs began to emit low-level piano melodies, the music lively but not eager, dreamy but not soporific. Overhead air fresheners started to diffuse freshness. The mood in the terminal building was often likened to that of a tea parlor, flower shop, or spa. And, in fact, tea, flower, and hand lotion self-serve stations were positioned around the room. Herbal, black, white, red, and green teas in triangular satchels were displayed in open mahogany boxes on high tables. Next to the boxes were stainless steel carafes that held purified water at exactly a hundred ninety degrees Fahrenheit, the perfect temperature for steeping most teas, along with mini pitchers of milk, bowls filled with natural sweetener cubes and lemon wedges, and baskets of spoons and stirrers. At the flower kiosks, tiny rosebuds and daisy blooms were available to craft a quick bracelet, and white steph-

43

anotis to weave into braided hair. Lotions in tall pump bottles stood at the ready on wide pedestals. Soon, passengers would fill their palms with velvety streams of coconut-breeze or pineapple-heat and marvel at the instantaneous renewal of moisture without an oily or slimy residue.

TRACKZ

MONDAY 13:24

On and between the cabin and surgery decks, an intricate system of passageways lined with magnetic rails was installed when the boat was first outfitted with its surgical stations. Two deckmen had completed the monthly maintenance scan for Trackz hours ago. BECCA confirmed their report at 09:42. But one of the deckmen, Larry, returned on his break, slipping back in through the single-access door on Deck 8, a door disguised like the other crew-related doors and screens on the boat, here by reclaimed wood paneling. Like a tightrope walker, he made his way along a rail, at times hopping from one rail to the other, still spry and athletic though not nearly as young and agile as he would have preferred to be.

Not long before the first cruise, Dr. Heston decided staterooms would be used as recovery rooms. There, passengers might as well wake up once the anesthesia wore off, once the wound drains were removed, the medication pumps and IV towers no longer needed, surrounded by their things in these rooms of their own. There, the vacation could continue as though they hadn't just undergone surgery—major or minor and everything in between.

But they couldn't have beds in the hallways. They couldn't have gawking as a recovering passenger rolled by, a surgical technician in scrubs at the helm and another at the foot of the bed to help steer. They couldn't have hands clasped to open mouths as other passengers, still awaiting their excursions, took in the wrapped bodies. Nor could they have the patients, those who might be awake but sedated, mortified to be seen in such a state. The continuous "waking dream" the Captain and his crew hoped to create meant they needed another way to get the patients back to their rooms.

BECCA identified a construction company in Austin, Texas, for the project, and Dr. Heston welcomed a team from J. R. Daniels and Associates a month later. The team spent two weeks on the ship, building ramps, wiring switches, laying out lanes, and, most importantly, installing custom magnetic rails. Once they finished, BECCA tweaked and vetted an open-sourced version of the software used by Uber to manage passenger transport. The crew tested Trackz for a week straight, moving beds around and around, from Hydrangea to staterooms on Deck 5, from Lilac to rooms on Deck 6, and so on. Everything worked precisely as it was designed to, and BECCA patched the system-level vulnerabilities she identified—except for one: the disruption caused by the magnets used to power the rails. The magnets enabled a smooth ride but interfered with the connection between BECCA and the bed's sensors, which monitored a passenger's vitals while she was in it. This meant that for three-to-four minutes, depending on traffic in Trackz and distance between station and stateroom, the passenger was offline, her vitals recorded but not able to be transmitted. BECCA ran a risk assessment, which reported that if a passenger were comfortable and stable, the chance of a bad turn during transport was extremely minimal: less than 0.8 percent. The Captain signed off, and Trackz went into operation.

Here's how it worked: During a passenger's final excursion, while she was still asleep, her bed would arrive in the station. Once she had been extubated but before she woke up, and as long as everything looked the way it should, she would be transferred to the bed—"Lift and slide on three, two, one." Then the bed would be scanned to confirm its destination, and off it would go, making its way through the passageways and up, up, up to the stateroom levels, where it would slide in through a panel in the wall. The bed would ease into its footboard, which in turn would activate a locking mechanism, which in turn would activate the wall panel's closing mechanism, which in turn would activate the room's wellness sensors to begin transmitting vitals to BECCA again.

Only twice had passengers been returned to the wrong cabins. Both times, the mixups transpired because the women's names were exactly the same—first, middle, and last: Shannon Marie White the first time and Claire Elizabeth Sommers the second time. While in transit, sleeping passengers were buckled across their shoulders and shins, and retractable railings surrounded the entire exterior of the bed. Beds moved at exactly four miles per hour. Not a single crash had occurred.

The women themselves had no recollection of the rides they took when their itineraries were complete. With their prolonged sedation, the smoothness of the ride, and the short time it took to move from operating room to stateroom, they might retain, at most, the sensation of movement. But this was easily enough explained by the ship itself, a phantom sway some passengers swore they could feel but only when they lay supine on the floor, as they might for a corpse pose at the end of Midmorning Yoga on Deck II.

LARRY

THE LAST SIX MONTHS

Larry had discovered Trackz when his team assignment changed. Back then, as the tedium of his daily to-do list wore on him, he found himself staring down other deckmen in hopes of provoking a response—a returned glare, a *what are you looking at?*, a punch, even. BECCA flagged his account for Conduct Violation after he landed a shoulder to the nose of a petite crewmember named Bryson, and Larry was reassigned to Rocco's team. Rocco and his partner were responsible for scanning the rail system each month, and during their first scan, Larry learned all about the system. Sure, he brushed off a few social engineering tricks to get Rocco to open up, but Rocco was all too eager to share. His new partner had been in grad school for statistics, Larry had learned, which Larry took to mean he probably read operations manuals for fun. So Larry asked questions while they swiped rail temperature readings and tested friction, and Rocco answered. While conducting a magnetic resonance study together, Rocco had launched into a detailed overview of the mechanics.

"I bet you could write a book about this," Larry had said.

Rocco had gushed, "The magnets are really something." Then he added, "Just don't get hurt. We're off the grid here."

"Really?" Larry had said. "How interesting."

Larry first visited Trackz alone when he had been looking for a crew bathroom. The boat was designed to sustain the illusion that it was built for passengers and only passengers, and Larry struggled to memorize the locations of the camouflaged doors to crew-only spaces. The access door to Trackz was right around the corner. *That* one he remembered, and Rocco had taught him how to open it.

Just as he swung the door open, a bed moved past, carrying a figure wrapped like a mummy, eyes closed. Larry had never accessed the system when it was actually transporting passengers. He just about peed his pants.

The roomy tunnel was dark but not cave-dark. Once the door closed behind him, Larry could still make out the rise of the rails, the beds as they moved along. The rails hummed lightly, and the pitch rose as a bed glided closer. The passengers themselves: silent, motionless. Long lumps sliding toward then away from him. The air was cool but comfortable, fresh smelling, even.

For a few moments, Larry observed. Then, just as a fourth bed rounded the corner, he zipped up, a puddle now sitting between the twin rails. He watched one more bed come and go, and then turned back to the door. It was locked. Or it might as well have been since he couldn't figure out how to turn the interior handle to reopen it. Larry tugged and pulled and twisted, but the door wouldn't budge. He watched another bed pass, then another before he realized what he had to do: ride back to a room with a patient, on the bed next to her unconscious body. Then he would need to sneak out of the stateroom before getting caught.

So that's what he did. He anticipated a Space Violation for the wild ride, for ending up in a stateroom—a place off limits to all crew except for assigned room stewards and excursion personnel when necessary. But none came.

So he did it again. Again, he accompanied an unconscious patient, perched at the foot of the bed like a boat's figurehead, the breeze on his face light and cool. The rails purred as the bed moved slowly along, farther into the constant gray dark until the end, when the room's back door started to slide open and the light from the stateroom revealed itself inch by widening inch.

And again. Again, he ducked through the maintenance door. Again, he boarded a moving bed, but this time, he rode astride the passenger. A cowboy on a comatose bronco.

And again. Always to feel the rush of the wait as he counted beds, holding out as long as he could. To feel the rush of the leap onto the moving, already occupied bed. To feel the rush of the final escape from the patient's stateroom, which could be harrowing. For as soon as the bed locked into place, the link to BECCA and all the ship's many sensors was restored. He had to get out of the bed before that happened. And he did. Every time so far.

Though sometimes it was close. After those rides, he would lie in his room, recovering as his break came to an end, and breathe and breathe, his skin a thousand pinpricks, a thousand micro-incisions, blood pulling in the drumbeat behind his ears.

But now, before the women boarded, before the excursions began, before beds began moving on the rails, Larry made his own way through the dark tunnel. He would have to return soon, along the rails the way he came, back to the access door, which Rocco had showed him how to open from the inside during one of their monthly scans. Against the door, to mark its location, he had propped one of the glow wands they offered passengers heading into the Cemetery at night. For now, he continued on, whistling to himself. The sound echoed in the enclosed space, carrying down the rails sweetly, like birdsong.

ALL ABOARD

THE PASSENGERS

MONDAY 14:00–15:15

Who were the passengers filing up the gangway on a Monday afternoon, the first weekend of March, for *PILGRIM*'s 52nd voyage?

For one, they all identified as female. The women ranged in age from twenty-five to eighty, though the majority were thirty to fifty years old. That meant the bulk of the passengers coming up the gangway in their shorts of varying lengths, wedge heels, and off-the-shoulder tops grew up to mantras like "be your best you" and "you do you," reading *Wild* and watching *Gilmore Girls*. Now, as adults, they took self-care seriously. They were committed to rigorously managing, even mastering, their life experiences. Their skin was sun-kissed but not tan, their parents having slathered them with paraben-free sunblock. They had been taught to be a boss and meditate, lean in and care less, demand consent and say no. They knew how to work hard and when to call in reinforcements. They came alone or with a friend from the gym or the office or Bible study or book club, or in a group of sorority sisters. These women who swept glossy strands off their foreheads and behind their ears worked or raised kids or did both or did neither. They were single, married, divorced, or not at all interested in partners. They were housewives and work-wives, partners and players. The spring sun, ever warmer it seemed, and warmer still from the height of Deck 10, encouraged them to remove their three-season jackets, cotton cardigans, and linen shawls. Levels of insecurity fluctuated among the boarding passengers. Most had money, some had a lot of money, and others couldn't afford *not* to come.

Once, a group of older women traveling together came on board without realizing the sort of excursions offered on this particular ocean liner, without noticing its itinerary was entirely customizable and lacked ports of call.

"It's a *what* sort of cruise?"

"The boat doesn't stop *anywhere*?"

"Oh my. How did we get here?"

"I could *never*."

But they did, all of them, especially once they understood there would be no volcanoes to explore, no city tours to disembark for, not even a beach. They wouldn't have the chance to strap neon belt bags around their hips, so instead they signed up to have their lips plumped, their teeth whitened, and the bruise-colored veins, cracking down the backs of their legs like fault lines, zapped away.

The wind had picked up, and a steady gust tore across the bay. BECCA raised the wind shield. Now only the hint of a breeze remained, and on it, passengers toward the stern could smell the rosemary and thyme from the bite-sized pot pies sitting on a nearby table, hot but not too hot to eat. Meanwhile, women just off the gangway caught notes of butterscotch, peppermint, and vanilla bean from the dessert tables.

The ocean air all of them breathed stimulated serotonin production and the release of endorphins. The moment reminded them of an endless teenage afternoon, lying on a lake dock in late summer, wood warm beneath bare legs and arms, clouds combing across the blue above and below. Precisely this moment or one just like it.

ROCCO

Rocco quietly fumed at his station, still cutting limes, still stocking drinkware, still making his way through the preboarding checklist though boarding was already underway. Lively music played. The scents of citrus and sizzling bacon mingled with the ocean air. Alone at the outdoor bar on Deck 10, Rocco counted and grumbled. He refilled and grumbled. He considered the things he'd like to say to his partner Larry, who had ghosted him for the third departure Monday in a row.

But Rocco wasn't much for confrontation. Even as the sentences flowed through his thoughts, he knew he couldn't tell Larry to "get his fucking act together" or even ask him, "What the fuck, man?" He had never in his life cursed at someone out loud. He knew when Larry showed up, if Larry showed up, he would nod and Larry would shrug, and that would be that. Graduate school in statistics hadn't exactly enhanced his interpersonal skills. He could, deftly in fact, talk to colleagues and clients about numbers and what they meant. But expressing himself personally to a peer? He'd rather have waste-disposal detail every cruise.

"Hey, man, what did that lime ever do to you?"

Rocco looked up and saw Larry leaning on the counter. But as he was looking up, he was still slicing. The knife came down, taking off a sliver of Rocco's thumb before continuing on through the lime.

"Whoops," Rocco said, putting his thumb into his mouth. He tasted blood immediately.

"You gotta be careful. Knives are dangerous," Larry said with a smile and not the least bit of concern.

Ignoring him, Rocco bent down to retrieve the med kit from behind the bar. He could do this: refuse to be baited by Larry. He could keep his cool, proceed as if nothing had happened, nothing at all. His last year in graduate school, while working on his dissertation and applying to every statistics and applied mathematics faculty position he could find, he'd had an office mate like Larry. The kid, as Rocco thought of him, had been fresh from an undergraduate degree and come in on a fellowship, and he never let Rocco forget that he was smarter than him.

Larry said, "Hey, toss this in there, will you?"

When Rocco looked up, a brass pen was coming his way. He caught it right before it hit the ground.

Rocco was confused, and his finger wouldn't stop bleeding. He popped his thumb out of his mouth, wiped it dry with a gauze square, and sprinkled some coagulant on the cut. "You want to add a pen to the med kit?" Next he pulled out a Band-Aid.

"Just want to keep my latest treasure safe. She's a beauty, huh?"

"You're talking about a pen?" Rocco asked, fitting a thumb cap over the Band-Aid to keep it secure. "We don't even need pens here." He tucked the pen next to thin tubes of hydrocortisol cream and bacitracin and zippered the kit closed.

"It may just be a pen to you, but to me, it's a prize."

Rocco shook his head. He stood and turned to the station's tablet to log an incident report with BECCA for his cut finger. Already he had engaged Larry too much, asked two too many questions. He clicked to submit the form, then tacked left. "You know," he started, picking up another lime, "you are more likely to cut yourself slicing a fruit than a vegetable, statistically speaking?"

Larry rolled his eyes as he shouldered a tray of drinks. Then he moved off, merging into the growing crowd of passengers.

BECCA

MONDAY 14:30

BECCA played music. The sound seemed to come from everywhere and nowhere, emitting from a system of tiny speakers embedded in the deck itself, the railings, and the retractable canopy that—when needed due to heat, high winds, or rain—she could deploy to cover as much as two-thirds of Deck 10. The sound system and canopy installations were part of the deck redesign last winter. Each pea-sized speaker was colored to match its surroundings, and BECCA had programmed them to be responsive. Music softened when conversations started, then picked up again during potentially awkward silences, so no strained moments occurred on deck, just a pleasing ebb and flow of conversation and soundtracks carefully curated to be appropriate for the situation at hand: for instance, passengers sharing favorite sheet-pan meal recipes, a woman recounting the recent demise of her marriage to a few sympathetic ears, a group discussing the latest superstorm to hit the East Coast and the imminent loss of the Outer Banks.

Yet automatically adjusting volume and ambient sound selection wasn't enough to overcome social discomfort entirely in the first few cruise hours. When they first met, BECCA noted, the women didn't have enough to talk about. They would exhaust introductory, professional, maternal, and domestic inquiries, burn through current events and pop culture, and encounter all too soon the end of discourse. They were not yet buzzed enough to ask, "So what are you having done?" The deck-men, too, reported on the unfortunate nature of such moments: all the darting eyes, the reaching into pockets or purses for a phone that wasn't there but instead was safely stowed in a harbor locker, the desperate steps toward the table-sized cheese board, a lounge chair, the restroom, movement the only way to fill the vacuum.

One woman set off and, encountering no satisfying destinations in her path, committed to exploring the various levels of the ship. By the time she returned to the deck, the party and even dinner service had ended. A deckman escorted the tearful passenger to her room, patting her arm and cooing, "Let's order room service. You'll feel better after some food. Then you can join the party at bingo tonight. Everyone makes a friend at bingo."

BECCA sent white lasagna to her room, steam curling up from its perfectly seared cheese top, and she made sure the woman won hardway bingo for double payout, which amounted to two spa treatments. By the end of the night, the wanderer had plans to meet up with two ladies for Punch Boxing with Pals the next morning.

LARRY

MONDAY 14:48

Larry chuckled as he made his way around the deck, his drink tray perched on a lightly bouncing shoulder. He couldn't help himself. When he saw more than three folds in a single elbow, he wondered what that skin felt like, the skin deep in the fold, dark and tucked away. He took a nearly empty glass from the woman of many folds and replaced it with a full one from his tray. She didn't notice the swap, nor the chuckles. Larry moved on quickly. He stalled near a flock of women with their heads bent together like baby chicks trying to keep each other warm. Growing up on his family's farm in Texas, he had sometimes envied the animals the company they kept, especially when the weather suddenly turned and stayed cold for weeks. Even under two blankets, Larry would go to sleep shaking, and to trick himself into falling asleep, he would think about baby chick fluff covering his body.

But Larry knew these women weren't cold, not on this sunny eighty-degree afternoon. Two had sweat rings growing down the sides of their bodies, like balloons inflating upside down. These women certainly had enough insulation. All five were most likely here to be downsized.

Larry returned to the drink station and took up another tray, this one with blue teas in mason jars that Rocco had garnished with lime slices. He made his way back to the flock and tapped the wide shoulder of a woman wearing an even wider bonnet. He tapped softly, not really wanting her attention yet. He leaned in until he could hear the conversation, which, of course, centered on Grandma Barbie:

"Sue. It's Sue, right? Sue said she saw her by the dried fruit alcove. Sue's a portrait artist. She specializes in faces."

"That's right," a different woman said. "No one's face is that symmetrical. Not even *Denzel*. We're talking perfect mirroring across the sagittal plane."

"The what?"

"Think butterfly wings."

"Oh."

"Is that her?"

Larry took a quick step back as the woman turned, her bonnet just about clipping him in the nose. The teas started to slide as the tray tilted, and Larry caught the tray with his other hand, righting it, but not before one of the teas toppled, sending a stream of blue shooting out at Larry.

"What have we here?" one of the women said.

"Oh, my," said another. "You're all blue."

"Ladies," Larry greeted the women who were now staring at him. He could feel liquid drip from his face onto his shirt. He smiled wide, then licked his lips. "I have some very tasty—and very blue—blueberry pie teas. Care for one?"

All but one woman nodded. While the others took their first sips, she explained, "Last week I ate a whole blueberry pie after dinner. Makes my stomach go wrong seeing blue now. Haven't even looked at the ocean."

"I'll leave you to it, then." Larry flipped the tray on its side and tucked it under his arm. Blue dripped, puddled beside him as he reached a hand around the woman in the wide, wide hat and nodded.

He dropped off the tray at the bar before heading back to his quarters for a fresh uniform. Rocco didn't say a word, just frowned as he poured another round of drinks.

Later, the woman with the bonnet would make her way to her stateroom to change for dinner. She'd take off her hat and frown at the line of sweat along the brim. She'd ball up the shirt she wore to the launch party and toss it into the laundry bag hanging in the cabin's closet. She wouldn't notice the two parallel blue streaks staining the fine linen until she got home.

But by then it wouldn't matter. She would need a whole new wardrobe to accommodate her new size and shape.

ANNALIE

MONDAY 14:55

During the party, Annalie became obsessed with Grandma Barbie. She had teacher ears, and as she picked up a plate from the end of a table-length charcuterie board, she overheard two crewmembers talking about a particular passenger, the oldest in age though not appearance, a woman who had returned for her eleventh cruise. Eleventh! If this woman could reinvent herself so many times, surely Annalie could do it once. She ventured closer and latched onto this bit of lore. Her stomach growled. She'd had biscuits and tomato juice on the plane and nothing else today. Near an edible art display that depicted a cheese sun setting behind a grape-and-berry mesa, she stopped to listen. Her students would love this story, she thought.

The crewmen, it seemed, weren't sure which passenger was Grandma Barbie. The one nodded toward a woman at the shellfish station, but the other said, "No way." They both glanced at a woman at the railing in a short pink dress, gauzy and bright as cotton candy, with white-blond ringlets falling to her waist. Annalie marveled at the height of her glossy nude pumps. No wonder she was standing at the railing, holding on.

"A strong suspect," the first crewmember said after a time, and the other nodded.

They went back to delivering bite-sized treats—crab sliders and mini quiches—in exchange for crumpled, crumb-filled napkins. Annalie, who'd picked up boat-shaped gouda slices, rolls of shaved meat, and a dozen or so berries, made her way toward the railing, toward the suspect, but a group of women coalesced in front of her, blocking her path. One wore a tiara and pink sash. By the time Annalie skirted the squealing bridal bunch, the blond at the railing was gone.

She set down her plate. Already Annalie could feel her stomach turn, hunger replaced by curiosity. She decided to follow the railing, trace a perimeter around the growing number of passengers now on board the ship. Off the ship, before coming to the Port of Los Angeles, Annalie had spent months, almost a full year tracking a phantom. In certain spaces she thought she could feel her sister's presence, and she would turn abruptly only to find another woman blinking back at her, or to discover that she was alone. So alone. She saw features and mannerisms in other bodies, other faces, and that recognition of her sister—there but not there, impossibly absent—would cause a sudden vertigo, and she'd have to sit down, wherever she was, a Midtown sidewalk, an aisle at Whole Foods, and count her breaths.

Halfway around the deck, her eyes scanning the crowd, she collided with someone. The woman was staring off across the ocean, a hand up to keep the glaring afternoon sun out of her eyes. Annalie apologized. In a rush, she explained her mission to locate a doll-like mythical passenger. She said, "She's here somewhere. I can feel it."

"Where?" the woman asked, turning to follow Annalie's gaze across Deck 10.

"Look! The hair on the back of my arms is standing up."

The woman looked, nodding. "How will you know when you find her?"

"Maybe it's you?" Annalie asked in return. "Are *you* Grandma Barbie?"

"Grandma?" the woman scoffed.

"Of course not." Annalie laughed.

"I'm Lyla." Lyla held out her hand, which Annalie shook.

"Annalie."

"Annalie: graced with God's bounty. Pretty name."

"Thank you, but how did you know that?"

Lyla bit her lip, then said, "Research."

"My parents said they closed their eyes, opened up a baby-name book, and pointed. My mom's finger landed on my name. My dad's finger on my sister's."

"What's your sister's name?"

"Aimee." She didn't say anything more. Her therapist at home reminded her weekly that not everyone needed to know she was a twin and had a deceased sister, and that bringing it up, especially within the first five minutes of meeting someone, was, in fact, a form of self-sabotage. When Annalie pointed out this meant there *was* a wrong way to grieve, her therapist had only pinched her lips together.

"You both lucked out then," Lyla said. "There are some awful names in those books."

"They said I would have been Amoeba if they had aimed a bit higher."

"Amoeba's not in any baby-name book." Lyla looked serious now.

"I figured that." Annalie said. "They're research scientists, my parents."

"C'mon," Lyla said. "I'll help you look for this Grandma Barbie."

Annalie smiled. "Let's go."

GRANDMA BARBIE

MONDAY 15:00

But they wouldn't find Grandma Barbie at the party on deck. Ever since her seventh cruise, she opted instead for a quiet tea in the small private library just off the Captain's Quarters. Dr. Heston stopped by each time, to welcome her aboard personally.

"We'll get it right this time, Bennie," he teased, taking her wrinkle-free, baby-soft hand in his.

"I hope not," she said, giving his hand a light squeeze and returning his smile with a sly one of her own. "How else will I spend my ex-wife's annuity?"

"I hear they're opening up seats on Meili Four later this month." Dr. Heston picked up the kettle to refresh her empty teacup.

"Oh, honey. I only want a one-way ticket to space. And not for at least a dozen more years." Bennie plucked three sugar cubes and dropped them into the cup.

Dr. Heston chuckled. "You know you always have a stateroom on my ship."

"Good. I'm not getting any younger."

"That's not what it looks like to me," Dr. Heston said with a wink.

LAUNCH PARTY

Talk of Grandma Barbie began at every launch party. Each cruise, the rumors were different. Someone heard she was eighty years old but looked thirty. Someone else heard she'd had her voice surgically altered to sound like Celine. Another woman insisted she'd been cruising for a year straight, but that woman's friend heard it was more of a rotation, six weeks on the boat, six weeks off. Annalie wasn't the only passenger to wonder if she were here now, to actively scan the many faces, the bodies, in an attempt to discern who among them had taken this plastic-surgery-cruise thing to the next level.

BECCA, meanwhile, knew it was the deckmen who initiated such rumors each cruise, but whether their idle chatter was designed to involve the passengers or was simply serendipity was unclear. What *was* apparent was the rate of rumor diffusion across Deck 10, spiraling outward from the dessert display, a single narrow table featuring an exquisite assortment of goodies, all bite-sized, all made with the freshest genetically modified ingredients to keep the calories and fat content low, low, low.

As expected, approaching women said the sweets looked too good to eat, but the deckmen staffing the table assured them that everything they saw was sensible as well as delicious. "Take," they said. "Eat," they said. "Enjoy," they said.

And the women did.

At the mini-quiche bar—featuring bright platters of options like cranberry turkey, lobster cream, jalapeño papaya—a deckman offered tongs to a passenger and asked the banal question, "Is this your first time cruising with us?"

The woman raised an eyebrow without the skin on her forehead wrinkling at all and nodded.

Perhaps, many cruises ago, that deckman grew tired of smiling and saying in response to that nod, "In that case, welcome!" so now said instead, "Can you believe there's a passenger who has cruised with us two dozen times? She may even be here now, but it's hard to say since her appearance is always changing."

Or perhaps he heard a different answer, something like, "No, silly. Why must you ask me the same question every time? Do I really look all that different?"

LYLA

MONDAY 15:07

Before Annalie ran into her and they started off together on their quest to find Grandma Barbie, Lyla had made her way to the ship's railing. The deck felt crowded, what with all the women spilling off the gangway one after another like dolls on a conveyor belt, and the crew members walking around with this drink or that drink, all bubbles and foam and frost. Here a plate of puffs piped full of mushroom mousse. There a tray lined with devilled eggs, topped with cracklin' bits and fresh herbs.

Lyla could handle bustle. In her labor-and-delivery ward, any shift had the potential to turn into a chaotic mess: extra family members sneaking into rooms, monitors going off, the lab calling, surgeons texting, nurses ordering people to fill the tub, to walk, to push, to not push, women yelling to have the epidural, to not have the epidural, to get their partners, to get their partners the hell out of the room. During those times, Lyla skated on the raised voices, prioritizing on the fly with a single objective: get the baby out. The sooner that happened, the less time she had to spend with those huge bellies proudly boasting a capacity hers couldn't manage. Here, though, on vacation, Lyla wasn't sure what the objective was, nor did she know how to navigate this sort of bustle, amid so much mingling and meandering. She would have preferred to skip right to her surgery.

While she stood at the railing, looking out across the water, she played the game she always played in moments like these, moments she stole or retreated into for this purpose alone: to visit the alternate universe she had created for herself. In this imagined place, she had the family she wanted—two boys and a girl, all under the age of six. They were happy children, these mind phantoms. The youngest still woke up once or twice a night to nurse, but Lyla didn't mind. Nursing soothed them both back to sleep. The middle one, the girl, was determined to stay four forever. This afternoon, Lyla pretended she and her daughter were out together, shopping for new spring clothes. Maybe they'd stop for a special treat on their way home. Drive-thru ice cream or convenience store candy, a box of sour worms or Skittles big enough to share. In seconds she was lost in the conversation she conjured, her attempt to get the mother-daughter dynamic just right.

"When you and your siblings are older, we'll all go on a cruise. And to Disney World. Won't that be fun?"

"Mom." Her daughter's voice was stern. *"Don't you know I'm only going to be four? I won't be older, silly."*

"Then I'll take your brothers. They'd like the boat's ice cream parlor."

"I could stay home with Daddy. I'm going to marry him."

"Is that so?"

"He's going to be king, and I'm going to be queen."

"Who can I be?"

"Silly. You can be Mom, Mom."

But it wasn't at all silly to Lyla. Not the kids, not the conversation, not even the cookies she had imagined baking yesterday with these apron-wrapped, flour-spattered imaginary children. In her mind, she had let them each lick something: bowl, spoon, or spatula. Lyla recognized the absurdity, but that didn't stop her. She conjured lists of Christmas presents—wooden teething rings, blocks and trains, nightlights that projected stars and sheep onto the ceiling. She imagined ear infections and what it might feel like to hold a feverish infant, *her* feverish infant, and whisper over and over and over again, *It's all right. Momma's here. I got you. I got you. I got you.*

A week before the cruise, she'd almost walked out of Target with two boxes of diapers. She didn't remember putting them into the cart. To the clerk at the self-checkout station, she'd apologized. "Apparently you *can* have too many diapers," she said and handed them over. She walked out with only what she had come for—face lotion, deodorant for her husband, foil, and fabric softener.

She sat in the parking lot then, trying to muster up the courage to return to a home where diapers were not needed. By the time she turned the key in the ignition, she had to head straight to the hospital for her next shift.

NICOLE

Nicole plopped into a rattan rocker beneath a white leaf-shaped canopy and pulled out her knitting. She had been on the boat for less than fifteen minutes. What would Justin say if he could see her now? Or Jane? Or Semra? Here she was, at a party on a cruise ship, knitting a sweater for her son that he wouldn't need until Richmond grew cold enough to warrant wool, and that wasn't for another eight months, if ever. She should have a drink in her hand. She should be relishing the ocean air. Instead, she hunched forward and threw a couple more loops. And she would keep throwing loops and counting until she forgot about the door to her craft room. Behind that door were all her unopened B+L boxes, stacked into a counter-height table. Now, fresh off the gangway, she couldn't remember if she had locked the door or not. She finished another row of the sweater's back and started on the next, red yarn snaking from the would-be garment into the bag in her lap. Not that Justin ever ventured up to the third floor . . . but what if, in her absence, he did? Perhaps he might hunt there for a checkbook to pay the sitter she had arranged to watch Max for the next two weeks. Perhaps he'd want to occupy her space while she was away. She imagined him sleeping next to *her* nightstand, using *her* sink in their en suite bath, and climbing the stairs to the attic room she had claimed as *hers*, now a holding bay for hundreds of beauty products she couldn't move. She jerked a needle, and the next loop went in lopsided. She'd have to pull out the whole row and start again.

Products she couldn't move *yet*, she corrected herself. After the cruise, she would have no problem selling her supply. Hell, she'd probably be able to sell mud from their backyard after filling up her social feeds with new photos. The cruise, of course, she wouldn't mention.

The craft room's key was at the bottom of her purse, attached to a key chain Max had made for her, a lumpy giraffe molded out of clay. Had she dug out the giraffe, put the key into the slot on the knob, and turned it before she left? She didn't keep the room locked when she was home, despite the room's contents. Too suspicious. Surely she'd remember if she'd had. She tried to summon the image of her right hand on the brass knob, the key clicking the tumblers closed, but it wouldn't come.

Somewhere in her yarn bag, a knot had formed, and when Nicole tugged, the line remained taut. It would take her ten minutes of pulling, pinching, and plucking to clear the tangle.

BIANCA

MONDAY 15:35

Bianca marveled at the young woman knitting. In Sea Pines, Bianca saw whitehaired ladies knitting on the front porches of their condos when she walked home from the club, but never someone this young. She had always considered activities involving yarn to be a grandmotherly pastime—knitting, crocheting, cross-stitching—any of which she might pick up once her tennis days were over, her girls settled and starting families of their own.

"What's it going to be?" she asked, walking up.

The woman looked up and smiled. "Sweater," she said. "I hope, at least. I'm still pretty new to this." She nodded at the needles she held, the red yarn winding out of a hole in the bag on her lap.

"For you?" she asked. Bianca had a couple cotton sweatshirts and a fleece jacket. She had never lived anywhere cold enough to own a cable knit sweater.

"For my son," the woman said. "My little boy. Red is his favorite color. Or at least it was when I left this morning."

Bianca thought about her daughters, the way their favorites, too, had been so changeable and Bianca always one step behind, still serving spaghetti and red sauce after the girls had moved on to angel hair and alfredo.

"I'm Nicole, by the way," the woman said, collecting both knitting needles in one hand and extending the other.

"Bianca," she said, returning the handshake. "Nice to meet you."

"You, too," Nicole said. "It's nice to know I'm not the only woman here alone."

"Honestly, I can't imagine coming with someone or in a group. I needed to get away. Fresh start, you know?" Or desperate panacea, but she left that unsaid.

"God, I hope so." Nicole had gone back to her knitting. "I still can't believe I'm here."

A deckman approached with a wide tray of bright drinks, fizzy blue ones and icy pink ones. Bianca took two pink drinks and offered one to Nicole, who wrapped the start of the sweater around her two knitting needles and tucked the whole thing into her bag.

"To fresh starts," Bianca said, raising her glass.

Nicole clinked her glass, and they each took a sip.

"Do you have any kids?" Nicole asked.

"Two," Bianca said. "Two girls."

"What's that like?" Nicole asked. "Having girls? Having two? One is plenty for me."

Bianca said, "Oh, it's fine. They're great," and then she sipped her pink drink until it was gone. Their conversation moved on from there to sundry topics—the drink they were drinking ("Too sweet," Bianca said, wrinkling her nose), the deckmen ("My, aren't they a sight!" said Nicole), their hobbies (knitting for Nicole, obviously, as well as reading books for her book club; tennis for Bianca, though did it count as a hobby if she pursued it professionally?), and the cities they came from. But part of Bianca's brain was still stuck on Nicole's early question—*What's it like having two children, two girls?*

After a few minutes, Bianca waved goodbye to Nicole, leaving her to her knitting, and continued to walk around the party. What's it like? What's it like?

She didn't know. She had no idea.

DINNER SEATING

BECCA

BECCA handled all seating assignments. At first, her algorithm responsible for these decisions had taken into account data from a passenger survey as well as the internet. It had considered factors like alcohol consumption, exercise regimens, past experience with stress eating, and interim fasting rates, as well as factors like net worth, brand preferences, club affiliations, and subscription services. With so much data, BECCA was highly successful at putting together women with enough similar interests *and* enough differences to keep conversation interesting, to make them feel that, yes, they belonged here, with these people in particular.

Only rarely did the algorithm lead to less-than-desirable interactions: saccharine smiles, rolled eyes, or under-the-breath commentary, for instance. But the situation never escalated beyond snide exchanges when two of the women would get up to go to the bathroom:

"Diane complains, but she's enabling her son. How does she not see that?"

"I stopped listening when she said she bought her own Christmas gift from him."

"When she said that, I threw up a little of that delightful clam chowder in my mouth."

"I tell you what—when my kids are adults, that won't be me. They're going to have to charge their own Teslas!"

Recently, BECCA had started to experiment. She was waiting until *after* the launch party to finalize assignments. She was taking into account who the women met on Deck 10. She was listening to their conversations.

She had predicted that these early encounters might carry significant weight and reduce awkwardness later, at the first dinner, where passengers sometimes fumbled for something to talk about. This way, women would sit next to a friendly face, pick up where they left off, and feel as though destiny had driven them together.

"No way," they would say. "The same table? What are the chances?"

Then they'd continue on about how they were *so* over juice cleansing and true crime podcasts.

So naturally on this cruise, BECCA put Bianca and Nicole together and paired them with Annalie and Lyla. All four women had checked the box for "life-changing" when asked to describe their hopes for the cruise.

Beyond arranging these likely fast-and-forever friendships, BECCA engineered the dining room itself to respond to passenger anxiety, excitement, insecurity, and longing in pleasing and productive ways. In other words, BECCA cultivated an atmosphere antithetical to the middle-school lunchroom or social media roast, environments that bred mean girls and outcasts, queen bees and followers. From time to time, BECCA called for minor adjustments to adapt the room's climate to the ever-changing cognitive and psychological climates of women. Most recently, bird and cloud wallpaper replaced the gold, textured walls, and antique dough bowls were filled with moss and succulents for centerpieces, which replaced the fresh flower petals strewn across wide circular mirrors that doubled as lazy Susans. BECCA was also constantly tweaking the chemical composition of the room's nondistinctive scent, but these minute changes were imperceptible to passengers and crew alike.

CEDRIC

MONDAY 18:42

The dining room doors opened at 19:00 sharp for dinner. Cedric picked up another wine glass. He rotated it slowly on the flour-sack towel balled up around his right fist. After his conversation with Kali, he just wanted the night to be over already. How was he going to bear so many new faces, so much smiling, the constant effort to make each woman he served feel completely satisfied? Already he was exhausted. He inspected the glass for fingerprints and water spots, then set it on the table and moved on to the next place setting. At his current pace, his tables would not be ready in time.

Too soon, the passengers assigned to his zone would arrive, and he'd pull out chairs and slide napkins onto laps. Cruise after cruise, more women came in, and for a moment every two weeks, just before the first dinner, Cedric would hold his breath and wonder if Kali might walk through the door in her black stilettos and that green shimmery dress she'd bought for their honeymoon. What if! If only!

Kali never came. Some women, though, were similar enough to his ex-wife that he'd hang on every word they said. Others, he knew, Kali would hate, and so he hated them, too, even as he smiled while refilling their water and patiently answered every question they had about the menu. When they complained about anything—food temperature or portion size or water spots on wine glasses—he muttered vegetable names under his breath as he walked away.

"Broccoli rabe."

"Sweet potato."

"Leeks, leeks, leeks."

TABLE 34

At Table 32, Annalie, Nicole, Lyla, and Bianca were still getting acquainted —with each other, the room, and the menu. They had covered all the basics, so now they sat reviewing the appetizer and entrée options. From the table to their left arose animated banter, so the four women at Table 32 listened. This quiet, this listening, BECCA knew, was fine, was good even. It would give them something to talk about. Women loved to talk about other women and the things they had to say.

This is what they heard from Table 34 as they sipped their water, their wine, eyes scanning the menu again (Bianca and Lyla), or else gazing out past the floor-to-ceiling windows at the ocean beyond (Annalie), or else tracing the paths of servers as they moved throughout the room (Nicole).

"The burrata is rather runny. Wouldn't you say?"

"What brings you here?"

"Signed up on a whim over winter break. The kids were whining, and I was staring at these heaps of dirty clothes. I just *couldn't*. We went to Target to buy us all new underwear, and by the time we got home, the kids were sleeping in the car. I just sat there, scrolling through Facebook, checking email. Before I knew it, I was booking the cruise on my phone."

"Oh, heavens, the focaccia melts in your mouth. You must try some!"

"I asked for this for my fiftieth birthday."

"Same here."

"I didn't know a plastic-surgery cruise existed until I came across the website."

"Me neither."

"Just genius. My friend had a tummy tuck last year. She had to empty her own drains. Spent two weeks in a recliner, day and night. No, thank you."

"I'll pass on the pickled shrimp, too. There's dill, and there's *dill*."

"Rapid recovery under prolonged sedation is what sold me, too."

"What do they call that again?"

"Days at Sea."

"Sounds dreamy."

"Oh, it is."

NICOLE

MONDAY 19:26

Across the bottom of the menu, a note to diners was inscribed in sprawling cursive, almost too fancy to be legible: *Please enjoy a five-course dinner. All options are healthful, fresh, and delicious, low in calories and saturated fats. Eat what you desire. Enjoy.*

Nicole ran her fingers over the words, the type bold and raised. Even with the extra weight she was hanging onto after having Max, she couldn't bring herself to worry about calories. Years ago, girls in her dorm at Hamilton College had outlined the perpetual diets of their mothers, not even a thousand calories for the entire day. Her roommates had scoffed at such austerity and laughed about all the ways their mothers had cheated, the little bites that didn't count. They groaned, too, about their mothers' wardrobes, divided into skinny clothes and fat clothes, no doubt contributing to the dysmorphia they now saw in the mirror. Nicole had blinked from the periphery. Her mother had died from an aortic dissection giving birth to her, so she didn't have a mom to laugh with, let alone at. And needless to say, her mother never had the chance to *let herself go* after having a kid. She was only gone.

On the ship today, Nicole had seen women like herself, women who didn't count bites and clearly didn't have gym memberships, their bodies beginning to soften and melt like ice cream cones in toddler hands.

Nicole assumed these women were on board for excursions like hers, liposuction and other fancier fat-removal, body-shaping procedures. Surgicom had pages devoted to all the possibilities, which she had scrolled, awestruck, while preparing for her trip. *LipoDisolve. LipoPulse. LipoVaporize.* Each procedure had a different degree of invasiveness, and all could be used to shrink varying amounts of flesh wherever shrinking was desired.

Nicole reached for her water and took a long sip while scanning the menu yet again. She wasn't good at decisions—big or little. Generally, she ordered what her friends were having. "That sounds good, Jane. I'll have the same," she'd say when they went to lunch. Even this cruise and the excursions she was signed up for hadn't been up to her. Her preference was to glide along the choices others made, their nods and head shakes a smooth ride on a slight downward grade, at times slippery but always moving her along.

The only decision she had made firmly and absolutely was to have just one child. She had risked enough with Max, had been so fearful that something terrible would happen to her in the delivery room. Or worse, to her baby. When her anxiety started to bring up her blood pressure, her doctor suggested a scheduled C-section with general anesthesia.

"Usually, we prefer our mothers to be sedated but awake during delivery, but I think in your case, this birth plan makes the most sense."

Nicole had agreed, and the next day, her blood pressure was back to normal. Yes, the plan had worked. Yes, she and her son survived the ordeal and came home together. But she couldn't do it again, not with Max in her life. She'd made it through one birth, which was more than her mother had, but she wouldn't take that risk again. The stakes were too high. Max needed her, and she would be there for him, the way her mom wasn't able to be, the way her dad refused to be, too sad and then too busy with more clients and projects, his construction company unable to break his heart.

"Miss? Your selections?" their waiter, Cedric, asked Bianca, who was sitting to her left.

"I'll have the spring roll, tomato soup, spinach salad, and cod. No shallots in the soup. No cheese in the salad. No capers on the fish."

Cedric nodded. "Yes, of course." He turned to Nicole. "Before you order, miss, if I may," he said. "I forgot to share this evening's chef specials."

Now that he was standing right next to her, Nicole could see that he was quite attractive. He looked to be around her age but in better shape. She imagined he rode a Peloton, if the crew had access to one, at least five days a week. His features were intense, all angles and hard lines, his eyes brown and deep. His hair, eyebrows, and beard were all dark and trimmed with nearly military precision. He looked nothing, nothing at all, like her husband.

Nicole closed her menu before he could say more, delighted to not have to make a string of decisions, to just say yes, yes, please, to this intriguing man. "That sounds good. I'll have that."

BIANCA

MONDAY 19:40

Once the food started to arrive, the women at Table 32 started to open up. When someone at Table 34 said a quick prayer over her lamb sirloin—"Lord, thank you for bringing me here. For making this dream come true. And bless this beautiful food."—Bianca, already nursing a second glass of wine, spoke up.

"At home, I have the same dream all the time. In it, all I do is run. First, I'm in a long white corridor." Bianca didn't consider herself a talkative person, but between the wine and maybe something in the air, she felt almost compelled to share more. "The corridor becomes a sandy beach, and I can feel my feet sink in, but I'm still running, just not as fast. Then the beach becomes a cornfield, and I can't see anything except green husks and blue sky." Bianca set down her glass of wine. "I have to keep my hands up—" She held up her hands in front of her face, fingertips pointing to the ceiling, elbows tucked in tight. "—like this to keep the stalks from scratching. And I'm running this whole time. Eventually the field spits me out onto a tennis court, but it's miles long and littered with busted rackets and balls ripped open at the seams, and I have to climb over slumping nets every seventy-eight feet." Even now Bianca found herself rushing, speeding through the words before cramming a bite of spinach salad into her mouth, and then another.

Bianca's dreams returned with predictable regularity. They stayed with her. Retellings, too, affected her physically—the rapid speech, her hunger, her heartbeat.

"Seventy-eight feet?" Annalie asked. "Is that significant?" She slid two cherry tomatoes off her fork and into her mouth.

"The length of a tennis court," Bianca said. Her salad now finished, she took a long sip of wine.

"I never remember my dreams when I'm away from home," Lyla said, bringing a forkful of crispy kale to her mouth.

"I do," Nicole said. "But nowhere near as much as when I was pregnant."

"Mmm." Lyla nodded, chewing and pointing to herself.

"So vivid! Every night after the first trimester," Nicole continued.

Lyla wiped her mouth with her napkin. "You wouldn't believe the number of women in labor who come in as ready to stop all that dreaming as they are to have their babies."

Bianca didn't say anything, though her experience had been the opposite. Her dreams had calmed during the first trimester and then seemingly disappeared. They returned the first week home from the hospital, even when she only closed her eyes for an hour, even as tired as she was. "You're a nurse?" she asked Lyla.

"Labor and delivery for over ten years now."

"Does it get old?" Bianca asked. "It must. The babies. After a time. Then it's like anything. Unremarkable. Like walking on the beach when it's your front yard."

"It hasn't," Lyla said quietly. She plucked her napkin from her lap and started to weave the fabric through her fingers. "The best time on the ward is at night, on a slow shift, when it's mostly just me and the babies in the nursery."

"What causes the wild dreaming?" Nicole asked. "I read somewhere it's a hormone thing."

"Progesterone," Lyla said, nodding.

"In my dream last night, I was at this bar," Nicole started. "I was the only one sitting there. There wasn't even a bartender, just glasses and alcohol." She placed her hands flat on the table in front of her. "When I

looked down at the counter, which was smooth and black, I saw someone. A man. But when I looked up, it was still only me in the room . . .
only now there was this face reflected in all the bottles. He was everywhere. Then I felt a hand on my shoulder. The thing was—" She leaned
forward, paused. "—it wasn't the man in the bottles. It was our tax man
asking for my 1099-miscellaneous."

"How about that," Bianca said. She was only half listening while trying to see where their server was. Finally, she saw him behind Nicole, on
his way back toward them. She raised her wine glass, pointed at it, and
flashed him a thumbs up. He pulled his arm out from behind his back,
revealing a wine carafe. She laughed. She felt the other women turn to
look at her. "Sorry," she said. She tapped her wine glass and puffed out
a breath of air and willed Cedric to walk faster.

ANNALIE

Annalie's mouth was full of bread. Continuing to eat gave her an excuse to keep quiet. She was done sharing dreams. She had shared enough with her sister over the years. Too much and not enough. When they were in elementary school, Aimee would climb the ladder to Annalie's top bunk, and there they would press their fingertips to the popcorn ceiling and stay up for hours, whispering and plotting the rest of their lives. At breakfast, over bowls of Cap'n Crunch, they would take turns telling the other one where they went while they were sleeping. They didn't like to be apart, not even in their dreams. Proximity, their mutual preference.

Annalie chewed slowly. She sipped her water, her wine. She listened. She didn't say that in her dream last night, she had been standing in a closet. All around her hung clothing in duplicate: two pink blouses, two blue tees, two white tanks, two pairs of dark-washed jeans. On the ground, double pairs of identical shoes sat in a long, neat row: sandals, then boots, then flats and heels. There was only one pair of sneakers, tossed to the back of the closet, laces stretching out like tentacles. Behind the sneakers, at the very back of the closet was a full-length mirror. Annalie had walked toward the mirror, but as soon as she looked into it, she woke up.

"If I may, Annalie?" Cedric stood next to her chair. Annalie leaned back, and he took away her empty salad plate and replaced it with a bowl of lobster bisque while the other women continued to share their dreams, their dreams of dreams. Into the steaming bisque Annalie slid her spoon, and she was thankful for the biting heat on her tongue.

CEDRIC

MONDAY 20:04

Tonight, like every first dinner of a new cruise, the number of pretty passengers surprised Cedric. He noticed more as the weeks went on, as the time since his divorce stretched out, despite the radical hope he had held onto until today, until his phone call with Kali.

Take the four women at Table 32. None of them were what he would consider overweight. Or wrinkled. They were all well-proportioned, all on the younger side. Bianca's shoulders and arms looked strong in the strapless dress she wore. Annalie was waif-life, but not in an unhealthy way. More naturally willowy. Lyla and Nicole appeared average in terms of height and build, like women who enjoyed bagels and French fries, just women with curves and substance, and what was so wrong about that?

Each of the women in his zone presented the same puzzle: *Why are you here?* For some, he could not imagine the work they wanted done. Other times, he thought he knew, or at least he could guess. He spotted crow's feet as he set down bowls of golden beet soup. When he dropped off honey halloumi and hummus bowls, he saw leathery skin, veiny skin, blotchy skin, even in the soft dining-room glow. He noticed buttocks indistinguishable from thighs and arm flaps swaying between shoulder and elbow. He picked up on facial features many would consider imperfect: large noses, thin lips, jutting chins, sagging jawlines, and foreheads as wide and dimply as blocks of cheese. Usually, Cedric spent the first night trying to tease it all out, but tonight he turned this question on himself: *Why was he here?*

Still, Cedric smiled as he approached Table 32 with entrées on a tray in one hand, a portable tripod in the other. "You're in for a treat," he told the women. With an expert snap of his wrist, he popped open the tripod, then smoothly guided the tray down. He heard clapping and looked up. It was Nicole, applauding. Another week, he might have bowed, hammed it up a bit. But not tonight. Tonight, he turned his attention back to the tray and started passing out plates. The clapping stopped.

"Looks divine," Lyla said.

"It better be," said Bianca. "The chef is a James Beard Award winner. His San Francisco restaurant has a three-Michelin-star rating. He won the final season of *Top Chef*."

Annalie asked, "How do you know all of that?"

Bianca shrugged and moved her arm to make room for a plate of pan-seared cod. "I was playing around with the mirror screen in my bathroom before dinner and found a page listing crew accolades."

"Everything looks amazing." Nicole leaned into the steam curling up from her dish. "And smells amazing."

Cedric had heard those words before, the exact same sentiments. Nearly every meal, in fact. He stifled a sigh and folded the tripod shut. Time felt cyclical, repetitive: the cruise's loop, each day's three successive meals, each meal service and reset. The women having work done, on the other hand, came out of recovery bruised but refreshed, swollen but shining; meanwhile he stayed the same, proving nothing by being here. He was no closer to Kali than he'd been three hundred days ago, when he first joined the crew.

He should have told the women, "Enjoy. I'll be back in a little to check on you." He should have offered some fresh ground pepper or an anecdote about the chef's beard, his tricks with liquid nitrogen, perfected on *Top Chef*. No, tonight he was not in a generous mood.

Even when Nicole called, "Excuse me? Cedric?" as he made his way back to the kitchen, he didn't turn around, didn't stop. He asked Andy to cover his tables and, when he got back to his cabin, logged a migraine into BECCA. He didn't bother to take off his apron, his server uniform, just crawled into bed and pulled a pillow over his eyes.

CONSULTATIONS

THE PILGRIM DAILY
FIRST TUESDAY

Where do you want to go today?

WALKING PATHS.
HOURS: 09:00–24:00

Park .... open
Mall .... open
Cemetery .... open

DINING.
SEE HOURS BELOW.

Breakfast 06:00–09:00
Lunch 11:30–15:00
Dinner 19:00

SPA. HOURS: 09:00–19:00

DAILY SPECIALS

Warming Herbal Scalp Treatment
Cooling Cucumber Body Wrap
Hot Oil Rub for Hands and/or Feet

Book now on your room screen or talk to your room steward to schedule a visit.

ON-BOARD ACTIVITIES. HOURS: 05:30–22:00

Wake Up Meet Up, Deck 12 .... 05:30
Punch Boxing with Pals, Deck 10, Starboard Parlor 07:00
Orientation to *PILGRIM*, Deck 12 .... 08:00, 09:00, 10:00
Bring-a-Friend Bingo, Deck 8, Bingo Hall 10:00
Beach Party & Karaoke, Deck 12 .... 14:00–16:00
Mixed Drink Mixer, Deck 10, Starboard Parlor............................. 16:00
Flow Yoga, Deck 10, Mint Canopy.. 17:00
Champagne Toast, Deck 12 .... 18:00
Horoscopes Under the Moon, Deck 12 .... 20:00

CONSULTATIONS. HOURS: 07:00–18:00

A reminder to first-time passengers: consultations are mandatory. For our returning passengers, we strongly encourage booking a consultation to review and update your itinerary. Appointments are still available and may be booked directly on any screen in your stateroom. Room stewards are available to escort you to the Consultation Station.

EXCURSIONS.

For passengers embarking on itineraries today, we look forward to welcoming you to your assigned flower suite. Room stewards are available to escort you.

BECCA

BECCA required first-time passengers to attend a consultation early in the week. Returning passengers were always welcome to book a session, too, and while some did, others preferred to start their itineraries first thing Tuesday morning.

During a consultation, each patient discussed with their assigned consultant their itinerary for the cruise. The consultant would pull up the passenger's file on Surgicom and review their scheduled excursions. Then, the consultant would share her story—all consultants were women, women who had had work done, women who had cruised on *PILGRIM*. She would share before and after photos. She would narrate in detail the degree to which plastic surgery had changed her life. Then, the consultant would say this, or some variation: "You can ask me anything. I'm not just an employee, you know. I've been where you are. I've cruised. I've gone on the excursions. I've recovered, and look at me now."

Originally and up until Cruise #28, these sessions had been led by the on-board team of physicians. But BECCA determined that this arrangement was not optimal for a number of reasons. For one, the doctors constantly complained about their hours: the consultations, the surgeries, the post-op visits, and the dictations. BECCA's data confirmed that the doctors were, indeed, working hours that increased the risks for burnout and fatigue, and thus error. Upon crunching more numbers, BECCA made an important finding: Doctors as consultants did not increase the number of procedures patients were electing to have while on board. It had been assumed that the suave and handsome, if arrogant, medical professionals hired by Dr. Heston would be persuasive. Surely these silicon-loving, beautiful-women-loving, highly educated men could reel patients in and convince them to shoot the moon, or at least add a little tuck to their excursion list. But no. Some passengers even decided not to go ahead with their previously scheduled itinerary, despite the steep cancellation fee.

BECCA once recorded a doctor railing at a passenger: "Yank up those eyelids and look, really look, in the mirror. You'd be a fool not to get this work done. That cutis laxa isn't going to tighten itself!" In the recording, the passenger had said up front she wasn't interested in adding another excursion. She said she wasn't interested in a hard sell. And the doctor, who had since been asked to find a new practice, took that refusal as a challenge, and he sold with everything he had, as hard as he could.

With previous passengers as consultants, sessions became friendly, more casual, more effective. "You know," a consultant would say, "I've heard that this new facial reconstruction procedure is *everything*. On the last cruise, these two passengers booked it as an add-on, which carries a bit of a discount, and they were *raving*. You go to sleep and wake up with a brand new look! And after, you're guaranteed ten years until you even *start* contemplating the need for Botox. With our updated 3D imaging studio, you can see and customize your face ahead of time. Nose like the Duchess of Cambridge? Yes, you can!"

Some passengers, of course, couldn't be swayed. The percentage of women opting out of add-on procedures fluctuated between 32 and 47 percent. The opt-out figure had been a lot higher when consultations were doctor-led—as high as 87 and usually around 65 percent.

Needless to say, investors were happy with this rate change, and they appreciated that it continued to drop. BECCA's algorithm for generating passenger-consultant pairings became more refined each week. Figure skater with pageant queen. Private-school board member with Upper Eastsider. Cardiologist's wife with Orange County lifestyle influencer. Real estate mogul with former telenovela star. Women, BECCA had learned, wanted what other women liked. They wanted that greener grass over there, just across the fence. They wanted what they didn't even know they wanted until another woman, one similar enough to them and *happy, happy, happy*, had it. They wanted and they trusted. Trusted and craved. And because of these linked impulses, they added on excursion after excursion. They opted for more innovative options, more complete packages. Statistics showed that if one woman announced at book club that she was having her kitchen done, the next month, three others would have scheduled meetings with contractors and at least one would also be in the throes of demolition. Extrapolating, BECCA forecasted that in the next six months, the opt-out rate would fall below 20 percent.

LYLA

TUESDAY 10:42

Lyla waited for her mandatory consultation in a room that played the same sort of music she used to hear in her reproductive endocrinologist's office, the same weepy instrumentals. Pictures of beautiful women hung on a wall, matted and framed and arranged in a grid, three across, four high. All the women—previous passengers, Lyla presumed—laughed at the camera as though they were having the best time. At her RE, one wall was a giant cork bulletin board displaying birth announcements two layers deep. Baby pictures hung on the other walls, so that everywhere you looked, you saw evidence of smiling, sleeping, living, breathing infants. She'd imagined the wall décor was meant to remind patients of what they were struggling for and the success that was bound to be theirs, too. The goal literally in sight. But eventually, those birth announcements and photos came to haunt Lyla. All those babies started to mock her and her fertility woes. *Look at us*, they laughed. *You can't have us! Not with Clomid. Not with IUI. Not with IVF. Not ever.*

Lyla had arrived early for her consultation, but now she wished she hadn't. All she could do was think about the bad news she'd received in a place like this: *I'm not sure why you're not ovulating regularly. Your lining isn't thick enough. Could be a hormone thing. Or tissue buildup. We'll need to abort the cycle, but you can try again after your next period. Miscarriage miscarriage miscarriage.*

Now at least she understood her recurrent pregnancy loss, even as she had to reckon with the completeness of her infertility. But that understanding meant she could do something about it. She'd keep a wait-and-see mentality for adoption, but she had waited long enough to stay pregnant for ten months. That's where Dr. Heston came in. He'd promised her not just a belly but an *experience*.

Lyla closed her eyes. She turned her attention elsewhere, to children whose births she could not announce, whose bodies couldn't be wrapped in muslin and tucked into tutus or barrels for newborn photo shoots. She wondered if her imaginary kids wanted to play I Spy while they waited.

"Can we? Please, please, please?"

Lyla laughed. "I suggested it, didn't I? Now, who wants to go first?"

Joshua and Lacy let their younger brother go, and Lyla was proud of their maturity.

"I spy something yellow," Tyler said. "No, something green."

"Are you sure?" Lyla asked. "Something green? Like the flower stems in the vase on the table?"

"Mom! Why'd you have to get it right on the first try? I wanted it to be my turn a little longer."

"You'll get another turn. It's good to take turns. It's nice."

"But sometimes it's not fun."

"At least you get a turn. Be thankful for that."

Satisfaction was so hard for children. They always wanted to watch one more show, eat one more piece of candy, play for just a little while longer.

The door behind Lyla opened, and a woman walked in. "Hello, Lyla! Sorry you had to wait. Shall we?" With a welcoming smile, she held open the door, motioning Lyla into the consultation quarters.

"What a space," Lyla said as she crossed the raised threshold. Around the room, consultations were in progress. Some pairs of women sat in booths, others at tables, others at a long bar.

"I'm Christina," the woman said as they made their way past the other pairings. "It's nice to meet you, Lyla."

They sat in a booth that had a purple drink on the table.

"I hear this is your favorite," said Christina.

"I had one yesterday at the party. Delicious," Lyla replied, taking a sip.

"They're quite popular." On her side of the booth, Christina touched the table, and suddenly a screen appeared. She began to type on it. "Now," she said. "Can you tell me what led you to Canterbury Cruise Line? Were you referred by anyone in particular?"

Lyla thought back. After her parents' tearful confession, she had wanted only to be alone, away from not just her parents but her husband, the adoption process they were starting, away from work with its hordes of fully-functioning female bodies. On any cruise—Norwegian, Princess, Royal Caribbean—pregnant women weren't allowed onboard after twenty-five weeks of gestation. When she had stumbled across the Instagram feed for Canterbury Cruise Line, she knew she had found her vacation. No pregnant woman would take a plastic-surgery cruise.

Then she had scrolled through the entire grid and had seen what Dr. Heston, the Captain as he was called, and his team could do. In *two weeks*. Remarkable. It had seemed too good to be true. Surely the images were Photoshopped or fake from the start. She dropped the idea for a time, but the bellies continued to haunt her. Expecting women were everywhere. In the grocery store, she confronted baby bumps and swollen ankles aisle after aisle. At the bank, at her fitness center, and of course at work: midsections swelling and hair so shiny and full. She found Canterbury Cruise Line's website and started to wonder. She filled out a contact form with a question for the Captain. *Can you do this?* she had asked. The Captain had replied, *Yes. Yes, I can. I can make you look and feel pregnant.* And now here she was.

"Instagram," she said. "That's where I learned about this cruise."

"Wonderful." Christina tapped the screen. "And I'm sure you know by now that the images we post are a hundred percent clean. The befores and afters are Instapixs a crew member takes as patients board and prepare to head home. Some passengers send in their own after photos once they are home and finish healing. But those are clean, too. We conduct full pixel analyses to confirm."

Lyla nodded. "I was impressed."

"Wonderful, wonderful. Now, I have a few questions for you. I've got a list they gave me, so please bear with me, okay?"

Lyla took another sip of her purple drink.

"How many cycles of IVF did you go through?"

"Four. Then two frozen."

"I'm so sorry, hon. That must have been awful."

"It was," Lyla replied, though what she really wanted to say was *you have no idea*.

"You've conceived seven times, is that correct?"

"Eight."

"Eight miscarriages, then? And all pregnancies terminated by week nine?"

"Yes, and this is relevant how? It's all in the patient history forms I submitted online." Lyla pushed her drink to the side. She folded her arms.

"I know, hon, I know. And I'm sorry. It's just I have this list of questions."

"Can we skip to the part where you tell me the risks and I give consent?"

"Actually, you'll do that in your flower station. I believe, yes, here it is, you'll be in Hydrangea, the newest station. It's positively breathtaking."

Lyla sat back, kept her arms crossed. "Then what is this meeting about?" she huffed.

In their booth, a single picture hung on the wall between them, and in it, a woman leapt through the air, her legs stretched and straight and lean, toes pointed, skimming the tops of wildflowers in a meadow. The pose seemed impossible, the midair split defying the limits of gravity, exceeding the hip joint's torque.

"Here we'll review your itinerary. Make sure you're satisfied with the excursions you've selected. See if there's anything else we can do. Anything else you'd like to have done while you're on board. Right now, we're prepared to offer you a special add-on discount."

Lyla watched Christina tap the screen, and a menu appeared with a list of procedures in one column, then a column for their original prices, then a column listing the discounted prices.

Christina continued, "We're not in the business of hard-selling anything. But you're already here, right? So why not do a little more?" She pointed to the procedure list. "This list is customized for you. We take into account the work you've already scheduled, as well as information from your passenger survey."

Lyla scanned the list. Some names she recognized, others she didn't. She shook her head. "I just want to be pregnant," she said. "Look pregnant," she corrected. "That's all."

Christina leaned in. "This isn't in my script, but I would like to be the first to say congratulations. I think what you're doing is very brave. Every woman who wants to be pregnant—look pregnant—should get the chance. And the Captain's the one to make it happen. He's extraordinary." She winked at Lyla. "That last part is in the script."

Lyla sighed. "I hope so."

"Now, I'll need you to sign here to confirm that you would not like to add on any of these procedures, but before you do, might I recommend the third one down, Toe Color Treatment? It's a fun one! You pick a set of four polishes for your toenails, and then your nails will cycle through the colors you've selected, changing once per season. Especially when you have that big old belly in your way, you're not going to want to be bending down to paint your toes, are you?" Christina raised an eyebrow.

Lyla considered. Now that Christina had mentioned it, not having to worry about her toenails for a year sounded kind of nice. The cost of the procedure as an add-on was only a little more than she might spend annually on pedicures at the Asian Nails in the strip mall two blocks from the hospital. Plus, her parents were paying.

"Let's do it."

Christina clapped her hands. "This is going to be so great for you." She tapped the screen in front of her. "I'm planning to get it done on my next cruise," she admitted. "If you'll just—" She pointed. "—initial here, check here, and sign here. Yes, just like that. And one more signature here. This will authorize us to add the charge to your account. Yup, right there. Terrific."

Lyla moved a hand down to her stomach. "I can't believe it," she said. In the wake of her early frustration, she was feeling giddy. She'd felt the shift as soon as Christina had offered her congratulations. Finally, it was her turn to celebrate something. She was used to family and friends, everyone she knew, expressing condolences. All the downcast eyes. The arm squeezes. The *I'm here for you*s. "This is really happening, huh?"

"It is," Christina said, reaching out to take Lyla's other hand in hers. "It says here to tell you that by next Wednesday night, your system will have enough HCG for you to test positive. I'll put a note in to have your room steward set out a box of pregnancy tests for you."

"This is really happening," Lyla said again.

"Later today, you might want to attend the mixed-drink mixer. After your excursion, you'll want to avoid alcohol. You'll also want to pass on uncooked fish, hot dogs, lunch meat, and certain cheeses. You know, I'm sure, all the foods to avoid."

Lyla frowned. "But those restrictions are to ensure the health of the fetus. I thought—"

"Of course, yes. But the Captain worked the typical pregnancy dietary concerns into the hormone therapy protocols. Anything that would normally compromise fetal health can affect the viability of *your* pregnancy."

Lyla started to smile. "So it will be like I'm really pregnant."

"Precisely. Except for the birth, of course, the experience will be as real as it gets."

"Morning sickness and all?"

"All of it." Christina nodded. "That's what you wanted, isn't it?"

"Yes," Lyla said, without hesitation. "Yes, that's it. That's it."

DR. HESTON

TUESDAY 11:02

Dr. Heston, in full surgical gear, pulled the pig-liver cells he had ordered from a medical engineering facility in Atlanta out of the coolbox in his on-board lab.

"Good, slow now, steady."

One of the Atlanta-based engineers was on Zoom, so she could consult with Dr. Heston and walk him through the procedure. A diagram was projected onto the lab bench beside the equipment tray. Today, they were building a pig-liver balloon.

At first, Dr. Heston could do with a scalpel and suction what women used to only fantasize about when they bought treads and weight racks for their homes, participated in hunger games with work colleagues, or signed up for boot camps in unused mall parking lots with ex-military instructors who shouted, "Do you want to die? If not, you're not pushing hard enough!" until they did, indeed, want to die. Dr. Heston could do more, so much more, than any over-the-counter or prescribed or dark web serum or lotion or tincture or cleanse. Women wanted wrinkle-free knees and elbows. They wanted muffin tops no more. They wanted breasts that shook, but not too much, when they ran. They wanted eyelashes that blinked a breeze. All without diet and exercise. Without any more steps to their bedtime routine. And they certainly didn't want to settle. They needed him. "Quit with the makeup. *Be* made up," he urged in an audio clip attached to his profile on Canterbury Cruise Line's website. "Plump, sculpt, tone: let *me* do the work for *you*."

Now, with 3D printing and pig-liver cells and myriad other tools and technologies, Dr. Heston could perform procedures that smacked of science fiction. Bodies were so complicated, the female form endlessly intriguing. He could push past the surface, push deeper than skin and adipose. He could penetrate fasciae. Rework musculature. Reimagine organs. Alter chemical composition. Maybe initially he had imagined he would be augmenting breasts and buttocks, lifting faces, and tuck, tuck, tucking on the boat day in and out, but that was a long time ago. Certainly before Rebecca created BECCA, and he saw the wonders she could create from code. If she could do what she did with lines of text, what could he do with tissue? Then he lost Rebecca: his muse, his idol, his everything. Since then, he'd found the harder he pushed, the closer he felt to her. She had lived and worked from one "Can I?" to the next, responding each and every time with a resounding "I can!" . . . until she got sick. Now he wore her mantle. "Can I?" he asked himself about new excursions, however challenging, however particular to one specific patient, regardless the cost. Always, the response: yes, yes, yes. Each innovation, each attempt to advance his knowledge and skill, was a love letter he wrote to his dead wife.

Take, for instance, a recent request. "I long to experience pregnancy, though I cannot conceive," a woman had written to him a few months ago. Fortunately for her, he understood pregnancy not as a matter of fertility, not as a product-driven process, but as a journey involving a series of systems, reactions, interactions. Yes, yes, yes! A friend of Rebecca's operated a medical farm in Georgia. He made a call.

Now that passenger was sailing on *PILGRIM*, and he would give her what no one else could. He would turn pig liver cells into a balloon capable of expanding slowly over a period of ten months.

"Okay," the biological engineer on the screen said. "Looks like you're ready for fusion."

BIANCA

"You'll see, Bianca. We're going to play a little trick on your mind, tell it it's younger than it is to help reset the clock a bit during your Body Rejuvenation itinerary."

"And this is a noninvasive procedure?"

"Excursion. Yes, completely. It's a newly developed osmosis therapy. We'll apply the compound to your scalp as a liquid and then conduct targeted massage to stimulate the movement of the liquid across the epidural tissue."

"That's it?"

"That's it. The treatment should have no effect on your memory or cognition, except you might find that you are a bit sharper and you might remember more. When they say the mind's the first thing to go, they're not kidding. But that won't be the case with you, Bianca. Not at all. If I'm honest, and I like to be honest, the worst part of this excursion is the liquid can leave your hair on the oily side. We'll be sure to have your room stocked with a clarifying shampoo to restore it to a clean radiance."

LARRY

TUESDAY 11:25

Some passengers considered the cruise a deeply personal journey and preferred to keep it that way. For first-timers in this category, consultations were quick, perfunctory affairs. *Yes, yes, no, please and thank you.* Bip, bop, boop. These women didn't enter the dining room again after that first night. Instead, they ate in lounge chairs on Deck 10 or in their rooms or at a table tucked into a corner of a common space for just this purpose. There they would find a book they had been longing to read, or playing cards (perfect for solitaire). Some might go the entire week uttering only a handful of words. The crew brought them food and drinks and anything they could think to ask for before they thought to ask for it, so what was there to say?

Lately, Larry had been having a little fun with these passengers. Today, for instance, he pulled the books BECCA had recommended—for one passenger, a beach read by Emily Giffin, and for another a Stephen King thriller—and swapped them. Instead of a matcha latte, he brought a lounging passenger on Deck 10 a chai. He set it down on the side table while she slept on a daybed, head and body nestled among at least a dozen pillows, book tented open near her right hand. Larry put his hands on his hips, surveying the scene. He imagined this woman waking up in ten, twenty minutes, refreshed but disoriented. She'd find a new drink waiting for her and smile, picking up her book again, scanning to find the sentence she last read. But she wouldn't find it on either page open before her. Where was the fun in that? Larry reached for the book, flipped forward a few chapters, then replaced it near the woman's hand. Again, he imagined her waking, returning to those tented pages again and again. She'd take a sip of her drink and frown, expecting the nuttiness of matcha and tasting the spiced notes of chai instead. Good, pleasant, but too sweet and not what she would have picked.

Eventually, Larry imagined, she'd find her place in her book and read on. She'd finish her drink, too. And only when setting down her empty tumbler would she notice that her ring was missing, a moissanite stone in a gold setting she had gifted to herself after her second divorce was finalized. But, she would have to wonder, had she worn it out here? Maybe it was resting safely on the ring rod in the bathroom of her cabin? Or in the tray on her nightstand at home? Or still stashed in her travel-jewelry roll in her suitcase? It could be anywhere, and anyway she was starting to doze again, the breeze warm and soporific.

After his shift, Larry would add the ring to his souvenirs, which he kept in his dopp kit on the shelf by his bed.

ANNALIE

"That's what Dr. Heston recommended for me? All of those?" Annalie stared at the screen built into the table before her.

Her consultant, Claire, smiled proudly. "He personally reviewed all of your information. I think you'll find, as I certainly did, that Canterbury Cruise Line goes above and beyond for its passengers. Dr. Heston especially—but the entire crew, no doubt—truly, truly, *truly* wants what is best for you. They want to see you happy."

"I don't know. It seems like a lot. And you said that follicle treatment is fairly new?"

"We can always stick with a more traditional weave, if you'd prefer. The Captain is offering you a hair procedure and teeth whitening at no additional cost. But it's what you want. He's terribly sorry about the loss you have experienced. It says here to tell you that."

Annalie watched as Claire's eyes grew wet, as she blinked rapidly.

"I don't know. It's a lot to think about." She used to cry, too, as soon as anyone mentioned her loss or her sister or asked her how she was doing. But in the past two months she had felt her well drying up, her sadness no longer the leaky fluid sort.

"Good thing my makeup isn't going anywhere." Claire ran her pointer finger along both bottom rows of eyelashes. "I'm a cryer, but now I don't have to worry about turning into a raccoon."

Annalie gave her a small smile. "Good thing."

Leaning forward, Claire took Annalie's hands in hers. "Listen. You're right. It *is* a lot to think about. But I'm here to tell you you don't have to. You can let us—and by us I mean Dr. Heston—take care of you. You check this box here, accept the Captain's recommendations, sign, and be on your way. Easy as pie. Blueberry pie. Not pecan. Pecan's hard."

Annalie smiled wider this time. She liked Claire, she realized. She appreciated her forward yet easy demeanor, the quick cadence of her speech, how she moved from heavy to light in the blink of a wet eye. She was surprised, too, at how comforted she felt by this woman and her squeezing hands, her ready tears, her absolute faith in the Captain.

Annalie asked, "Is that what you would do?"

Claire nodded. "Yeah, honey."

Annalie clicked and signed.

ROCCO

Rocco's nearly limitless patience made him an excellent candidate not just to work with Larry but also to escort first-time passengers around the ship from one activity or amenity to another. *Gopher shifts*, he called them. Before reaching a passenger and after leaving her at the spa or her room or the Consultation Station, Rocco traveled the boat alone, and this quiet time enabled him to recharge his social battery so he could engage other passengers, face Larry, and interact with the rest of the crew. As he wound his way down the crew ladders to cut from the Fiber Arts Studio on Deck 9 to the Grand Staircase on Deck 5 where Nicole was supposed to be, Rocco considered an alternate reality, the one in which he had landed the job after his only on-campus interview (despite the seventeen applications he'd submitted); the one in which he was now living in Pullman, WA, where the likelihood of rain on any given day approached 60 percent, teaching Introduction to Statistics and Statistical Thinking for Humanities Majors while also starting up his Tourism Data Lab for the School of Hospitality and Tourism Management; the one in which his doctorate—and the seven years he had spent on it—meant something, in which he was called "Doctor" earnestly by colleagues and students and not only by Larry, who used the designation to mock him;

the one in which he was probably, if he were being honest with himself, lonely and miserable.

He spotted Nicole, paused about halfway down the stairs, about to turn and head back up. He called to her.

NICOLE

"This is nice." In the Consultation Station, Nicole sat on a barstool across from Marie, a woman in a flowing linen dress. They both leaned on the bar top between them, both cradled the mugs of mocha in their hands. Anywhere but here, she and Marie would be two friends, young mothers with young children in a three-day-a-week preschool, grabbing coffee before carline formed, when they would drive their minivans up behind the other minivans already waiting, the line stretching across the parking lot and around the block.

"It just gets better. Believe me."

"You've cruised?"

"Twice already. Once on my own, and the next time with my best friend."

"How nice."

"It was. The perfect girls' getaway."

Nicole almost started to tell Marie this trip was supposed to be that for her, too, but she didn't want to explain the misfortunes that befell her best friends in the days and hours leading up to their departure. "Maybe next time."

Marie smiled. "That's great that you're already thinking about next time. I like where your head's at."

Now Nicole smiled. "It's hard not to. I don't even need to ask for a drink, and a deckman appears, holding just what I want before I know I want it. The waiters, too, are so accommodating. So thoughtful."

"They're all rather dashing, aren't they?"

"They are." An image of Cedric popped into Nicole's head. Clearing her throat, she took a sip of her drink.

Marie tapped her hands along the bar, and a screen appeared. "I'd love to review your itinerary and then share some ideas we had that might be the perfect complement to what you have planned."

"Oh, good. I have some ideas also." On her shuttle to the Port of Los Angeles, and before putting her phone in a locker in the terminal building, Nicole had been on Surgicom, perusing the possibilities. She had made a list.

"Excellent!" Marie was all smiles. "Before my consultation, I thought for sure I would stick with the tummy tuck I wanted and the boob job my husband requested. But no. You are way ahead. Good for you!"

Nicole saw it differently. She was way *behind*. Way behind getting her pre-baby body back. Way behind on having regular sex with her husband. Way behind selling B+L products. Way behind on a balanced budget for their family. "I need this," she said quietly, pulling from her purse the water bill envelope on which she had written a few excursion names.

Marie squeezed her hand. "Oh, sweetie," she said. "You *deserve* this. And you'll see. Everything will be different afterward. Better. I promise."

Nicole blinked away tears. "I hope so." So much was riding on this trip. She had to get it just right.

Twenty minutes later, Nicole had added on skin firming and smoothing injection therapy, a permanent weave, and new eyelashes.

"What about the risks?" she asked.

"Of course. Though I should warn you—I warn all the women I consult with—reading the side-effect literature might not be the best thing. We have to document all possibilities, so you can imagine. But I'll say this: Your itinerary is safer than flying from Richmond to LA. And you've already done that."

"What about recovery? Days at Sea, I think it's called? What's that like?"

"You'll recover in your room under sedation until you're pain free and ready to get out and about again. It's delightful, honestly, to wake up feeling so rested—and with the body you want. I see here—" Marie pointed to the screen. "—that your itinerary is scheduled for Hydrangea Station Saturday morning. That's the best time, really. That way, you can enjoy all the on-board activities for a few days, and you'll be well-rested and healed before you head home."

"And that's it? Do I need to do anything?"

"When you disembark, you'll receive a Treatment Management Plan. All passengers do. Otherwise, you'll need only to enjoy your brand new you."

It wasn't until Nicole had hugged Marie goodbye and was on her way to the spa (for the Warming Herbal Scalp Treatment, a perk to prepare for her permanent weave) that she remembered she'd wanted to review the anesthesia for her itinerary. She'd meant to ask how long she'd be knocked out, what the odds were of something going wrong. Once she and Marie started talking about eyelash length and the amount of shine she wanted in her hair, all that had slipped her mind. Now, on the stairs between Decks 5 and 6, the questions returned in a dizzying flood.

She turned around. She would go back. She would apologize but say she had to speak with Marie again.

"Nicole! There you are!"

She spun toward the voice. As a deckman approached, she saw his nametag read Rocco.

"I'm here to escort you to the spa. Allow me." He held out an arm.

Nicole hesitated. "Well, actually—" Now she was torn. Should she try to go back? Maybe some pampering would soothe her anxiety more than answers to her questions. Answers wouldn't have saved her mom from her aortic dissection after all; sometimes bodies behaved in unforeseen and unfortunate ways. She lay a shaky hand on Rocco's arm. "Thank you."

AMENITIES

THE PILGRIM DAILY

— FIRST WEDNESDAY —

Where do you want to go today?

WALKING PATHS. HOURS: 09:00–24:00

Park .... open (breezy with cool but pleasant temperatures expected)
Mall .... open
Cemetery .... open

SPA. HOURS: 09:00–19:00

DAILY SPECIALS

Reflexology for Cellular Regeneration
Wine Soak and Cabernet Hot Stone Massage
HydraFacial

Book now on your room screen or talk to your room steward to schedule a visit.

DINING. SEE HOURS BELOW.

Breakfast 06:00–09:00
Lunch 11:30–15:00
Dinner 19:00

ON-BOARD ACTIVITIES. HOURS: 5:30–22:00

Tea Meditation, Deck 12	05:30
Essentials about Essential Oils, Deck 10, Starboard Parlor	07:00
Yoga in the Sun, Deck 12	08:00
Caring for your Crystals, Deck 10, Starboard Parlor	09:00
Rainforest Zumba, Deck 10, Mint Canopy	10:00
Ballroom Dancing Lessons, Deck 10 Starboard Parlor	11:00
Lady of the Sea Pageant, Deck 12	14:00
Water Painting Class, Deck 10, Citrus Canopy	15:00
Mixology Mixer, Deck 10, Starboard Parlor	16:00
What To Read Next, Deck 10, Mint Canopy	17:00
Happy Hour Bingo, Deck 18, Bingo Hall	18:00
The Zodiac & Cordials, Deck 12	20:00

EXCURSIONS.

For passengers embarking on itineraries today, we look forward to welcoming you
to your assigned flower suite. Room stewards are available to escort you.

ROCCO

Wednesday morning was busy for Rocco and the rest of the deckmen. Though some returning passengers had been on excursions yesterday and were now recovering in their rooms, and the flower stations were running full schedules today, plenty of women were still waiting for their itineraries, and whether anxious or excited, they needed things to do.

Fortunately, *PILGRIM* offered a plethora of amenities. Every day as passengers cycled through health and healing, activities were scheduled from predawn to well after dusk. In large part the day started early to accommodate women in the throes of menopause who couldn't sleep past 04:00, despite wine, despite Benadryl, despite crime procedurals they downloaded on their tablets and listened to with headphones under the covers lest they disturb their partners or pets. So beginning at 05:30 today, Rocco and Larry facilitated an hourlong tea meditation on the ship's topmost deck. Brandon, a surgical technician with a background in osteopathic medicine, guided passengers through a series of mindfulness exercises while Rocco steeped tea and Larry passed out cozy lightweight blankets and extra pillows. At 07:00, the three of them would hold an Essentials about Essential Oils class in a Deck 10 parlor. Women would munch on scones slathered with clotted cream and meanwhile dab their wrists and necks with dozens of scents. The day's offerings and timings changed each week in response to participation data from the previous week and passenger preferences as identified through both observation and surveys. One week, the flower-arrangement class might focus on succulents, and the next on seasonal blooms. Some weeks, yoga was offered twice only on Tuesdays and other weeks three times a day, every day.

Rocco marveled at the customization BECCA offered passengers, the complexity and responsiveness of her algorithms, and tried to discern the underlying logic. Even now, for instance, he considered the types of passengers in attendance at this hour for this activity and tried to identify correlations between each passenger-type and their tea preferences, categories and connections BECCA surmised deductively, no doubt. This morning, his data supported three passenger-type categories:

The first, the Nervous Newbies, came aboard with a single friend, a sister, or a mother. They signed up for minimally invasive work and stuck to their plans even after their consultations. They attended early morning activities every morning they could, and they talked about *next time* with varying degrees of confidence while sipping English breakfast tea finished with a drizzle of honey and a splash of milk.

The second type, the Motivated Marathoners, aspired to be like Grandma Barbie, whoever she was, and paced themselves accordingly. These were women who tried out a full D cup and then decided a year later to revert to a more reasonable, less lively C. They had their faces lifted again and again. These shape-shifters like Mary this morning, sipping her macchiato with oat milk—fascinated Rocco. Their body composition likely approached a ratio of 50 percent carbon to 50 percent silicon. Yesterday, a rumor had spread about Mary—how she had charcoal sketches of the work she desired, labeled in neat cursive, an entire notebook full, kept in her navy leather tote—the one hanging from the purse hook on the back of her chair now. Another woman was rumored to cruise once a month for an entire year, changing a feature here, a dimension there. She supposedly suggested the Captain start a Frequent Cruiser Program, which he did following Cruise #30. And another was thought to be the Captain's mother, cruising periodically since the first voyage at a 50 percent discount.

Finally, there were the women who wanted a complete transformation, all at once. They wanted to go home different people entirely. These passengers Rocco thought of as the Other Seekers, and they drank organic teas—peppermint, chamomile, and occasionally Earl Grey. They tended to be quiet, contemplative, and sad, like Annalie, who tucked her teacup into her chest like she was guarding it and who, when the wind picked up off the leeward side, turned to face it, closing her eyes, surrendering herself to the soft morning breeze, hoping it might, bit by bit, pull her apart.

BECCA

After the first two nights aboard, the dining room hummed at breakfast. Passengers were feeling refreshed. All who required and wanted consultations had had them, so a nervous excitement bubbled in the air. The women were chatty. Eager. Some would embark on their excursions today. Today! Even if they had come alone, and even after just two nights, the women felt settled and comfortable. They remarked on the strange sensation that they'd been gone much longer. "Was it really just Monday we set sail? It feels like a week since I changed my last diaper."

Solo travelers who wanted to make friends usually did. BECCA made sure of it. By breakfast Wednesday morning, women had latched onto their new friends, their people, and they filled the morning meal hours with bits and pieces of their lives, information and experiences they usually kept to themselves. Here, away, so very far away from their jobs and responsibilities and routines, they opened up over bacon and egg tarts and cereal milk mousses. With old friends or new ones, they felt that what they said here, what they shared here, mattered, that the other women were listening, that they cared. They couldn't remember the last time they felt that way. Already, the cruise seemed like the most glorious idea. Already, it had been good for their souls.

Yes, Wednesday's morning meal seemed to last hours, as though every divulged secret, each revealed detail, in the act of surfacing, created its own timescape. The women shared and shared. Most of them. But a few were careful not to share too much. Some things they couldn't talk about. Not yet, anyway. Not yet.

NICOLE

WEDNESDAY 07:44

Waking up Wednesday morning, Nicole remembered how the women in her knitting circle had talked about cruise toilets. "The flush is something else. Like someone strapped a lawn mower under the toilet bowl." None of the knitters had heard of Canterbury Cruise Line until they asked the host's Alexa at their February gathering. Instead of the responses Nicole had been expecting—judgments, incredulity, awkward silences—the other women had expressed only jealousy and enthusiasm for her upcoming trip. They spent the rest of the meeting barely knitting, comparing notes: what they had done, what they would do, what they would never.

As it turned out, Nicole didn't even need to flush. The toilet did it for her, and when it did, the sound—a minute gurgle—barely registered. If she hadn't been paying attention, the waste removal process would have seemed magical. Sit down to a clean bowl; stand up to a clean bowl. Even in a public bathroom, which she made a point to visit, she found the same quietude, a whisking was all.

When she showed up for breakfast Wednesday morning and found that she was first to the table, she decided to ask her server about it. Not exactly a mealtime subject, but then Cedric appeared with a tiny cinnamon roll, a morning *amuse-bouche* he called it, and she said, "Can I ask you something?" just as he said, "I'm sorry about Monday night."

Then she said, "What happened Monday night?" just as he said, "You can ask me anything."

They smiled then.

"I don't recall anything you need to apologize for . . ." she trailed off, suddenly awkward, wondering what she'd missed.

Cedric looked away. "I left dinner. Early. It was pretty abrupt—and rude. And I'm sorry. It was a tough night. A tough day."

"Is everything okay?" She felt the same alarm she felt when she saw her son's school's number pop up on her phone.

"Yeah, I think so." Cedric took a deep breath. "It will be."

"Soon, I hope," Nicole said. "But listen. There's nothing to be sorry about. We all have tough nights. Heck, it's been a tough year."

"Thank you," Cedric said, finally meeting her eyes. He widened his stance and crossed his arms over his chest. "Now, about that question? Or do I need to sit for this?"

Nicole felt herself blush. She shook her head, then blurted, "What's the deal with the bathrooms?"

"You could throw a party in the one on Deck 9, and I believe women have."

"Sorry, I mean the toilets."

"My understanding is that they are impossible to clog, but if—"

Nicole shook her head, her cheeks growing hotter. "No, no. I mean the sound. I thought the flush was supposed to be louder on a ship. A lot louder."

"Oh, that." Cedric grinned. "Were you expecting a roar?"

"I was, in fact."

"Apparently, the updated septic system has this whisper technology. Cutting-edge waste disposal."

"No kidding."

Around them, the dining room was starting to fill with people and their accompanying sounds: the tinkling of glasses, the rush of coffee into mugs, good mornings and hellos and the flap of napkins unfolding.

"We're cutting-edge everything around here," Cedric said with a wink.

"Is that so?" Nicole replied, canting her head with a sense of absurd enjoyment. It was ridiculous. Shocking, even. One minute she was asking about toilets, and the next she was *flirting*.

Cedric excused himself to check on his other tables, but she was aware of him glancing at her from time to time. There had been a shift, one he seemed to sense, too. Moments ago, he had been her server, a man with a handsome face and sad eyes and answers to her questions. But now, it was like he had imprinted on her, his smile wired to her own, his eyes seeking hers. She was keenly aware of his location in the room, the distance between them. Already she wanted him to return and also to never come back. If another server took over for the duration of the cruise, she would be both relieved and devastated. She lifted the menu to study, though she already knew what she would order: some eggs and a crepe, a little something savory, a little something sweet.

CEDRIC

Nicole's mannerisms, the way she spoke, the way she tucked her hair behind her ears before gathering it up and laying it along her left shoulder: all of it reminded Cedric of Kali. He had thought so the first time he saw her, too, and yesterday's meals had convinced him.

"This is my first cruise," she was saying now as Cedric set down her plate, offering her salt flakes for her eggs. "I'm a little nervous about the surgeries."

"Excursions," Cedric said. The Crewmember's Handbook had a whole section on providing passengers with preferred terminology. Not *surgeries* or *procedures* or *work*: *excursions*. The idea, he had read, was to minimize concerns commonly associated with medicine and surgery, like pain and complications.

"Right." Nicole looked down. "Excursions make me nervous, too."

Cedric took a step closer, placed a hand on her shoulder. "You don't have to worry. Everything is going to go smoothly. Before you know it, you'll be back in here telling me all about your itinerary, looking even more beautiful." He had only intended to reassure her, but she looked so much like Kali, the words tumbled out.

Nicole continued staring at her food, but her mouth curved up. Cedric cleared his throat and headed back to the server station, trying to concoct an excuse to return. Fresh herbs for her eggs, perhaps? But he had plates to bring to other tables, coffee to refresh. By the time he made it back, the rest of Table 32 would be there. He could have stayed to talk for another minute, another two. Instead, he had turned and walked away.

NICOLE

Nicole felt fidgety in Cedric's wake, and she hadn't even had a sip of her coffee. Why a compliment from practically a stranger had this effect on her, while her husband's many affirmations made her cringe, she couldn't say. She only knew that for the second time since she'd left home, she was grateful to be here alone, without Jane, without Semra, unmoored from their companionship with its prescribed ways and means for being in their company. Jane was the flirty one, after all; this was her domain. Nicole reached for her coffee.

She would only manage two small sips before the other women started to show up. They would ask how she slept, how she felt. They would sniff the air and say, "French roast? Smells good." They would look around for Cedric, but he would already be beside them with a tray of steaming mugs, explaining which little carafes held cream and which oat milk.

"I slept well, thank you," Nicole would say as she replayed her conversation with Cedric in her head, felt the pressure of his hand on her shoulder.

For the rest of the meal, she would feel this fracture of attention—trying to participate in the conversations around her, all the while attuned to Cedric's movements, his interactions with other passengers.

Perhaps, though, she laughed too loudly or smiled too broadly or responded to questions too late, distracted by her racing heartbeat, Cedric's compliment once again looping through her mind. *Beautiful. Beautiful. Beautiful.*

ROCCO

The walking paths were scheduled to open at 09:00, but some passengers, of course, showed up at the shared entrance early. So Rocco outlined the three paths to the growing number of passengers gathered and gathering, the group looking more and more like a three-dimensional catalog for a high-end fitness brand. He had the scripts in the Crewmember's Handbook memorized, though some days, depending on what he saw on the faces staring back at him, he trimmed a bit here and there and other days he embellished with a fun detail or two:

"The Mall is wide, the route tiled, with a soundtrack of nineties pop music. Escalators carry walkers up and down between the two levels, each with storefronts, kiosks, and big-city charm. You might make your way to the Forge, a jewelry boutique on Level 2. There, you'll also find a three-tiered fountain, the perfect spot to toss a coin or a bobby pin for luck. Pretzeltown, another favorite, is on Level 1 by the kiosk that sells Canterbury Cruise Line merchandise. You can stock up on waxing wands, pocket mirrors, reusable grocery bags, and mugs. No space in your luggage? No problem. Anything you buy, we can ship. You heard that right—we're a shipping ship.

"The Park path is less open, secluded even. You can hear birds calling in the high foliage, the crunch of leaves underfoot. You'll want to breathe in the woodsy scent. Among the many trunks, you'll see ferns and shrubs, a dense array of greens and golds. Leaves rustle in the breeze, and Spanish moss hangs from sprawling branches.

"You might think Park, with its gurgling stream, dirt trails, and wild-flower walls, is the most peaceful place to walk, but no. That's Cemetery. You can explore headstones, statuary, and monuments. Here, the markers commemorate the women who have been reborn on the ship, thanks to the Captain. There's Molly Rae Hightower, passenger on the twenty-first cruise, who asked Dr. Heston to return her to her thirties. Her inscription reads, *Bloom long, bloom strong / Time like sun and rain / On petals ever fresh.* Be on the lookout, too, for Sammy Jane Haversham, Dr. Heston's first completely custom facial transformation. Her marker reads, *In the mirror / Unmasked and unafraid / At last know thy self.* Jennaca Claudette Jones . . . now her itinerary was remarkable, avant-garde even for us. See if you can guess it from her inscription. That's a fun little game."

The passengers thanked Rocco and retied the laces of their Brooks, their HOKAs, their Allbirds. Once the gates opened, they started off in clusters of twos and threes. At first, Rocco suspected, they'd look around, eyes wide and conversations minimal, but soon enough, they'd start talking, exchanging personal histories, doling out anecdotes one after another. They'd tread thoughtfully on the spongy, clover-covered turf of the Park, the glossy ceramic tile of the Mall, the crunchy gravel of the Cemetery. Before they knew it, lunch service would start in the main dining room, or it would be time for another round of ballroom dancing lessons in the Starboard Parlor on Deck 10.

Rocco still remembered the first few months of cruises, when the ship's decks and public spaces resembled those of ocean liners boarded by the vacationer, the family, the retiree: several saltwater pools, no canopies, towel bins that resembled dumpsters, a putt-putt course, bocce court, stage, and one simple walking path—a three-lane track in a half-mile loop. But back then, few passengers, if any, swam in the saltwater. No one played putt-putt. Women chipped their newly reinforced Quick-Grow Keratin nails playing bocce. They grumbled about the track. "You have to wake up at five to walk in peace," a passenger huffed. "After that, it's a constant stampede. Should have packed wrist guards or signed up for the Strong Bones excursion!"

So a few months later, the boat sat in the harbor for an entire week while Decks 9 through 12 were redesigned. A steel scaffold around the boat was draped with thick black sheets. Space Genie trucks moved in and out of the harbor at odd hours, never during daylight. Flatbeds carried wide wooden crates that a rented crane hoisted up, up, up, over the scaffold, and onto the ship. None of the renovations were seen nor heard by harbor crews or passengers on other cruise ships. At the end of the week, the scaffold and black fabric were gone, and from the dock the boat looked the same. But it wasn't.

The renovation necessitated certain changes to the services and comforts, so Rocco and the other deckmen returned to the boat for two days of intensive training before the next cruise embarked. When they welcomed women aboard, immediately they witnessed the exceedingly positive, if awestruck, reactions of the passengers to the changes. As women dipped their toes in the Epsom salt ponds on Deck 9, deckmen distributed fuzzy towels that wicked away moisture and prevented excess UV light from seeping into skin tissue. From an array of stylish kiosks, they served cold brews in tall tumblers that kept drinks suitably chilled. And they directed and sometimes escorted passengers to the entrance to the three new walking paths: Mall, Park, and Cemetery.

LYLA

Bianca stepped up to the railing, breathless and hurried. "I'm not late, am I? We said nine, right?"

"We did," Lyla said. "You're fine. I came early. I just like it up here. The breeze. The waves." She was looking out into the distance, one hand shielding her eyes from the rising sun and the glare coming off the water.

"Are you walking in those?" Bianca asked, nodding toward Lyla's HOKAs, a pair designed for stability and comfort, which Lyla required of her footwear to make it through a twelve-hour shift.

"Of course. Most comfortable pair of shoes I own." Lyla looked down at her shoes, which admittedly looked like boats, the white now whitish gray, the rubber outsole now generously scuffed. She told herself she couldn't afford new ones—not with two imaginary children in spring soccer, not with shin guards and cleats to buy. Whenever possible, Lyla sought opportunities for her imaginary family to interact with objects and impinge on situations in the real world, if only to justify a pair of worn shoes—though only and always to herself. Now that she was here, so far from her childless life with Timothy, the explanation tumbled out: "The kids need shoes more than I do." Then she couldn't stop. "The two older ones are starting soccer this spring, and they both need cleats, shin guards, balls, and jerseys." The words felt delectable on her tongue.

She marveled at how they had sounded. The best part was she couldn't return them like a box of unneeded diapers. There was no going back now. Here, on the cruise, she had three children, and later this week, it would appear as though she had one more on the way.

"I think I had a pair of clunkers like that when I was in middle school." Bianca bent down to double knot the laces of her Nikes.

"These," Lyla said, wrinkling her nose, "are like walking on air."

"I'll take your word for it." Bianca smiled. "Maybe Mall this morning?"

"Perfect," said Lyla. "I can look for souvenirs for my littles."

DR. HESTON

The Mall was Dr. Heston's favorite path, and the one passengers spent the least amount of time in. He liked to walk it when it wasn't too crowded, like now. BECCA reported just six women in the Mall. In his office, he traded his scrubs top for a deckman button-down before stepping onto the escalator. On the way down, he pulled on a Canterbury Cruise Line ballcap, the bill tight and low over his eyes.

Dr. Heston had designed this walking path himself to capture the pomp and pleasure of the American Mall circa 1998. Its easy-to-navigate two-story layout, in the heart of Decks 10 and 11, boasted iconic features—the cinnamon-sugar-pretzel station, the calendar booth, a department store's perfume counter—without ascribing affiliation to any particular store, chain, or brand. So no Bath & Body Works *per se*, though a store sold lotions, candles, and soaps. And everything was on sale, to reduce anxiety about capitalistic overindulgence. Though the Mall was in some ways forward-looking—purchases easily made by tapping one's cabin card to smarttags on the items themselves—here, the past returned in pleasing ways. According to BECCA's passenger data, the Mall elicited keen feelings of nostalgia, which in turn boosted happiness and alleviated stress one sniff, one purchase, one doughy bite of pretzel at a time.

Dr. Heston had insisted on this path despite the high cost of construction and inventory and the hassle of restocking. Before they started the cruise line together, Rebecca had had a strange fascination with the mall down the street from where they lived. She would pop over on her way home from work, and sometimes in the evening, instead of settling down on the couch to watch a show with him, she'd slip out the door with a wave. *I'm just going to look*, she'd say. *I'll be right back. Need anything?* When the first stores started to close, Rebecca had been distraught. *Soon they'll all be gone, and we'll have to get everything at Target or online.*

Subscribe-and-save underwear isn't the worst idea, he had said, trying to lighten the mood.

Don't, she told him.

The Captain couldn't stop malls from closing, and he couldn't bring back his wife, but he could resurrect a mall in Rebecca's honor. He could invent stores that carried her favorite things: wool socks from Ireland, tea towels with bold screen-printed graphics, succulent planters in suggestive shapes, bangles and bracelets of every size, style, and material. Then he could keep the storefronts lit, the shelves stocked, and the escalator carrying passengers from Level 1 to Level 2 and then back down.

Off the escalator, he did a loop. He sniffed scented candles with names like garden party, rainstorm, and peach grove. At the sunglasses bar, he tried on a few of the latest styles: aviators with mirror lenses, thick wayfarer frames with midnight-blue lenses, and light-weight purple frames with matching purple lenses. Then he picked up a pretzel, which he chewed slowly on his turn around Level 1 and back up. The pretzel's thick salt grains stung his lips and dissolved on his tongue. Today's cases were routine, nothing fancy or new, but he had a big week ahead of him, and he needed his mind clear and focused. A pig-liver balloon sat in his lab, its cells curing in the cool, sterile air. Two full arrays of 3D-printed facial implants were laid out on nearby trays, wrapped and stacked, ready for installation. Pretzel gone, he sucked a bit of oil off the tips of his fingers as he cleared the top step of the escalator. He balled up the wax paper and shot it into a garbage can designed to look like a giant red-and-white-striped fountain drink cup, complete with plastic straw. Slipping through a door that led to the crew-only gangways and quarters, he pulled off his ballcap and made his way down to Hydrangea Station.

ROCCO

WEDNESDAY 09:14

"Tell me, Dr. Rocco, who would you prefer to sleep with: a face or a body?" Larry asked. He closed the cabinet doors and stood up. The two deck-men were refreshing towel stations before Rainforest Zumba. "Or one of the trolls before she has her spine straightened?"

Rocco just shook his head and kept folding towels. To Larry, Rocco knew, there were three types of passengers: those here for facial proce-dures, those here for bodywork, and those, like the ones he referred to as trolls, who were here for the works. Each week, it seemed, Larry's disdain for the women grew. He was complaining more, scheming more, making more snide comments behind their backs, however hunched.

"If you were as charming as me, you wouldn't have to choose," Larry quipped.

"Ha!" Rocco barked before he could stop himself. But he knew that was true. Larry was the smoothest deckman on the ship. His recommen-dation ranking was so high, Rocco sensed BECCA tolerated more of his shenanigans, his sly whispers, his rude remarks veiled behind a strange compliment or offer: "My, how the fluffiness of your towel suits your waistline"; "I shouldn't, I *really* shouldn't, but can I bring you another croissant?" Women loved him.

Rocco stood up and activated the towel-station tablet. "Did you enter the counts from the leeward side into the system?"

"Who pissed in your coffee? I'm only having fun. Something you could try, you know."

"Who's to say I'm not having fun?"

Larry raised his eyebrows. "Right. I forgot." He took the tablet from Rocco. "You're a math guy."

Nodding, Rocco said, "Counting is my *jam*."

Larry scoffed, "Do you even know what fun is?" He punched numbers on the screen, entered his four-digit crew code, and swiped to close.

"I had this one proof in grad school," Rocco said with a smile. He picked up the lotion refill jug and handed it to Larry. "Now that was a good time."

"What is this shit? Honeysuckle?" asked Larry, wrinkling his nose.

"Almond Sunrise. Don't you read the memos?"

But of course Larry didn't. That had been one reason Rocco listed in his petition for a new partner. One of many. He needed to get away from the man. They had been working together since BECCA had assigned Larry to his team six months ago. Early on, Larry had entertained him with his observations, but back then Rocco wasn't really listening; he was still trying to come to terms with his life: where he had been and the choices that led him here, to *PILGRIM*, so far from the future he had envisioned. Now that he was listening, was forced to listen (thanks to their enduring partnership), he couldn't stand the man. Larry seemed like the frat-boy sort before the Greek houses rebranded themselves as clean-living communities a few years back. The sort who would strap a backpack on a fellow brother so the kid could keep drinking without drowning in his own vomit.

Last night, Rocco finally heard back about his petition: BECCA granted his request. He'd have a new partner for the next cruise.

BIANCA

WEDNESDAY 09:18

The brightness and bustle of the Mall walking path reminded Bianca of Harbour Town with its waterfront boutiques and eateries stretching from the lighthouse and back along the yacht basin. A deckman told her yesterday that Mall was the least crowded walking path, and this surprised her. Cemetery struck her as morbid, though it supposedly celebrated those reborn on the ship. Still, she didn't see the appeal. Park seemed boring despite rumors of little treasures hidden in bark, sudden downpours like wet symphonies in the leaves, and branching paths that might, just might, lead to a mineral hot spring said to reduce the appearance of wrinkles, cellulite, and varicose veins. Besides, the quiet—any quiet, really—opened up space for a series of what-ifs she'd prefer to keep at bay: *What if this Hail Mary didn't work? What if her tennis career was over? What if all the years away were for nothing? What if she wasn't as good as she wanted to be, as she thought she could be? What if her family didn't want her back? What if she was fine with that?* Walking the Mall with Lyla, she hoped, would curb the questions. Maybe coffee, conversation, and sensory overload would drown out her doubts.

"I used to drink a lot of coffee," Lyla was saying. "It fueled me through nursing school and night shifts early on. It's been a while, though. Years. Only decaf tea now."

"No coffee? I couldn't. Not for a single day. Mornings of big matches, I need it to calm my nerves. Drives my coaches crazy."

"It's the bitterness. Even with loads of creamer and sugar, I can't get past it." They rode the escalator down to Level 1.

"My first year living on Hilton Head, I started going to this one place every day after my morning workout. Just part of the routine. Owners are real sweet. Older couple. Left the corporate world decades ago. Always asking me about my backhand, what tournaments are coming up. You can tell they like the slower pace of the island but they miss some of the action."

"So you play tennis and live at the beach? That must be something."

"It sounds more glamorous than it is." The last time she had gone to the beach was the day she lost to Bruce and booked the cruise. But before that, it had been months.

"My kids love the beach. I'm sure they'd want to go every day if we lived on the coast."

"Mine, too. Little beach babies when they were younger." Bianca didn't say anything about now, and she hoped Lyla wouldn't ask. She didn't know Lyla well enough to reveal what she had given up for her shot at a career. And the woman had three kids! She wasn't sure how sympathetic Lyla would be. For a time, the two women quietly took in the full storefronts, the bright kiosks, the mesmerizing glow and glimmer of the displays.

"Is it hard to play and raise kids? Do you travel for tournaments? Though they probably love that, going with their mom to different places. I bet they love watching you play."

Bianca thought, *Not yet*. That life—raising kids and pursuing her tennis career at the same time—still eluded her, but it's what she wanted, the unicorn she had chased here even: to have Vivian and Rowan with Anthony in the stands at her first US Open. "The girls stay with their father when I travel," she explained, which was a true answer, if not thorough. They walked past a store with open sample jars lined up on a stand. They could smell the soft pretzels ahead. "One day," she added, "I'd like that very much." Bianca didn't share her next thought: *I'm not good enough yet, and I might never be.*

"That must be tough for you."

Bianca didn't know what to say. Taking a long sip of her drink, she settled on "It is." Because it was. Because she could have been wrong about everything. Having the girls. Leaving the girls. Thinking she could make it. Thinking she needed just a little more time to make it. She slurped at the coffee that remained at the bottom of the glass.

ANNALIE

WEDNESDAY 10:02

At dinner last night, Annalie had asked Nicole if she wanted to meet up in the morning. Lyla and Bianca had made plans to walk the Mall, but Nicole admitted that malls made her sad, and Annalie agreed. The last time she had walked through a mall had been with Aimee—Lenox Mall in Atlanta. It was that way with a lot of things, even still, a year after her sister had died. The last time she flew on an airplane had been with Aimee. The last time she'd been to a restaurant was with Aimee. Instead, Annalie had suggested she and Nicole find a set of comfy deck chairs and sit in the sun.

Her therapist had given her a goal a few months back to make one plan each day. That simple directive, a goal a day, had been a "game-changer," she announced two weeks later, and her therapist had beamed back at her. She couldn't believe how accomplishing a single task every day moved time along.

Now she could map out a whole week at a time. Monday, she had planned to board a cruise ship. Yesterday, she planned for her consultation. Today she planned to sit and relax with Nicole. Tomorrow she would play bingo with all the ladies (Cedric highly recommended it). On Friday, she was scheduled for her last on-board therapy session, and her itinerary would begin on Saturday. Sunday, she would be sedated, recovering. A day she didn't have to worry about.

And there, just like that, another week gone.

On Deck 12, she spotted Nicole. The woman had her glossy black hair tied in a knot, and she was wearing a white maxi dress with a bandeau top, the brightness radiant against her skin. She was knitting something red as Annalie approached.

"Hey," Nicole said over her knitting needles, "you're the yin to my yang." She nodded at Annalie's dress, which was the same style as Nicole's but in black. "We could be twins."

Annalie cringed at the word. *What she was. What she wasn't. What she could no longer be.* She was tempted to turn around and head back to her room. A few months ago, she would have. Now, she imagined her feet rooted to the ground. She let her canvas tote slide off her shoulder and sat next to Nicole, who didn't know any better.

A deckman appeared, holding out a towel. "For you, dear," he said. Annalie took the towel, unmistakably almond-scented. "I'll be right back with a couple refreshing drinks."

"Thank you, Rocco," Nicole said sweetly. "Rocco is the greatest," she told Annalie.

"I try," the deckman said with a shy grin as he turned away.

Annalie sat back, using the towel as a pillow. "How nice is this." She found the nutty aroma soothing. She breathed deeply. When she returned home, she would have to remember to look for almond-scented products. A candle, perhaps. Then she smiled. Her therapist would be thrilled to hear she had planned for something weeks away.

"What's so funny?" Nicole asked, winding yarn around one of the purple needles she held, then, without waiting for an answer, "Do you have any sunblock on you? I'm terrible about wearing it. I never burn, but I know I should wear it."

"Sorry," Annalie said. "I can run down to my room and grab you some?"

As she rose, however, Rocco returned and set down a tray with two tall glasses of something pink and frothy and two little bottles of sunblock. "Ladies," he said as he retreated. "Enjoy."

"Wow," Nicole said.

"Would you prefer unscented or coconut soy sun crème?" Annalie asked, reading the labels.

"Coconut," Nicole said. She rested her needles in her lap as Annalie passed the bottle.

Nicole untwisted the cap. "My one friend, Jane, buys stuff like this all the time to try." She brought the crème to her face and inhaled. A tiny dollop of white clung to the tip of her nose. When Annalie giggled and gestured to her own nose, Nicole opened a little mirrored compact and grinned, watching her reflection as she carefully smoothed the crème over her features.

Annalie couldn't remember the last time she had so much as glanced at her reflection. Before Aimee—an early-morning runner—had been hit by a car speeding along a city street, mirrors were just mirrors. The day after the funeral, Annalie had sat in front of the full-length mirror in her bedroom for hours. She had fallen asleep there eventually, curled on her side in a tight roll, staring into her own face like it was Aimee's. Like they were kids again and huddled together in one of their beds, almost forehead to forehead, dreaming the same dreams. Like they had all the time in the world to make them come true. After waking up alone and stiff, Aimee barely gone, she'd avoided mirrors as much as possible. Here on the boat, she kept her bathroom mirror on screen mode. "What are you knitting?" she asked, taking the bottle back from Nicole and rubbing some of the creamy white lotion along her arms.

Nicole tugged more yarn out of her bag. "Sweater," she said. "For Max. My son. His skin's like mine, his hair, too. He's going to be a little stud in this red."

Annalie watched for several loops. She liked the tapping sound the needles made when they came together. "Do you have any other kids?"

"Just Max. I made it through one birth, and that was enough for me. But he's plenty. Love him to pieces."

Again Annalie thought about Aimee, how she felt when her sister didn't come home after that last run, would never come home: shattered, all shards and sharp edges. And now here she was. She had come so far.

She picked up a pink drink, took a sip, and said, "This is life." She had meant to say this is *the* life, but the drink was cold on her tongue, and she skipped a word.

"And our excursions haven't even started yet!"

Annalie relaxed as Nicole's hands moved, listening to the steady *click, click, click*. The air smelled like almonds. She put the straw back in her mouth and closed her eyes. She thought about asking Nicole what her plans were for the cruise. And she would after another sip.

NICOLE

After her morning in the sun, Nicole showered and spent entirely too long trying on different outfits before heading to lunch. Lyla was already at Table 32 when she arrived, and it looked like it would be just the two of them today. Even Cedric, it seemed, was elsewhere. Nicole listened while Lyla talked, surveying the room again, to be sure. In between bites, her eyes moved from table to table, serving station to serving station.

"Well?" Lyla asked at one point, halfway through her salad.

Nicole finally looked at the other woman. "Well what?"

"Who are you looking for?"

Nicole dropped her eyes to her black bean habañero bisque. The truth was banal, ridiculous—that she was looking for their server; oh, and, by the way, he had called her beautiful at breakfast and now she couldn't stop thinking about him. Lyla didn't seem like the sort of woman to entertain flights of fancy. As a working mom with three kids—*three!*—she probably didn't have time to daydream. She might even look down on women who did.

"Just distracted by a woman over there," Nicole lied. "She looks like the daughter of someone in my knitting circle."

"Is it her?"

"I don't think so? At least, her mom didn't say anything about it." Nicole dipped her spoon into her bowl.

Lyla shrugged. "Maybe she didn't tell her mom?"

"How could she not?" Nicole asked.

"Everyone has their secrets." Lyla forked more arugula into her mouth.

Thinking about all the secrets she had—from her best friends and from her husband—Nicole nearly choked on her soup. Primarily that even though she was a failing Baden+Lakes operator, she couldn't stop ordering more shipments. For the sake of appearances, boxes had to regularly arrive on her doorstep, only to be later stacked in her craft room beneath a fabric tarp. Justin had been so encouraging, so happy for her to have something to do when Max started kindergarten. Then so proud it killed her. Semra and Jane, too. They gushed about her at book club and celebrated her promotion from consultant to operator at one of their Wine Wednesdays. But the truth was her friends were her only clients. And if they knew about her debt, how large it had grown again, even after she'd liquidated Max's college fund. . . . If she could go back to the night when Semra hosted that first B+L party, she would stay in her oversized sweats and fall asleep next to Max after all his bedtime requests for more water, a snack, one more hug, another story, another sip of water, a hand to hold—his warm breath in her face, her right arm tucked under his body and tingling from elbow to fingertips. In that alternate reality, she never would have signed on to sell the products. She might not even be here. Or if she were, she wouldn't feel the desperate dread that bubbled around her. She'd be laughy, breezy, and honest.

"My mom booked my cruise," Lyla said.

Nicole set down her spoon and pushed her bowl away. "No kidding. And she didn't want to tag along?"

"She wasn't really invited," Lyla said. "It was kind of a long-overdue birthday present."

Nicole nodded. "Christmas present from my husband. Justin." Speaking his name only made her feel guiltier, reminded her of the two credit cards she'd used his name to get, cards he didn't—and couldn't—know about.

Salad finished, Lyla drew her pointer finger along the edge of her plate and stuck her finger, now coated with dressing, in her mouth.

"It's that good?" Nicole asked.

Lyla laughed. "I could eat it with a spoon!"

And when a server, who wasn't Cedric, appeared with a small cup of it, that's exactly what she did.

LARRY

Larry was in a good mood, despite Rocco annoying him. He was even whistling a bit as he brought a passenger he laughingly thought of as *Girtha* her drink, a sour cherry martini. "Time to pucker up," he told her as he set the glass down on the table beside the woman's sun couch.

"Yes, indeed. Come to Mama." Girtha reached for her drink but kept her eyes on Larry. It was a look he was used to, here and elsewhere. *Stay with me. Let me take care of you.* He was still a teenager when he'd discovered them—the women used to throwing money at what they wanted: the bodies they'd been denied, the royal treatment they thought themselves entitled to, the men their aging husbands weren't.

Larry was fine with being one of those men. Even as a kid, pedaling a Schwinn Roadster from Goodwill down the center of town, he was bound to get hollered at by the older ladies who sat on their benches with their newspapers, dogs curled at their feet. "Look at that hair, flying in the breeze," they'd say. "That's blood-boilin' hair there. Just you wait, little Larry John Jeffreys."

Now, Larry winked. "Try to keep me away." He headed back to the counter where Rocco was pouring a green smoothie into a tall glass.

"Is this one for her?" Larry asked, nodding to a woman ahead and to the right. "Spaghetti Hair?"

"It's for *Julie*," Rocco said, bending over the minifridge. "The sweet young woman in the checkered one-piece at your ten o'clock."

Larry turned to look. "Right. Like I said. Spaghetti Hair."

"Her drink—" Rocco stood and reached for the blender. "—is melting."

"Finish that frosted mocha for Man Hands over there, and I can take both at once."

Rocco stiffened. "Her *name* is Samantha."

Larry rolled his eyes. "You really need to lighten up, man."

"You really need to be more respectful."

"Thanks, Dad. I'll get right on that."

"We're all just toys to you, aren't we? The women especially," Rocco said as he poured equal parts ice and mocha mix into the blender.

"You have no idea," Larry said, a wide grin spreading across his face.

Before he came on the cruise, Larry had worked poolside at the Trophy Club Country Club in Dallas. He met Claudia his first week outside. The heat was nearly unbearable, even with the aquafans stirring a breeze and sending a fine cool mist into the air. But Claudia had a cabana and didn't seem to mind. He brought her a rosé and watched her swim laps, her body long and sleek and nearly naked in a bikini consisting entirely of straps. "How old do you think I am?" she had asked when he refilled her wine.

"Thirty-five," he had said at once. Then he offered to reapply her sunscreen. By the following weekend, her kids had returned to their northeastern college campuses for the new fall semester, her husband was abroad for work, and they were sleeping together.

Over the next two months, he lifted eleven pieces of jewelry and pocketed over a thousand dollars in cash. He hadn't planned to steal from Claudia in the beginning. At first, their affair was its own adventure. He would rip away her clothes and throw her down on her bed, where they could roll this way and that and never fall off. She was like taffy in his hands, able to be tossed and turned, supple and yielding. In the middle of the night, they'd make their way to the kitchen for food but wind up tangled together against the wide windows, then sprawled and sweating on the cool, hard tile. But too soon it became, like everything else, a drain, his energy and interest trickling away.

One morning while Claudia was putting on makeup at the vanity in her closet—a room of its own, with square footage comparable to his entire apartment—he took a bracelet pooled in the tray on her dresser, one of several there, glittery and delicate. And so a new adventure began.

Each time he walked out with a prize—extra cash clipped into his billfold, pearl earrings in his pocket—he felt euphoric for hours afterward, the breathless rush swallowing him whole. Claudia would ask him to bring her a robe after sex, to make and bring her coffee so they could sit on the veranda the mornings he didn't have to work. She begged him to be her sweet boy and fetch a towel when she climbed into the shower, and to then join her there. On these errands and when she lay sleeping at night, with drool dangling from the corner of her mouth like a string he might pull, he learned his way around the house, her belongings.

The letter from Canterbury Cruise Line arrived while she was downstairs in her cryotherapy tank, and he opened it. He had enough money now to leave Texas, and he thought *why not?* Why not pack a bag (with clothes from her husband's closet), hop a flight, and start over? He was tired of taking her things. Maybe this cruise line was hiring. There, he'd find another Claudia, a dozen more. No rent. Hardly any expenses. Los Angeles to explore on his days off. He booked a comm-car to the airport and called the club and his landlord. He made up a story about a sick family member out West. An emergency. He was mighty sorry, but his sudden departure couldn't be helped, thank you kindly for understanding.

And meanwhile he imagined Claudia emerging from the freezing chamber and calling his name. Then she would wander around her big house in her black robe, her voice echoing across the marble, floating across the bur oaks out past the second-floor veranda. She'd look for him at the club that afternoon and the next day. By the following week, she might even wonder if the affair had happened at all or if she had dreamed the pool boy into her bed during the long lonesome weeks with her children gone, her husband away.

"Why do you hate them so much?" Now Rocco capped the blender and turned it on high, which caused it to emit only a gentle purr while instantly pulverizing its contents.

"Hate women?" Larry frowned. "I love women," he said. "Love to tease them, have fun with them. It's not a big deal." The blender stopped, and Rocco poured the drink into the frosted mug Larry had pulled from the ice drawer. "We can't all be the serious, brooding, math-teacher type."

Rocco only sighed.

Larry then proceeded to pass out the drinks, but to the opposite women. He said, "No, you don't want what you *thought* you wanted. I'll show you what you want."

"Oh, will you?" Julie said, accepting the frosted mocha. "Yeah, I guess this is what I wanted."

"Please do," Samantha said, taking the green smoothie chock full of antioxidants. "You can show me anything."

BIANCA

"I just want to move forward with my career. Just make the tour. Just win. I want to stop using the word *just* all the time. To explain just about everything."

Bianca was in Wellness Room 3. She let out a heavy sigh and crumpled into the room's club chair, hugging her knees to her chest. She was a bit buzzed from dinner. In other words, ready to talk.

The voice in the room asked, "What does moving forward look like to you?" One of BECCA's auxiliary systems, THERapp, conducted all therapy sessions on the ship, as many as a half dozen at a time. From what Bianca had learned clicking around on her bathroom's mirror screen that morning, AI had been running therapy programs since one called ELIZA in the 1960s. Three-quarters of a century later, AI systems designed for dialogic sessions were indistinguishable from human therapists, except that they offered greater attention and focus during appointments, as well as the ability to customize an interaction in terms of language, tone, and conversational style to best suit the participant's own speech mannerisms and vocabulary. Bianca had to admit she instantly felt comfortable talking in this space, the voice warm, inviting, and concerned, like a friend, a grandmother, and her sports psychologist rolled into one.

"Moving forward looks like a strong showing in Miami. Then one at the Open later this summer."

"Anything else?"

"At some point, moving home. I could train during the day and pick up the girls from school. We could travel as a family to different cities for my matches. That would be nice."

"But tennis comes first?"

"Well. Yes." Bianca paused, then said quietly, "I'm running out of time."

"How so?"

"Soon I'll be too old to compete. Soon the girls will be grown and gone. But there's still time now. Just barely." Bianca could feel her heart racing.

"And if it runs out?"

"I fail." Standing, Bianca started to pace the small room. "All these years away and nothing to show." She shook her head. "That can't happen."

"Why not?"

"Tennis is the only thing I'm good at," she explained, "and it scares me that I'm just not good enough." Back and forth across the room she moved, eyes trained on her feet.

"What if you couldn't play anymore starting today? What would you do?"

Bianca stopped moving. "What do you mean?"

"If you decided to be done starting today."

"Why would I do that?" Bianca frowned, "I've invested so much." She plopped back down in the chair and crossed her arms. She refused to entertain this line of inquiry.

"Let's continue this conversation when we meet on Friday."

Bianca shook her head. She didn't want to continue this conversation. She didn't want to have it at all. "I'm not a quitter. That's why I'm here. I refuse to give up."

"Of course. Yes, of course. But you need to relax. Dr. Heston will take care of your body, and you've got the heart and soul. Now you need to work on your headspace."

"My headspace—" Bianca threw up her hands. "—is more a mess than ever."

"You might be surprised by how clear-headed you can feel after a game or two of bingo."

"Bingo?"

"Thursday's high-tea round is exquisite, I'm told."

Bianca pursed her lips. "Our server recommended it. I was planning to go with the other women at my table."

"It has a four-point-nine rating from former passengers. Over a hundred glowing reviews. I think it will be good for you to play a game that *isn't* tennis and have some fun."

LYLA

Lyla walked through the Park by herself after dinner. She liked her dining companions, but she also liked time to herself. The sky remained
bright despite the late hour, and she passed a few other solitary walkers
and walking pairs. She rounded a corner near a gurgling stream, and a
bird let out a cry. The sound reminded Lyla of when she almost walked
off the ward with a baby. Rosemary's cries had had that same wild, frantic pitch. A heartbreaking sound.

That night five years ago, Lyla had reached down to turn off the
motion-detecting sensor in the crib before lifting Rosemary into her
arms. The newborn's eyes were pinched closed, her mouth a gaping pit
of noise. The protocol was to soothe if possible and re-swaddle; if the
baby was still upset, she was to bring her to her mother to be nursed.

Lyla had held Rosemary to her shoulder and started to sway. She
patted the infant's back and cooed, "Hey, little one. What's the matter?
There, there. It'll be okay."

But still the baby had squalled. "You must be hungry," she told Rosemary, placing her back in her blanket and wrapping the soft cotton
around her squirming body. "Let's get you to your momma."

Before leaving the nursery, Lyla had scanned the baby out and entered the mother's room as the destination. The time was 2:14. Lyla was

two hours into a second shift. The ward was perpetually understaffed, and with a particularly high volume of births tonight, the shift manager had asked Lyla to stay until 4:00.

She had steered the bassinet down the hallway. For a moment, Rosemary lay still, perplexed by the sensation of movement. But even before they reached the mother's room, the tempest was back, the baby's arms and legs flapping as she hollered.

"Knock, knock." Lyla had pushed open the mother's door and rolled Rosemary up to the bed. "Someone is quite hungry," Lyla said.

The woman in the bed turned over but didn't wake up. Lyla pushed a button on the arm of the bed to turn up the lights in the room. "Rosie is here to see you," she said, louder this time. How the woman was able to sleep through her baby's incessant cries was beyond Lyla. "She's ready to nurse," she said, louder still. The woman didn't move. Now Lyla reached over and pushed the button to raise the top half of the bed to a sitting position.

"What is it?" the woman growled. "I was sleeping." She glared at Lyla, but already her eyes were closing again.

"I have your baby," Lyla said. "She's hungry and upset."

This wasn't the first time on her watch that a mother had struggled to wake up to nurse a newborn, but tonight Lyla was tired and her patience for this sort of behavior minimal. Before having a baby, women should understand and be prepared for what they'll lose. Sleep, for instance.

"I already told that other nurse. I have no interest in breastfeeding. I've seen what it can do. Can't you just give her a bottle?"

And then Lyla understood: in a different decade, this woman would have had an abortion, not a baby, but that hardly mattered in light of the vociferous reality in the bassinet. Still, Lyla's tone softened a degree. "Are you sure you don't want to give it a try? They say mothers can be soothed by it too." Rosemary hadn't let up. In fact, her riot had gained a rhythmic quality.

"Fine." With that, the woman had reached to the row of buttons herself, lowering the lights and reclining the bed once more. "Bring her back in the morning. When she's not crying. I'll try then." She pulled the blanket back up and rolled over.

At the beginning of a shift, Lyla may have tried to coax the mother again. The baby was hungry *now*. Lyla was fourteen hours' deep, however. She was tired, and Rosemary had already been crying for a solid thirteen minutes. The poor thing. Lyla couldn't imagine how a mother, however she came to be a mother, could ignore her own child. After wanting one herself for so long, after a handful of miscarriages, Lyla would give anything to have a baby wake her up at night. She would happily nurse any hour, at all hours. She'd do whatever it took to care for a child that was hers.

Her baby. Two impossible words, elusive words, but perhaps after two in the morning, after fourteen hours of labors and births, after thirteen minutes of squalling, perhaps they needn't be. Perhaps she could have a moment to pretend *this* baby was *hers*. That wouldn't be the worst thing. Perhaps especially not for Rosemary.

"All right, darling. How about that bottle?"

She'd pushed Rosemary back out the door, back to the nursery, but instead of scanning her back in, Lyla took two premixed bottles from the warmer and told the nurse now sitting at the desk that she was taking Rosie back out.

Bethany had been logging patient reports. "By the way, that mom in room 74 is at an 8, and I think the one in 78 is heading for a section. Dr. Smithfield is in there now with Mollie."

"Busy night," Lyla had said and walked out.

Since all the rooms on the floor were occupied, Lyla had wheeled Rosemary around to the refreshment station. At this hour, the chances of anyone walking in for a grape juice carton were slim. She pulled the baby up and out of the bassinet. "Hey, hey," she whispered. "It's okay." She rocked Rosie in her arms while shaking up the first bottle. "Momma's here," she said, the words chalky and coarse on her tongue. Again she tried: "Momma's here." She smiled at the baby in her arms as she slipped the bottle's nipple into her small mouth. The wailing stopped, and in the quiet that ensued, Lyla had let the dream consume her. She forgot Rosemary wasn't hers. She forgot she was at work. She forgot that leaving the delivery ward with an infant was strictly prohibited unless the proper authorizations had been made and release granted. She forgot about the chip implanted in Rosemary's patient identification band that would alert hospital security and the nurse sitting at the desk in the nursery. She forgot about her unexplained infertility and how painful it was to want something you couldn't have. She forgot the numbing ache she felt in her stomach, how hollow she had become. And she never, not for a second, considered what it might look like to the two security guards and Bethany when they met her at the elevator that let out at the parking garage, Rosemary bundled in her arms, peacefully sleeping at last.

"I'm so sorry," she had said as the other nurse snatched Rosie from her. "Please. I didn't mean. I wasn't. I would *never.*"

She knew, of course she knew, that she couldn't begin to explain what had led her to the elevator with Rosemary tucked into the crook of her elbow. She couldn't say that her imagination had bested her fatigued mind, convincing her that it was time to take her baby home—home to the crib that had stood vacant for the past four years in the nursery she had painted two weeks after her first positive pregnancy test and two weeks before her first miscarriage.

Instead, she had said she had been walking Rosemary to soothe her back to sleep at the mother's request, and being as tired as she was, she hadn't realized she was leaving the ward when she used her fob to unlock the double doors. Her body was on autopilot, she pleaded. She wanted only to comfort Rosie. That was all. She meant no harm. This would never happen again.

A hospital administrator had investigated for five days, during which time Lyla was placed on administrative leave. She told her husband she needed a break, that she was taking a few vacation days for self-care. She didn't want Timothy to know what had happened. Already he was at his wit's end with their timed, missionary-only intercourse and the vitamins and diet Lyla had him on to maximize the durability and mobility of his sperm. Pineapple at every meal!

Lyla had cried with relief when the administrator informed her she would not be fired. But as she walked out of the office, her relief started to lift, like a narcotic fading. Her steps grew heavy. Even though it had been mostly an accident, she remembered how it had felt to hold a baby and think it was hers. Her empty arms now ached. "It was only pretend," she told herself. "Just make believe," she said. "A story."

THE PILGRIM DAILY

Where do you want to go today?

WALKING PATHS. HOURS: 09:00–24:00

Park . . . . open (chance of rain showers)
Mall . . . . open
Cemetery . . . . open

SPA. HOURS: 09:00–19:00

DAILY SPECIALS

JointEase and Full Body Stretch
Energy Alignment
Glycolic Resurfacing Facial

Book now on your room screen or talk to your room steward to schedule a visit.

DINING. SEE HOURS BELOW.

Breakfast 06:00–09:00
Lunch 11:30–15:00
Dinner 19:00

ON BOARD ACTIVITIES. HOURS: 05:30–22:00

Coffee & Carpe Diem, Deck 10, Citrus Canopy. 05:30
Sunrise Yoga, Deck 12 . . . . 07:00
Debut Novels to Devour, Deck 8, Library. 08:00
Lady Boss Life Coaching, Deck 10, Starboard Parlor. 09:00
Influence Anything, Deck 10, Mint Canopy. 14:00
Wine Tasting, Deck 10, Starboard Parlor 15:00
High Tea Bingo, Deck 8, Bingo Hall. 16:00
True Crime Podcast Happy Hour, Deck 10, Starboard Parlor 17:00
Cocktails around the Campfire, Deck 12 . . . . 22:00

Cruise Counseling is still available this afternoon.
Book on your room screen or talk to a crewmember to schedule.

EXCURSIONS.

For passengers embarking on itineraries today, we look forward to welcoming you to your assigned flower suite. Room stewards are available to escort you.

ANNALIE

THURSDAY 11:42

Annalie was scheduled to meet with the on-board therapist before lunch today, and again tomorrow, before her excursion on Saturday. Theresa, the therapist she had been seeing at least once a week since her sister died, thought continuing therapy while away would be a good idea. "And be sure to report the medications you're taking. The anesthesia team might want to switch things up for you."

So Annalie registered for the Cruise Counseling excursion, which meant she was entitled to up to three hour-long sessions on the ship and two hour-long phone calls in the month before or after the cruise. A deckman escorted her to Wellness Room 4, but when Annalie opened the door and walked in, she was surprised to find herself alone.

The room was cozy, softness everywhere: a daybed covered in fluffy throw pillows, next to which sat a small round table with a single woven coaster. On the coaster sat a mug of tea. Annalie could see steam rising, and she smelled peppermint. On one wall, there was a floor-to-ceiling window looking out on the ocean, which was choppy now, riddled with whitecaps. The sky, too, looked unsettled. Clouds formed a rough patchwork quilt of white through which rays of sunlight poked to form spotlights on the sea.

"Please. Sit down," a voice said, and Annalie turned around. "Get comfortable," the voice said.

"And you are?" Annalie asked.

"Your on-board therapist. You can call me Irene."

"Where are you?"

"Here with you. Just not visible. If you'd prefer, I can project an image onto the wall."

Annalie sat on the edge of the daybed. "What do you mean you're here?"

"I am present with you." The voice was melodic, even.

"I don't understand."

"I am one of the ship's auxiliary systems. An artificial intelligence. You can call me Irene."

For a moment, Annalie considered getting up and requesting a refund. But she was curious. What would a conversation with a computer be like? She sat back. "Hi, Irene." She felt the skin on her forearms prickle.

"Shall we begin?"

Annalie nodded. "Let's." But where to begin? She picked up the steaming mug of tea. She took a sip and pulled away quickly. The scalding liquid burned her tongue.

"I'm sorry about your tongue. And your sister."

"Thank you." Annalie still wasn't sure how to best respond to condolences. Expressing gratitude was the simplest way, though the one that made the least sense to her.

"How are you doing?"

"Fine. And also not fine. What you'd expect, probably."

"Are you enjoying the cruise so far?"

"I think so? The ship is lovely."

"What would you like to talk about today?"

"Can I ask you a question?"

"Of course," Irene said. "Please."

"How do I move on?"

Theresa didn't like this question. She wouldn't tell Annalie what to do. She said her job was to help Annalie understand her grief and move *herself* on. But maybe Irene would be more prescriptive.

"Moving on is a process. It's ongoing and never-ending."

"At least tell me this trip will work. My itinerary. Tell me I'm not crazy."

"You are not crazy. You are grieving a terrible loss."

"Will this work?"

"I don't understand your question. What do you mean?"

"Will all this help me feel better?"

"According to available data, itineraries similar to yours carry a high likelihood of improving overall outlook. Greater than 74 percent. Unfortunately, we have no statistics on the effectiveness of any excursion as a coping mechanism for the loss of a loved one. Based on my risk-assessment algorithm, I predict a favorable outcome. Appearance changes are not a new phenomenon, and they are becoming more prevalent, but as you can imagine, human identity is complicated, and there is still a great deal unknown about the relationships among identity, appearance, and well-being, especially in the case of multiples."

Annalie exhaled. "So I'm heading in the right direction."

"Do you think you are?"

"Maybe. No. I don't know." Annalie took another sip of tea. "I mean, a plastic-surgery cruise? Is this really the answer? How did I get here?"

"I imagine a plane."

At that, Annalie started to laugh. She couldn't help herself. Tears flooded and flowed from her eyes. She laughed so hard she couldn't catch her breath until BECCA picked up on her distress and released more oxygen into the room. Then she sat there, breathing deeply and yawning. "I think I'll just close my eyes for a little."

"Of course. Naps are a powerful but underutilized form of self-care."

Annalie closed her eyes and slept the rest of the hour away, curled up on the daybed, one hand lightly bent around her mug of tea, now tepid.

NICOLE

THURSDAY 13:07

The ship's spa was a "natural" oasis, carefully designed to activate serotonin production and inhibit the release of epinephrine. Temperature-controlled bamboo floors extended to walls painted to look like fields of lush spring grass. Waist-high pillar candles, as wide as the wheels of an SUV, sat in the corners, and all the seating areas were padded with fringed pillows and tufted cushions.

When she walked in, Nicole tucked her clothes in a locker and wrapped a fluffy—the fluffiest she had ever touched, in fact—robe around her bikini-clad body. In the courtyard lounge, Nicole basked in a scent that combined the brininess of the sea, the serenity of an alpine mountain, and the coziness of a library. Dappled sunlight filled the space, along with a light piano melody.

Nicole had booked a dermaplane facial and myofascial release massage, both recommended to her at her consultation. As she breathed, she imagined each inhale filling her, each exhale pushing out her worries, her dread, her deception until she was just a sensory being. When her wellness engineer appeared to escort her to a private treatment room, she was so relaxed that she found it merely ironic that he shared a name with her husband. Maybe it would even help her think about her husband while this Justin's hands kneaded her skin. She took off her robe and lay down on the long, padded table in the center of the room, pulling the sheet up, up, up. Maybe, but probably not. Who was she kidding? She'd be thinking about Cedric. She'd give herself this flight of fancy, she decided as Justin's fingers started to comb her shoulders, the pressure warm, soothing. And she wouldn't feel bad about it. The list of all the things she had to feel bad about was long; the well of all the guilt she harbored, deep. This one thing, this crush, she'd allow. It was harmless, after all. And finite. A mental excursion.

BINGO

CEDRIC

THURSDAY 16:02

Cedric's attention sharpened when he saw the women from Table 32 arrive for Thursday's High Tea Bingo.

Lyla was humming a tune, and the words ran through his head: *There was a farmer had a dog, and Bingo was his name-o.*

"What's double pay?" Nicole asked, pointing to the digital billboard.

"You win twice as much," Cedric explained, stepping out from behind the women.

When Nicole's eyes widened at the sight of him in his pristine white tuxedo, he couldn't help beaming.

"Ladies," he said, "it's lovely to see you." He held Nicole's gaze as he spoke, watching the color creep into her cheeks.

"Now—" He held the door open for the women. "—the game is electronic and automated. You don't have to worry about missing a number on one of your cards. Your game tablet will handle everything for you. All you're required to do is sit back, enjoy the tea and scones and company, and watch as you win."

"So you do nothing?" Bianca asked. "Just sit there?" She rocked on her toes.

"And win money," Nicole offered. "I like how that sounds."

Cedric was having a hard time dragging his eyes away from her. He wanted to tell her he liked looking at her face, but he knew how awkward, how awful that would sound. But he meant it. She had a lovely face, and he couldn't stop staring at it.

"Come and see for yourselves." Cedric ushered the four women inside. "Come, come." When Nicole walked past, he breathed in deeply. She smelled like peaches and marshmallows, so fresh and sweet. Her shoulder practically brushed his, and he wondered if he would have felt an electric shock if it had. "Feel free to sit anywhere."

The women walked to an open table, and Cedric followed. "Since you're sitting in my zone, I have the pleasure of serving you. Get comfortable, okay? I'll be right back with your game tablets."

As he walked away, he thought he heard Nicole say, "Put a good-looking man in a tuxedo, and my word." She added quickly, "Don't tell my husband I said that."

THE BINGO HALL

"Welcome! Welcome to everyone! The four o'clock session is about to begin."

On a dais at the front of the rectangular room, a man in a black tuxedo stood, microphone in hand, white teeth gleaming. He nodded, and around the room, the lights dimmed.

On the left wall screen, a giant bingo board appeared, but blank, an empty grid. On the right wall screen, a spinning sphere materialized. The screen at the front of the room remained blank.

"We'll start with two-way bingo," the man in the black tux said, and as he spoke, the words TWO-WAY BINGO flashed on the screen behind him, along with an explanation of the round. After asking if there were any questions, he gestured to the image of the giant spinning ball. "One table at a time, I'll invite you up here to the dais, and you'll take turns picking the next number. Then you can relax while the magic happens. If your board is a winner, your tablet will start to flash and vibrate, and you'll see yourself here."

Turning, the man nodded to the screen now showing the room they were in, the women they were sitting with. Nicole appeared next to Lyla, Bianca, and Annalie. Then the hidden camera panned away, moving to capture other pairs and groups. Around the room, little shrieks rose and faded as the camera, wherever it was, continued its course, and more women found themselves cast onto the screen.

"We don't even look real," Bianca said.

"HD really is something," Lyla replied.

"Shh," said Nicole. "I want to hear this."

Their host was explaining the winnings. "Since this afternoon tea is a double-pay session, the winning row earns double. And as always, power numbers are in effect for each round. With a power number, the winning board earns six times the payout." A few whoops could be heard around the room. "But even though not every board can or will win," the man continued, "we promise to make this experience a treat for all of you. The staff is at your beck and call. We'll start pulling numbers with table one."

"So that's what this eight means," Annalie said, pointing to their table number, showcased in a small ornate gold frame.

"You would think that even the ball-pulling would be automatic, what with all this fancy technology," Bianca said.

"I'm sure you can opt out and not go up," Lyla said.

By the time their turn came, there were no thoughts of opting out. They could barely stand to wait any longer. Already they had seen seven tables of women approach the giant two-dimensional spinning ball, hold up their hands, and pluck a three-dimensional wooden marble off the screen.

"That can't be!" someone in the crowd had gasped.

"What in the world?!"

The crew, milling about in their tuxedos, just smiled and offered by way of explanation: "It's magic."

When they'd arrived for bingo, the four women were prepared merely for a diversion, an afternoon of company, tea, and treats. The prospect of winning provided an added element of fun. As the grandeur of the game was revealed, however, a feeling of gratitude swelled among them. This was more than diversion, more than distraction. Here they might, for a time, forget a parent's deceit or a financial strain or a personal disappointment, or a grief so vast it was its own ocean.

All around the room, women marveled over the spectacle of the screens, the men in their tuxedos, the miracle of pulling a marble from a moving picture. They drank tea, partook of savory biscuits and quiches, assorted breads served with hard and soft cheese; they chatted and waited for their tablets to announce they had won. For some of them, over the course of the afternoon, their companions became another sort of elusive prize for women of or nearing or edging past middle age: friends.

LYLA

THURSDAY 16:37

Lyla took a bite of quiche.

"Did y'all know Bianca is a professional tennis player?" she asked.

"Like Serena?" Nicole asked, eyes widening. "I watched her play when I was little. She destroyed everyone."

"Well, no," Bianca started. "Not like Serena." She paused. "Not yet."

She left it at that, and Lyla recognized the strategy. It was a non-answer answer, she realized. A clever dodge. Bianca had done the same thing earlier when Lyla asked about her career.

"Your girls," Lyla said.

"Who?" asked Nicole.

"Bianca's," Lyla clarified. "Your girls. You said this morning they lived with their father? In Florida?"

"They do." Bianca picked up her teacup and took a sip.

"Divorce is terrible," said Lyla. "I'm sorry. You must miss them terribly."

"I do," Bianca said, but too loudly. Then, clearing her throat, she explained, "But we're not divorced. Just living apart while I train." She lifted her cup higher, as though she could hide behind the delicate porcelain painted with pink flowers.

Lyla was confused. "I don't understand," she said.

"I have to stay away," Bianca explained. "Dedicate myself to my come-back. If I go home now, all the sacrifice will mean nothing." Her voice turned imploring. "It has to mean something," she continued. "If not, then I would have missed so much to be exactly where I was when I left." Bianca was blinking rapidly, breathing rapidly, and meanwhile bingo numbers continued to appear on the screen at the front of the room.

"Oh, Bianca," Nicole said.

"I'm sorry." Bianca lowered her teacup, and her gaze, to her lap. "I've never talked about this before."

Near them, at Table 6, a woman's tablet started singing, and now all of the women around her were clapping and calling out, "Bingo! Bingo!"

They appeared, their delight effervescent, on the screen at the front of the room.

"I don't understand," Lyla said again as the commotion began to fade. "How long have you been away?"

"I used to split time between Florida and South Carolina. But then I signed with an agent, and it was harder to get back." Her voice dropped to a whisper. "It's been . . . years."

At the front of the room, the host explained, "Now we'll continue on to any two, hardway." An explanation appeared on the front screen and on their tablets: *Bingo in two straight lines without the use of the free space.*

Nicole and Annalie watched the screen, but Lyla kept her eyes on Bianca. She felt feverish. She remembered Rosemary's mother that night so long ago, how the woman had refused to wake up to nurse her crying baby. She remembered her last ultrasound, how at nine weeks her baby no longer had a heartbeat. These memories spiraled into other memories, other miscarriages, an endless spinning series, wild and furious. Who was this woman? To have children, a gift twice over, and then walk away? And for what? Tennis?

Before Lyla had started imagining the family she longed for, she'd play a game in her head. She'd ask herself, *What would I sacrifice for a child? To make it full term and give birth and hold my own baby?* The list was long, twisted:

their dishwasher and garbage disposal
vision in one eye
travel anywhere outside her town
every show on any streaming network
hot showers
watching one last snowfall

Who was this woman, this *mother*?

BIANCA

The balls began to bounce again. The game resumed. Cedric poured tea for Bianca from a fresh pot. "It's very hot," he warned. "Be careful."

Nicole turned to Bianca. "What about your husband?" she asked. "What does he say?"

Bianca shook her head. "We haven't talked for a while."

"But you can go back to your family," Annalie said. "It's not too late." She plunked a second cube of sweetener into her now empty cup and nodded to Cedric, who filled it. He picked up several crumb-filled plates and retreated.

Bianca shook her head again. "I've tried. I've packed a bag, grabbed my keys, and tried. I get as far as the bridge before turning back." Steam rolled off the top of her tea. Too hot to drink. She brought the cup to her lips anyway and burned her tongue. She cradled the cup in her hands, but the heat was there, too, the burn leaking into her palms, along her fingers.

"Try harder!" Lyla said, her voice loud, sharp, and insistent, the tone Bianca imagined she'd use to coach a woman through pushing after twenty-four hours of labor.

Before Bianca could respond, before she could return the hot, hot cup of tea to the table, there was a sudden burst of noise, and Bianca's tablet started to jiggle and flash and sing. They all startled.

"Bianca, you won," Annalie said. "And the power number. You got the power number."

"Shit," Bianca said. With the sudden eruption of song, her hands shook, her burning hands. The shake caused tea to slide over the rim of the cup and slosh into her lap. "Shit," she said again, and in her desperation to get the hot cup out of her hands and the scalding tea out of her lap, she spilled even more, nearly the entire cup before she at last settled it on the table. "*Shit*." The hot liquid had soaked her skirt, and now all she felt was a radiating pain. Trying to ease the fire eating at her skin, she pulled the linen away from her body. She pushed her chair back and stood up.

Cedric appeared at her shoulder. He was muttering, "I told them we needed heat-resistant teacups." Then he soothed, "Bianca, allow me to help. We'll get you fixed up in no time. On *PILGRIM*, a burn is nothing, nothing at all."

AFTER HOURS

NICOLE

One minute Nicole's settling into her vacation, trying to leave her worries behind, and the next minute, there's Cedric: a nuclear flash consuming all other thoughts—past, present, and future—in one explosive burst. Once, on a walk with her friends back home, their babies bundled in strollers, Jane had confessed to her and Semra a crush on her eye doctor. *Out of nowhere*, Jane said. *Just poof, there. And such a nuisance.* She reminded them about the terrible stye she had—*When my eyelid was red for like a month? One eyelash follicle after the next swelling up?*—and how she had to see the doctor once a week until the infection cleared. *It went away*, she said. *Thank god.*

As she recalled Cedric in his white tux, Nicole couldn't agree with Jane. Her crush wasn't a nuisance at all; rather, she now considered it part of her whole cruise experience: another excursion tacked onto her itinerary. A free upgrade! All day today, she'd imagined an assortment of possible interactions that strengthened their undeniable connection. In one, she had a strange reaction to medication, and Cedric noticed, dropped his tray, and whisked her up into his arms, rushing for help. In another, he slipped a note under the door of her stateroom, suggesting a time for them to meet under the stars. And she did meet him under the stars. It was the stuff of movies, and she filled her head with it, pushing out the boxes of unsold products, the friends and family she has been lying to for months, the state of her marriage. Was it a bit disconcerting that here she was mooning over Cedric while at home she physically recoiled from her husband? Sure, of course. But. "It's just an excursion," she told herself after dinner as she pampered herself with the lotions and serums, oils and mists that filled her cabin's bathroom. "No adverse side effects," she read aloud, examining one label, and then, with her ring finger, she dabbed a little of the contents onto the soft skin below her eyes.

ANNALIE

THURSDAY 21:46

Annalie arrived at the entrance to the Cemetery just after a group of five passengers started down the path. The last two nights, she'd had the place to herself at this hour. Tonight, though, she followed, ten or so paces behind, and listened. She wanted, if only for the duration of her walk, to let the light chatter of these women wash over her, a balm to the terrible end of bingo.

"My girlfriend will never believe this."

"Neither will my coworkers."

"Would you if you weren't here?"

"I thought it was creepy at first, but once you're in it, it's so tranquil. All the lovely headstones. The quiet."

Despite her initial shock at seeing this particular path advertised on her bathroom screen night one, Annalie also found it peaceful here. She thought it might make her sad, but instead she felt calm, closer to Aimee. The neat gray markers, the dark green grass around them, leafy branches overhead. Clover and moss. A breeze and on it a hint of summer. A stirring restlessness and the promise of heat.

"I wonder if the names and dates are for real people."

"Rocco said they're the names of passengers, and the dates signal when they cruised."

"Passengers who *died* on the ship?"

"Sort of. Died in one sense and left as different women. *Reborn,* he said."

Annalie sucked in a breath, felt her head spin. Would her name be on a headstone after this cruise? If her itinerary were successful, she *would* leave a different woman. The thought comforted her, strangely: her name and Aimee's both on gravestones. A way to be together.

"What does that even mean?"

"You've seen the Captain's Instagram account. You know what he's capable of."

"But just because he *can* doesn't mean he *should*."

Two of the women nodded, two others shrugged, and one woman stopped, a hand flying to her chest. She explained, "I'm still not used to these and their bounce." Annalie stopped, too, waited and watched.

"Remember what Larry said? He said the Cemetery was haunted."

If so, Annalie wanted it to be haunted by exactly one ghost.

"He's full of it."

"But he sure is cute. Those dimples?"

"He said women in the Cemetery have felt something brush past them, or even through them. Can you imagine?"

"Like the sea breeze? Or air conditioning?"

"I'm just repeating what he said."

"Are we still planning to do Cocktails around the Campfire?"

"If we make it out of here alive."

"Not funny."

The women walked closer together now, shuffling as a pack, shoulders and hips bumping together from time to time.

"Are we the only ones out here?"

They started to turn, and Annalie panicked. She darted to crouch behind a tree stump. She could feel her pulse battering her ears. She was being ridiculous. She could have stayed on the path. So what that she was eavesdropping? So what that she was here, too?

"Looks that way."

"Larry said Mall traffic really picks up at night. All those bright lights and shiny objects."

"Where did the light here go?"

Annalie peeked around the stump and saw the women as gray outlines in the gathering dark.

"We're at sea. No light pollution. When the sun sets, night comes on in a blink."

"Where's *that* light coming from?"

"Me. I carry a flashlight in my purse."

Annalie watched a small bright beam dart through the area around her. But then, off to her left, she saw another light, hazy and unmoving. A lantern. Curious, she started to ease toward it.

"What about a taser?"

"Just mace."

"Did you feel that?"

"I'm sorry. I can't help it. I'm freaking out. Have any women died on board? Does anyone know?"

"I read on Surgicom that lightning has a higher chance of killing you than most of the excursions offered."

"But not all?"

The voices grew indistinct as Annalie stood and wound her way among headstones and more tree stumps, the golden light in the distance intriguing.

At last, she reached the lantern, hanging from the front of a stone mausoleum. The building was as big as a backyard shed. The wooden door had a metal ring for a handle, and it stood ajar. A few tiles were missing from the slate roof. Along the right wall, vines formed a dense green lattice.

Annalie didn't think. She unhooked the lantern and slipped through the doorway. Inside, candles glimmered in wrought-iron sconces. Above them, the ceiling was beadboard. The rest of the small room was constructed from gray bricks of varying shapes and sizes. Before her, a wide staircase led down into darkness.

Annalie crept forward, compelled to carry out this strange, strange quest. Down the stairs she went, step by step. At the bottom, her sneakers met a packed dirt floor. Down a short corridor, she saw more light, candles twinkling. And she heard talking. A man's voice. She wasn't alone here, wherever here was.

LARRY

Larry stood just inside the maintenance door on Deck 8, flashlight in hand, steeling himself for a ride. He had come to appreciate the parade of bandaged bodies that passed before him, Woman 2.0 or 3.0 or 4.0 or 11.0, the most recent version fresh from production. He'd expected the women to be covered with sheets, swathed in fabric. Instead, they were clothed only in bandages and dressings.

He studied the beds and their occupants as they passed, moving along Trackz from surgery station to stateroom. He discerned swelling. He traced the lines of IVs and catheters. He observed the fine texture of white gauze, its grid-like weave, at times wrapped tight, at times slack.

Part of the thrill of times like these was that he was the only one, so far as he knew, who saw women during transport. He was the only one who joined them for this part of their journey. He liked how vulnerable they were in the space and time between surgery and wellness, that gap at the threshold of recovery. His skin prickled and his pulse raced as beds moved past, excitement heightened by his restraint. He no longer climbed aboard the very first bed he saw.

At first, he rode only every few weeks. Then, weekly. Lately, he'd increased to two rides per week, occasionally three. The adventure was something else: the stealth required to access the door undetected; the leap onto the moving bed; the stateroom arrival and the desperate flight from the room to return to where he was supposed to be. If he could pocket a trinket on his way out the door, even better. He had quite the collection by now: some diamond-stud earrings, an eyeglasses case, a scrunchie, rings, an emerald-studded hair clip. He stowed these prized repossessions in his dopp kit, right in plain sight on the shelf next to his bed.

But the best part of the ride was the woman he would have all to himself for a few minutes. Just her and him there, moving smoothly along the rails, her body a gently breathing doll. He tried not to let his thoughts linger on the things he could do. If he were, say, to unbuckle the straps holding the woman snugly in place, then help ease her over the railings and watch as her body folded, tucked itself into the space between the wall—slipping slowly by—and the moving bed. Would she wake up before the next bed came along, disoriented and sore? Would sensors in the rails detect an obstruction and pause the whole operation? Or would a collision occur, one after which the passenger would need actual surgery, not just the plastic kind, if she were lucky enough to encounter a moving bed traveling four miles per hour along a magnetic rail system and still be in a condition where surgery was an option?

Larry watched one more bed pass. The next one would be his ride. He could feel his palms start to sweat. He waited for another bed to round the corner, his heart a churning propeller.

DR. HESTON

Annalie appeared in the open chamber, lantern extended before her like a crucifix to ward off the kind of trouble expected in a cemetery.

"Come in," Dr. Heston said, standing from the wrought iron bench and wheeling his arm around. "You are welcome here," he continued. "Anyone is, though I'm afraid not many make it here."

Passengers only came down if they were looking for a bathroom. That had only happened twice when he was there himself. The first woman asked if he were a ghost. The second fled in a hurry once Dr. Heston told her how to get to the closest restroom.

Usually, his twice weekly visits to Rebecca's memorial were solo affairs. He sat on the bench in the midst of the garden (thriving under solar lights), talked shop with her, updating her about the current cruise, his work, new excursions. He had to imagine she was proud of him, especially weeks like this one. Of the two of them, she had been the innovator, the paradigm-shifter, and he wanted so badly to honor her legacy. She was the seed, he reflected once, here in this garden, and he would see that seed germinate and leaf out and bloom and bloom and bloom.

He told her, too, about the passengers, the crew, how much he missed her still. Sometimes, he just sat quietly among the flowers, imagining the life they should have been living together, this the garden they would have shared.

"That's too bad," Annalie said quietly, her eyes on a lush rose bush, "that no one comes. It's beautiful." She set down the lantern and came forward, hand extended to touch a pale pink bloom. "They're real?" she asked, clearly surprised at the petal's softness, like a damp tissue.

Dr. Heston nodded. "Hydroponics and solar candles and, poof, indoor garden."

"In a mausoleum of all places," Annalie said, finally meeting his gaze. "I'm Annalie."

Dr. Heston already knew that. He just never expected to see her here, in this space. But here she was. Of course she was here. All at once, her presence made perfect sense. "So nice to meet you, Annalie. I'm Walter. Walter Heston."

"As in the Captain?" she said, eyes wide. "Dr. Heston?"

"Yes, but please call me Walter."

"I don't know if I can do that," Annalie admitted.

Dr. Heston laughed then, and the light sound echoed in the small space.

Annalie smiled. "I'll try."

Dr. Heston returned to the bench. "Care to have a seat?"

Annalie lowered herself next to him, and for a while, the two of them sat there on the bench together, breathing in the heady aroma of plants growing, flowers blooming, the space around them so alive with color.

After a time, Annalie asked, "Who's Rebecca?" She nodded to the stone plaque in the wall before them.

"She," Dr. Heston started, clearing his throat, "is my wife. *Was*. Was my wife." He blinked hard.

"I'm sorry," Annalie said.

Dr. Heston watched as she squeezed her eyes shut. When she opened them, she said, "I lost my sister recently. My twin sister."

"I'm sorry," Dr. Heston returned. They both took a deep breath and turned back to the flowers, to their own worlds of grief.

More time passed. Then Annalie asked, "Do you want to talk about her?" She glanced over and their eyes met, held. "I'll just listen. I'll just be here to listen."

Did he? Yes, found he did. He really did. He wanted to talk about Rebecca. "Okay," Dr. Heston said, a small, tight smile forming. "Okay."

THE PILGRIM DAILY
FIRST FRIDAY

Where do you want to go today?

WALKING PATHS. HOURS: 09:00–24:00

Park . . . . open
Mall . . . . open (pretzel bite samples available all afternoon)
Cemetery . . . . open

SPA. HOURS: 09:00–19:00

DAILY SPECIALS
Acai Peptide Treatment
Seaweed Wrap
FasciaFill

Book now on your room screen or talk to your room steward to schedule a visit.

DINING. SEE HOURS BELOW.

Breakfast 06:00–09:00
Lunch 11:30–15:00
Dinner 19:00

ON-BOARD ACTIVITIES. HOURS: 05:30–24:00

Matcha and Mantras, Deck 12	05:30
Advanced Barre, Deck 12	07:00
Barre for Beginners, Deck 12	08:00
Mimosas and Bloody Marys, Deck 10, Citrus Canopy	09:00
Fragrance Mixology, Deck 10, Mint Canopy	14:00
Jewelry Design, Deck 10, Starboard Parlor	15:00
High Tea Bingo, Deck 8, Bingo Hall	16:00
Hello Weekend Happy Hour, Deck 10, Citrus Canopy	17:00
Dancing after Dark, Deck 12	22:00

Cruise Counseling is still available for this afternoon.
Book on your room screen or talk to a crewmember to schedule.

EXCURSIONS.

For passengers embarking on itineraries today, we look forward to welcoming you to your assigned flower suite. Room stewards are available to escort you.

LYLA

When she couldn't sleep the night before her excursions, Lyla started to shop for maternity clothes. Earlier, after bingo, she had found a tablet on her bed. She tapped the screen, and a note appeared:

> *On behalf of Canterbury Cruise Line, I'd like to invite you to begin creating your dream maternity wardrobe. Please browse and order. This tablet has been preloaded with websites for maternity boutiques and $1000. Enjoy and happy shopping! Thank you for embarking upon this journey with us. We look forward to making this dream come true for you.*
> *Sincerely,*
> *The Captain*

So for hours into the night, Lyla browsed clothes from Storq, Seraphine, PinkBlush, and HATCH. She couldn't quite believe her belly would ever be big enough to necessitate a new wardrobe, yet she had seen the projections during her consultation. She knew where she was headed. She added items to carts on three of the sites. She entered shipping information. But in the end, she created accounts instead of clicking to purchase. She went back to reading reviews for jumpsuits.

BIANCA

FRIDAY 06:27

Bianca jogged around Deck 12 as the sun crested the horizon, a wobbly orange dome growing on the edge of the world. Instead of the three walking paths, she elected to circle the highest deck, fast along the sides, slower around the curves. Despite the breeze, sweat glistened along her arms and beaded and fell from her nose. At this hour, on this day, and especially after bingo yesterday, she wanted to see only sun and water.

She hadn't slept at all last night. Her burns were fine, but scenes from bingo kept coming back to her, and those led to other scenes. The last time she saw the girls. The morning she left for Hilton Head. The day she had taken the girls to the club to give them lessons and thought it might be time, *her* time. That maybe, just maybe, she could make a go of it. The intense heat of that day returned to her. The girls had looked destroyed after their hour on the court. They were still young then, eight and six, maybe. Damp, curling hair haloed their flushed faces. They had only wanted ice cream. Bianca remembered how her older daughter, Vivian, had stomped her feet. Any other day, that attitude would have driven Bianca mad. She would have reached out to squeeze Vivian's rail-thin arm and whisper savagely, *Do not talk to me like that. Do you understand? That is not acceptable*. But that day, she had brushed off the girl's tantrum like it was a band of sweat glimmering across her upper lip. She had taken a sip of water and then dumped what remained in her bottle on Vivian's frizzy, sweat-matted head. It had dripped down her face, along her shoulders. *Hey!* she had said, but she was smiling. *Mom!* Then Bianca had taken them out for ice cream. The day had turned out to be a good one. A really good one.

Bianca slowed to a walk to cool down, one arm sliding along the smooth railing. She smelled the salt in a breeze that cooled the short, dripping hair at the base of her neck. In two hours, she'd report to Hydrangea Station, and her itinerary would begin.

On her fifth slow lap, she spotted someone else on the deck. He appeared opposite her, across the width of the boat. He was crouched down, one hand holding a bottle of some sort, the other holding a cloth he used to scrub at the railing. She wondered if he had been there all along, stepping out of the way as she passed, then returning to his work. Had she been so intent on her run, her thoughts, her memories, eyes scanning the water for fins or another presence among the waves, that she had failed to notice him? Surely not.

It wouldn't have been the first time she failed to see what was right in front of her. She did it with her keys and coffee cups in the morning. Her glasses and toothbrush at night. When she had lived in Florida, Anthony would help her track down the items she sought before she could become frustrated, distraught. But on her own, she was always losing things. She could walk right next to her purse looped over the back of a kitchen chair a dozen times and not see it. Always, she'd react the same way when she couldn't find something: calm at first, then increasingly more frantic. Once, a few months ago, she dumped out half the kitchen drawers looking for a ladle before she found it with the rest of the cooking utensils in the wide stainless steel holder next to the stove, half hidden by a wooden spoon. After the find, her skin smoldered, little fires everywhere, her body sinking, a heap of ashes on the kitchen floor. There she cradled the ladle in her arms, tight to her chest, just breathing until she could feel the cold, hard tile beneath her, until her boiling pasta had crusted on the bottom of the pan and the sauce she had warmed in the microwave had grown cool. These episodes exhausted her, the pursuit of something that should have never been lost in the first place. But she couldn't think about it too much, what it meant, the mental mechanisms at play.

As she approached the deckman, she slowed her steps. Would he move? Should she? She felt as though she were trespassing, or invading space that wasn't hers. When she was fifteen steps away and closing, he still didn't look up or seem to sense her proximity. Five steps away. His scrubbing stopped abruptly, so she stopped. He stood, turning toward her.

"Lovely morning," he said, his half-smile tugging out a dimple in his left cheek. His nametag read Rocco, and she recognized him from the other day. He had the lanky, soft physique of a man who didn't play sports, except maybe golf. If she had to guess, he had held a nine-to-five office job before joining the crew.

"Is it okay that I'm up here?" she asked.

"Of course. Most passengers prefer the walking paths is all. But it's nice up here. Quiet."

"I like it," she said.

Rocco asked, "Excursion day today?"

Bianca nodded, reached back to tighten her ponytail. "The first day of the rest of my life."

She'd intended her tone to be light, to put a wry spin on the adage, but the words came out leaden, and hearing them, she cringed.

Rocco's expression was carefully blank. "Best of luck." He offered a small salute before moving out of her path.

LARRY

When not riding passengers back to their rooms, Larry thought about his most recent ride and the next one. That's what he was doing as he scooped eggs onto his plate in the crew dining hall; as he salted the steaming yellow piles liberally; as he stacked a rasher of bacon alongside the eggs; as he sat and shoveled his breakfast into his mouth, forkful after forkful; as he chased the plate of food with first a brimming glass of milk, then a smaller one of cranberry juice.

He dwelled on how it had felt when he hopped on the passenger last night. Her eyelids fluttered as he swung himself onto the bed, but she didn't grimace or moan like some women did as he struggled to position himself. Each ride, he tried different moves, different mounts, different touches, all while watching the woman's face to see her reaction. He didn't want to hurt these women, not really, but sometimes he couldn't help himself.

There was a certain beauty in a face tight with pain, and of course it didn't last long. The ride was a couple minutes at most. And the women were mostly unconscious, the pain not even registering in their morphine-induced dreams. Last night, he had opted to lie down next to the woman he traveled with. He stretched his body along hers and stared at her closed eyelids. He tilted her face toward him and felt her breath on his cheek, warm puffs like invisible cotton balls.

He never attempted to have sex with the women. He wasn't a rapist. There wasn't enough time for that anyway, and, besides, he had discovered that poking could be quite satisfying. So he explored bodies in that way. With his fingertips.

HYDRANGEA STATION

THE CIRCULATOR

BEFORE

Rebecca Heston—along with a team of two computer scientists and four nurses—built the Circulator, BECCA's first fully interactive software. When the project was in development, the nurses commissioned as consultants emphasized thoroughness, efficiency, and bedside manner, and the computer scientists coded empathy into the meticulous system. So when a patient mentioned goose bumps or the operating table detected shivering, the Circulator would say, "I'm sorry for your discomfort. Here, let me warm things up a bit." This line would then activate the thermostat to increase the current setting by two degrees Fahrenheit. The team also integrated the Universal Prevention of Wrong Site, Wrong Procedure, and Wrong Person Protocol into the system to make the surgical stations compliant with ASPS Operating Room Safety. Such compliance was unnecessary given the international waters in which the operating rooms were located when excursions were underway, but Dr. Heston insisted, and the credential was highlighted on the website. Once the team finished building a dense repertoire of responses and tones in expressing them, of specialized and lay vocabularies, and once they had scripted every possible scenario they could think of and committed them all to the database, it was Rebecca's turn. She spent a week with the system before announcing the upgrade complete, the Circulator system self-learning, fully responsive, and able to optimize passenger experience and safety. "God, she's glorious," Rebecca, sitting at her terminal, had said.

The Captain, next to his wife, was watching her, not her screen. Specifically, he was studying the line from her neck to her shoulder to her arm. Now he traced that line with a finger. Now he leaned in, kissed her shoulder, breathed in her skin, dryer sheets and dew and leather. "Yes," he said into the soft of her neck, "you are."

LYLA

The first thing Lyla saw in the operating room was a table lined with little smooth hills in a grid. Her implants. Her imagined sons would have raced over to them, seeing water balloons to toss at each other. They would have made sure to pop them all, laughing each time the liquid inside burst free. Their sister would have preferred the chair ride into the room. She would have asked to go again and again—*Again, Mommy, again!*—and each time, her little mouth would have fallen open to see the door swing wide on its own, to feel the warm light bathe her. *Again, Mommy, again!*

A man in full surgical dress stood beside the table. As the chair moved forward, Lyla could tell the man was smiling despite the mask he wore. After ten years in the hospital, she could discern expressions, even emotional states, despite caps and masks. She could read body language through the bagginess of scrubs.

The chair pivoted in its track, turning ninety degrees before rising a foot and locking into place. The man disappeared from view. Lyla looked around. She saw another table, this one lined with surgical instruments, neatly arranged by type and size. A tray of retractors sat behind the row of clamps, forceps, and needle holders, and to the left sat neat stacks of blue OR towels and Ray-Tec sponges. She saw a cautery generator, suction machine, defibrillator, IV tower, the anesthesia cart. And behind all the waiting equipment and supplies, Lyla saw floor-to-ceiling cupboards.

Whenever Lyla had been on her period or dealing with another failed pregnancy, she would request inventory duties at work. For hours, then, she could busy herself with restocking and ordering supplies. Instead of contractions and cervical dilations and baby bowel movements, she counted syringes, fluid bags, and antiseptic wipes in the closets and operating room cupboards. Counting provided the right amount of monotony, and she was comforted by the clarity that resulted. *Forty-five sixteen-gauge needles. Eighty-four sterile booties. Five bed pans. Two dozen catheter kits.*

"Welcome," a voice said, a female voice, not that of the man she'd seen. Lyla looked around, peering as best she could past the chair's wide, tall sides. If someone else was in the room, they were directly behind her. The voice, though, didn't seem to have a point of origin. It was like the room itself was greeting her.

"How are you, Lyla? I am the Circulator. Welcome to Hydrangea Station. We are so pleased you're here."

Lyla didn't know if she should say something, if the voice was interactive or simply a recording.

"Are you comfortable?"

Interactive, it would seem. "My feet are cold," she said.

"Here, let's warm them up a bit. I apologize for the discomfort."

Lyla continued to scan the room. "Thank you," she said. "Where are you?"

"I am here."

Lyla tried again. "What are you?"

"I am the Circulator, one of the ship's systems designed to make your excursions pleasing and safe."

At Lyla's hospital, nurses rotated through the circulator role, and sometimes surgeons made requests. She received a lot of those and preferred to be the circulator if she was going to be in the OR. Other nurses fussed over the patients. Early in her career, she had fussed, too, but now she kept things moving along.

"How do your feet feel now?"

Lyla wiggled her toes. "Warm," she said, a bit surprised. "Thank you."

"You're welcome, Lyla." A brief pause, and then, "Now, I will introduce you to the team who will ensure your care throughout your journey."

Lyla's chair wheeled around, and before her stood a row of four men.

"Your lead surgical technician, Jared." He was the same man she had seen earlier. He gave a little salute. "Two assisting technicians, Isaac and Kennedy. And Slate will be your anesthesia technician." These men took turns stepping forward or bowing slightly. "And finally, the lead physician, Chief Surgeon Dr. Heston. You might know him as the Captain. He is currently scrubbing in and will join us shortly."

It felt awkward on the patient side of things after spending so much time on the other, preparing women for C-sections and D&Cs, hysterectomies and tubals. She hesitated, then waved.

The Circulator spoke again. "Gentlemen, I would now like to introduce you to our passenger Lyla." In her soothing, steady voice, the Circulator described what they all already knew: the procedures Lyla would undergo today, including the installation of a Pregnancy Patch, as well as a series of seven implants at the hips, buttocks, waistline, and breasts to create Lyla's maternal figure, and finally a balloon made of pig liver cells that was programmed to stretch continually at the rate of 1 millimeter a day for ten months before returning to its original size at the rate of 10 millimeters an hour.

Meanwhile, a screen appeared on the right wall and on it the outline of a body, limbs outstretched. The location for the Pregnancy Patch was marked with a red light. Where each implant would go, a blue light appeared, and a green light indicated the positioning of the pig-liver balloon. Then the image zoomed in on Lyla's toes. "Lyla will also be having her toenails done today." The four shades Lyla had selected—a sky blue for summer, taupe for fall, a deep purple for winter, and a buttery pink for spring—appeared next to the toes on screen, now glowing yellow.

Then the Circulator said, "Lyla, while the technicians complete their final preparations, I would like to review and confirm relevant medical information as well as your consents for treatment."

Lyla nodded.

"Excellent. Let's begin."

While the men counted instruments and performed their final equipment checks, Lyla listened and agreed, listened and agreed. She had already read the literature. She knew the risks, death among them, as with just about any surgery, but she couldn't help but think ahead to her pregnancy. Her *pregnancy*. Soon she'd know what it felt like to be one of those women who skipped along into motherhood in a single straightforward line, without so much as a basal body thermometer, without pills and injections and blood tests. Just a belly that would swell. At the end, the Circulator thanked her for her patience and cooperation. "We pride ourselves on setting extremely rigorous safety standards. We hope this pleases you."

To be pregnant . . . without a single worry that it might end? She replied, "Yes." This had to be the excitement some women felt when they peed on a stick and watched two parallel lines appear. Even before the anesthesia technician placed a mask over her face, Lyla felt like giggling.

DR. HESTON

When Dr. Heston entered, Lyla lay sleeping peacefully and naked on the operating room table while Kennedy taped her arms to the armrests.

"Wasn't sure if you needed her shaved." Isaac shook the pair of clippers he held in his left hand. "We can have the hair gone in five."

Dr. Heston studied the body on the table. "Go ahead, then. It's not necessary for the sterile field, but it will give me greater visibility. And Rebecca, please add a NoGrow lotion to her post-op product recommendations."

Dr. Heston only called the Circulator by his wife's name. He couldn't respond to the sound of his wife's voice any other way, and in fact, the Circulator kept him in an operating room even when he wasn't performing impossible procedures. He regularly took on routine bodywork—plumping a chest or rebuilding a labia—procedures any of his team could perform, and he did so to hear the voice of the woman he loved so dearly.

The Circulator said, "Affirmative."

Isaac said, "Very well, sir."

Of course, today's procedure was anything but routine. When Lyla had reached out to share her story and ask for his help, of course he'd said yes. This yes to Lyla was really a yes to Rebecca, a yes to continuing this mad quest he was on to advance, always to advance. Inventing procedures had come to feel like injecting Botox, a way to attain a bit of smoothness, if only temporarily—to focus on something other than how much he missed his wife.

Now he felt a calm eagerness settle over him. In his mind, he saw Rebecca at her desk, fingers poised over her keyboard, cursor blinking on the command line.

THE PILGRIM DAILY

FIRST SATURDAY

Where do you want to go today?

WALKING PATHS. HOURS: 09:00–24:00

Park . . . . open (a light drizzle expected this morning)
Mall . . . . opens at 10:00 today
Cemetery . . . . open

SPA. HOURS: 09:00–19:00

DAILY SPECIALS
O2 Blast + Infuse
Cupping Therapy
Fermenting Facial

Book now on your room screen or talk to your room steward to schedule a visit.

DINING. SEE HOURS BELOW.

Breakfast 06:00–09:00
Lunch 11:30–15:00
Dinner 19:00

ON-BOARD ACTIVITIES. HOURS: 05:30–23:00

Herbal Tea for Early Risers, Deck 12 . . . . 5:30
Farmer's Market, The Mall. 07:00–09:00
Brunch Bingo, Deck 8, Bingo Hall. 10:00–12:00
Grass Weaving & Basket Making, Deck 10, Mint Canopy 14:00
Paint Fabulous Florals, Deck 10, Starboard Parlor. 15:00
Craft the Perfect Cocktail, Deck 8, Bingo Hall 16:00
Dance Like a Star, Deck 10, Citrus Canopy 17:00
Moonlight Yoga, Deck 12 . . . . 22:00

EXCURSIONS.

For passengers embarking on itineraries today, we look forward to welcoming you
to your assigned flower suite. Room stewards are available to escort you.

OUT & ABOUT SPECIALS.

The Float Tank has limited availability starting after 10:00 for hour-long Dark
Floats. The Cryochamber has Flash Freeze appointments available this afternoon.
Book directly on any screen in your stateroom or schedule with your room steward.

ANNALIE

SATURDAY 02:57

Annalie saw her twin everywhere on the ship. In the dining room, a blonde near the floor-to-ceiling windows with Aimee's hair, blunt across the shoulders. On the stairs, Aimee's smooth, tanned arm moving down along the railing a flight below. On deck, Aimee's body on a yoga mat, legs long and strong, toes pointing and flexing and pointing again. Once, just outside the bathroom, she saw ears with feather earrings, but then the head turned. There were sunken cheeks and a plumped, pouty mouth. Not Aimee. She had told Dr. Heston—Walter—about these phantoms, and he said Rebeccas haunted him, too.

After she returned from the Cemetery for the second night in a row, Annalie had fallen immediately into a hard sleep. She hadn't changed out of the joggers and tee she had worn to walk. She hadn't even brushed her teeth. The vials in her bathroom sat untouched.

Right before three in the morning, she woke to a soft *blip, blip, blip* in the night. She pulled herself up and out of bed, over to the porthole window. Looking out, she saw her sister, walking on the soft waves in the moonlight. Each step sent ripples out across the water, shimmering sine waves that came right up to the side of the ship and lapped the hull.

DR. HESTON

When he reentered his operating room in Hydrangea Station gowned and gloved, Dr. Heston checked the thermostat. Though the Circulator regulated the room's conditions, he wanted to make sure everything was just as it should be. Today he would transform a woman's face with 3D implants rendered from a series of photographs—photos he had taken, in fact—printed in the ship's lab. Today he would see nearly two years of lab work and grief play out. Before scrubbing in, he had even checked the carts and supplies laid out for the procedure, a task typically handled by a surgical tech under the Circulator's supervision.

Earlier, he had visited Rebecca's memorial once more. Cemetery had been quiet at six in the morning, his rose garden bountiful. He heard only the mausoleum door's groan, the dusty plod of his footsteps, the sizzle of mist on flower petals. The morning was so quiet, so still, and that quiet, that stillness reminded him of time stretching before him, years upon quiet years. For some time he'd known what he had to do, and he would do it today.

Now the doors were opening, and a warning whistle sounded, low but urgent, like air cutting sharply past a blade of grass. The patient was about to enter the room.

ANNALIE

The chair moved along a track through Hydrangea Station. For Annalie, the motion felt like that of a monorail. The slow and seamless gliding reminded her of a trip to Disney World their class had taken senior year of high school. There was a boy she'd been dating at the time. Aimee'd had someone, too, someone she liked and would start seeing by the time they left Orlando. Before she and her sister started at Pitt, though, they ended things with their boyfriends. To make things easier, Annalie had pretended to be Aimee, and Aimee had pretended to be Annalie. The boys never knew the difference.

At Pitt, Annalie had majored in English and had taken a theory course her junior year. She'd encountered Derrida that semester, and what had stayed with her, what she recalled now as her chair slid silently along its track, was the "knowledge of finitude" he described, the question around which an enduring friendship revolved: *Who will die first?* All friendships, Derrida had insisted, were constituted on the inevitability of mourning. All partnerships, hers and Aimee's included, came down to this: *Who would die, and who would mourn?* Now, of course, she knew.

Her chair rounded a bend, and before her appeared a pair of doors that started to yawn open at her approach. In the widening gap, a glow was spreading. Above the doors, a light turned from red to green. A female voice said, "Welcome, Annalie." The chair moved forward, and the soft glow surrounded her, swallowed her. She imagined coming back out, on the other side of her excursions, bandaged but breathing. For a quick moment, she also imagined not coming out and wondered, as she had wondered before, if that would be so bad.

NICOLE

SATURDAY O8:14

Nicole changed three times Saturday morning before breakfast. Finally, she settled on a strapless linen jumpsuit. The pant legs were flowing and forgiving, and the middle was loose above the waistband to hide any bulge. She was going for effortless chic, she told herself. She pulled her hair back and to the side in a low bun to keep her shoulders exposed. "There." She exhaled into her bathroom mirror screen before strapping on her wedges and heading out.

"I was starting to think I'd have the morning off," Cedric said as he pulled out Nicole's chair. "I was worried you were abandoning me."

"I would never!" Nicole returned, slipping right into their flirty repartee. All week, she'd had Table 32 to herself for at least part of breakfast. Before the cruise, she would have been mortified to sit alone at a café or restaurant for a meal. What would her server think? The other diners? What would she do while she waited on her food? But since her crush started Wednesday morning, she didn't mind, not one little bit, eating alone. Sometimes, too, Cedric would take a knee next to her so they could talk, share stories about their lives before this week. Nicole learned about his divorce, and Cedric learned about Max and her mother as Nicole's eggs cooled.

"I'm glad you're here," Cedric said with a big smile. And with a flick of his wrist, Nicole's napkin hopped off the table and onto her lap.

"Me, too," she said. "It's my last meal before—"

"—before your excursions," Cedric finished. "I know. I've put in a special request. The chef makes this insane crème brulée French toast. You said crème brulée was your favorite, so I thought . . ."

"Perfect," Nicole said, trying not to cry or kiss Cedric or run away or sweat too much. "Thank you."

Cedric bowed. "I'll be right back with your latte." He winked.

Nicole took a long sip of ice water, gulping down the cold and hoping none of the other women would show up, hoping for more time with Cedric. This hope, and her tingling awareness of Cedric moving around the room, kept Nicole from thinking too much about what was to come. After breakfast, she was to report to Hydrangea Station, and despite her consultation and her confidence in the safety protocols she'd read and reread on her stateroom screen, she was struggling to overcome her anxiety. If she could fast-forward to recovery, she would. Cedric was, she found now, a crucial distraction.

By the time he came back with a few freshly cut strawberries and a salted caramel latte, she had finished the water and was crunching on some ice.

"Don't worry, okay?" He stood with one hand on the back of her chair. His fingers were so close to her bare shoulder that she felt the back of her neck become a thousand needles.

"About?" she asked. She had so much to worry about.

"Your itinerary." Cedric picked up the water pitcher and refilled her glass. "You are in the best hands," he continued. "Before you know it, you'll be back here begging for more of this French toast I'm about to serve you."

Nicole laughed, a bright pop of sound. "It's that good, huh?"

"Mind-blowing." Cedric backed away from the table and flung his hands open, fingers spread in a faux explosion.

Nicole raised an eyebrow, and it was Cedric's turn to laugh. He waggled a finger at her before turning toward his serving station.

Nicole's wish came true: She had the table to herself. Cedric served her and only her. He had other tables, but he didn't seem to pay them as much attention. He even pulled out the chair next to her and sat while she cut into bites the gooey breakfast confection on her plate. Cedric's knee was inches from hers, his hands folded on the table near her bare arm, and as Nicole brought a bite to her mouth, her hand shook.

She found she didn't really like the dish—the consistency too much like pudding, and all of it entirely too sweet—but she ate it anyway, telling Cedric about the dog she'd adopted but had to return two days later (he was a biter), and the time she broke a wrist in aerial aerobics (falling from a ring eight feet off the ground). That class had been Semra's idea, of course. She talked about Semra, Jane, and even her "job" selling B+L, skirting the fact that she'd bought twenty thousand dollars' worth of products she couldn't move (despite following all of the company's trusted marketing strategies).

"You didn't save me any?" Cedric asked, picking up her dish when she was done and pretending to inspect it. His cheeks, she noted, were baby cheeks, hairless and smooth, with a slight dimple in the right one when he grinned, as he was doing now. "So good, right?"

Nicole brought her napkin to her mouth. "Mmm hmm," she affirmed.

Bending to clean the table with a handheld crumb vacuum, Cedric spoke quietly, his voice almost swallowed by the machine's gentle whir: "I wanted to do something special for you."

He turned his head to meet her eyes, only a whisper of space between them, and Nicole held her breath. An endless moment later, she exhaled. "Oh?" That was all she could think of to say.

Cedric just smiled, his eyes never leaving hers. Then he stood, shut off the vacuum, and asked, "Tea for the lady?"

She nodded, not trusting herself with words. She could stay just a little longer, she decided. Ten more minutes. She would have tea and then head straight for Hydrangea from here, replaying scenes from this morning on her way.

Cedric had stopped to speak to someone at the drink station, and now he was turning and coming back toward her. He wasn't carrying a cup of tea, though. His hands were empty, swinging lightly at his sides. So strange. He seemed to be moving in slow motion, each step longer than the one before it. He was shrinking, too. With each step, he grew smaller and smaller. Nicole yawned. Watching Cedric walk toward her was exhausting. Her eyelids grew heavy. She closed her eyes, giving in to the weight pressing down, then moving down, settling into her chest, her stomach, and expanding into a pit, growing, growing, now crawling down her legs, which she could no longer feel.

CEDRIC

SATURDAY 09:09

Cedric stood in front of Nicole, whose eyes were closed. Now her body started to slump and tilt to the right. He secured her with a strap and nodded to the crew member standing behind her—a surgical technician wearing a server uniform so as not to not alarm the passengers still dining. The man pulled a small metal object out of the pouch in the front of his shirt and bent down to release the chair's wheels.

"That was easy," Cedric said. "She went down fast."

"We've perfected the delivery system and the dosage," the other man said.

"How often do you do this?" Cedric asked.

"Often enough. There's no need for passengers with trauma to suffer needless anxiety. She'll thank us later. They all do." He grunted over the fourth wheel, which appeared to be jammed in its chamber. "All this technology," he said, "and these wheels stick every time."

Cedric asked, "Will she remember any of it?"

"Hard to say." A click, and the fourth wheel released. "Anesthesia is tricky. Some remember everything up until the final bite. Some barely remember even waking up for the day. Depends on the body chemistry of the individual."

"I see." Cedric hoped Nicole would be an individual who remembered more.

THE CIRCULATOR

SATURDAY 13:32

"3-0," Dr. Stalworth said.

"Let me get this vessel first," said the assisting surgeon, Dr. Keating, dipping the Bovie back into the open cavity. Kennedy slapped the requested suture on a needle holder into Dr. Stalworth's open palm. Isaac held three clamps looped through fingers on his left hand and pulled a retractor tight with his right. So it would go, the entire itinerary like this, holding here and there, metal moving from tray to Isaac or Kennedy's hand to a doctor's hand before joining the site, while another tech counted and recorded used OR rags and sponges, needles and threads, pulling out more of anything as needed, moving about in a wider circumference around the sleeping passenger. So much work to do! Instruments popped into gloved hands. Clamps clicked open and closed. Metz and Mayos snipped soundlessly. Black string knotted and pulled taut; once cut, the released ends flicked off gloved fingers into the surgical waste bin.

Meanwhile the Circulator sensed and listened—in this operating room, and the next one, and the next, and the next—monitoring four itineraries simultaneously.

Meanwhile Nicole slept, tube taped to the side of her mouth, vitals all in their normal ranges, her body still, pliable in its stillness, her abdominoplasty in progress.

"That old Caesarean scar was something," Dr. Stalworth said.

"Shoddy OB work, if you ask me," responded Dr. Keating.

"The materials those guys use? Staples and stitches?"

"Stone Age stuff."

"These scars. It's no wonder." Dr. Stalworth swapped the suction for a Kocher.

"If they could see what we're working with."

Dr. Keating held out his right hand. "Another 3–0, please."

"That new laser would blow their minds."

"It blows my mind, and I'm used to the crazy stuff we do."

"But sometimes, isn't it nice to just do tucks all night? Cut, please."

"I don't know. I can get tucked out. After a while, it starts to mess with my stomach. Heartburn like you wouldn't believe."

"I'll tell you what. A night of tucks is good for my waistline. Makes me drop the hamburger and opt for a salad."

"Have you tried the burger on the boat?" Dr. Stalworth used the Bovie to zap a series of vessels. "Not meat, but it's tasty. Even has the same heavy, greasy feel in your mouth, but it's good for you."

Dr. Keating lifted an eyebrow. "Good for you? C'mon. Even Beyond and Impossible burgers aren't *good* for you."

"Circulator," Dr. Stalworth said, his hand, then his arm dipping into the open abdomen to explore and evaluate before they continued. "Can you have a hamburger with the works in the lounge for my friend here when we close?"

"I am not able to assist with this request."

"It was worth a try."

BIANCA

SATURDAY

After a day to herself, Bianca had fallen asleep early, still dressed in her clothes, and dreamed not so much a dream as a memory from years ago. She'd been walking in the woods with Vivian and Rowan when a cloudburst had surprised them, soaked them. In the parking lot, the girls had jumped in puddles, shrieking with delight, and later, at home, after warm baths, they'd cuddled on the couch with her, watching a movie until they all fell asleep like that, heads on one another's shoulders. Anthony had tapped her knee to wake her. He was home late from work. She had uncurled herself from the couch, from the sleeping bodies of her daughters, and she and Anthony had each carried a girl up to bed, two sets of little limbs swinging gently as they climbed the stairs. She could have stayed on the couch. She could have slept forever with the girls like that, tucked in tight against the disappointments that would come.

"Fuck," Bianca said, the sound of her voice startling after so much quietude, only ambient noise—others' conversations, bird noises and breezes, dings and plops and rustling. She turned on the bedside lamp and used a control panel to bring the bed and herself into a sitting position.

Ever since bingo, Bianca found the thought of socializing fraught, perilous. She couldn't *unshare* what she had shared. She had left her family. What else was there to say? To other women, other mothers especially, she imagined she seemed a monster. So she didn't join her table for dinner Thursday night, and she kept to herself all day Friday and today, too. Meals she ordered delivered, and she picked at them in her room.

This morning, before her scalp treatment and massage at the Spa, she had walked the Park path. There, she thought she'd glimpsed Nicole ahead of her, her dark ponytail flapping against her back, pale yellow tee flashing through green branches heavy with spring buds, and Bianca had quickly turned down a narrow side path and picked up the pace. By the time she got back to the entrance with its wide wooden archway, Nicole, or the woman she thought was Nicole, was nowhere to be seen.

In the afternoon, she had followed her massage therapist's orders to rest in the shade outdoors. *Let the sea air work its magic.* She read under a pale blue canopy, whisps of honeydew and cut grass on the breeze. She napped, and when she woke up, poked around in the stack of magazines that had appeared beside her while she slept. Coastal decor. Celebrity athlete marriages. Perfect hoodies for all seasons. Smart fitness accessories and gear. She sat and listened to the water lapping against the hull, turning pages.

In the evening, she walked again, this time on the Cemetery path, where the growing darkness felt like a blanket stretching across her shoulders, pulling tight to her chest. Under her footfalls, the gravel crunched. She thought about the next day, and the day after, and the day after. In the morning, she would report to Hydrangea Station, and after she woke up from her itinerary, she'd be one step closer to becoming the person she knew she could be, winning on the court and elsewhere. Able to return home with her head high. Or she wouldn't be any closer. She'd lose more, languish, and then what?

Deep into Cemetery and a ways from the main path, she found a mausoleum. After pulling open the door, she stared into the hazy dark, waiting for her eyes to adjust. She shook her head. No, she thought. She didn't even cross the threshold. She turned back, retraced her steps. *No.* If she couldn't win, she'd retire. Put up her rackets for good. No more lessons. No more coaching. No more tennis centers in plantations or country clubs. Going forward, it was all or nothing. One way or the other, she'd return from the cruise a different person.

At the entrance to the Cemetery she let out a breath she hadn't realized she'd been holding. A deckman approached, offering a can with a tube snaking out of it.

"Interested in some oxygen, with a delightfully cozy basmati rice scent?"

Bianca started to shake her head. She started to insist that she was fine, didn't need any extra air—no, thank you, sir—then realized oxygen was precisely what she wanted right now. "Yes," she said.

The deckman smiled, passed the can and the attached line to Bianca, explaining, "Just hook that piece, yup, that one, called the nasal cannula . . . that's right, you got it . . . bingo."

Bianca inhaled deeply. Immediately she felt like she was in a warm kitchen, standing over a pot of creamy, comforting rice.

"Pretty great, right?" The deckman rocked back on his heels.

"Incredible," she said, and she meant it.

"And when you're done, you can recycle both pieces at any recycling station on the ship."

All the way back to her cabin, Bianca could practically feel her alveoli ballooning, her cells opening, her tissues renewing with this infusion of extra air. God, she felt great. And this was only the beginning.

DR. HESTON

SATURDAY 13:45

It was as though someone hit a baseball out of the diamond three years ago, over the county sports complex's metal fence. Out there, the ball hit the parking lot asphalt and started to roll, and it rolled out of the lot and down the road, gaining speed on the downward slope and skipping over the train tracks into downtown, where it bounced along the sidewalk, past the barber, three thrift stores, and a hot dog shop, and it kept on rolling past neighborhoods and parks and the wide swath of woods at the edge of town filled with chestnut oaks, shagbark hickories, and a tulip poplar, its golden blooms ablaze in the evening sun. The steep grade only increased the ball's velocity, and it continued rolling along the bypass on the outskirts of the city, under truck beds and minivans and Mercedes sedans. On and on it rolled, and as it rolled, it took on a will, a life of its own, skipping like a stone across rivers, bouncing off longleaf pines and white oaks, traveling quietly down dirt roads for a time, then into new cities, where it ricocheted from skyscraper to skyscraper like a pinball before falling down fire escapes and zipping along riverwalks and over bridges. Onward it rolled, through night and day, sun and rain, slipping past homes in a neighborhood where crepe myrtles bloomed and kids played on backyard trampolines and women walked with their babies wrapped tight to their bodies. The ball continued on until it struck a stone in the street and shot left, spinning down a cul-de-sac, bouncing, and bouncing again while picking up speed, finally bouncing so high and spinning so fast that it careened through the second-floor primary bedroom window of the Cortero family and directly—as if guided by some higher power—into Nicole Cortero's abdomen, where it had remained ever since, planting itself in its new environment of tissue and fluid, its presence indiscernible amid the symptoms women in their thirties experience before, during, and after having a child: cramps, nausea, fatigue, lightheadedness, spotting, more cramps, the midsection distending.

Or at least that's how Dr. Heston imagined the origin of the tumor he cupped in his gloved hand, a mass affixed to the lower wall of Nicole's uterus, wedged under the bladder and seven centimeters in diameter. He sighed.

"Finish this up, close, and hold the other procedures. This is all we can do, I'm afraid." The Captain nodded to Drs. Stalworth and Keating, who had called him in to consult. They understood the gravity of what they'd found. They would take great care. Exceptional care. This would be their finest tummy tuck.

Long after Dr. Heston scrubbed out, he would still feel the satin ball in his hand, and from time to time, particularly on hot and hazy afternoons when he recalled the long summers he had spent on Little League ball fields, chewing gum and spitting into the dusty red clay and smacking his fist into his glove—in retirement, even—he would think about the ball he'd seen in a woman's abdomen and wonder why it landed where it did.

THE PILGRIM DAILY
SECOND SUNDAY

Where do you want to go today?

WALKING PATHS. HOURS: 09:00–24:00

Park . . . . open
Mall . . . . opens at 10:00 today
Cemetery . . . . open

SPA. HOURS: 09:00–19:00

DAILY SPECIALS

Magic Eraser
HydroScalp Treatment
Kale Cream Contour Wrap

*Book now on your room screen or talk to your room steward
to schedule a visit.*

DINING. SEE HOURS BELOW.

Breakfast 06:00–9:00
Lunch 11:30–15:00
Dinner 19:00

ON-BOARD ACTIVITIES. HOURS: 05:30–23:00

Spiritual Awakening, Deck 12 . . . . 05:30
Farmer's Market, The Mall 7:00–9:00
Brunch Bingo, Deck 8, Bingo Hall 10:00–12:00
Sunday Funday Boozy Afternoon, Deck 10 . . . . 14:00–16:00
Weekend Wind Down Happy Hour, Deck 10, Citrus Canopy 17:00
Starry Night Sleep Training, Deck 12 . . . . 22:00

EXCURSIONS.

For passengers embarking on itineraries today, we look forward to welcoming you
to your assigned flower suite. Room stewards are available to escort you.

OUT & ABOUT SPECIALS.

The Pedicure Parlor has Signature and Luxe mani-pedi appointments available
starting at 15:00.

BIANCA

In one of the dressing rooms at Hydrangea Station, Bianca took a gown and matching robe out of an open closet. She chose a pearly blue set. Blue was the color she saved for the final round of a tournament, a ritual started at her first state championship when she was thirteen. That's what she kept telling herself this was: a championship match.

As she changed, flashes of the future she longed for cartwheeled through her mind. Her agent on the sidelines in Miami later this month. (She could hear his fiery chant after each ace: *C'mon, Bi!*) Her opponents dropping in nearly straight sets. A long shot, but a shot, at qualifying for the US Open this summer. This *summer*! Her girls and Anthony running outside when her car pulled up the drive. Vivian and Rowan insisting, *Don't ever leave us again,* and her reply, *No, my darlings. I'm back. I'm here.* Their hair in her face all strawberries and sticky heat. And her husband folding her into his arms, his murmur in her ear: *I knew you could do it.*

She left her clothes folded in the locker labeled with her name and pulled on the gown. Against her skin, it was cool, more sheen than material. She wrapped the robe around her and cinched the belt. Then she stepped into the fleecy slippers set out before her locker. She had no jewelry to remove, nothing valuable to secure in the available safe. She looked in the mirror. There, she already saw a younger version of herself, her reflection a palimpsest. There, traces of the young woman she was at twenty were visible in the freckles along the bridge of her nose, something shining in her murky brown eyes, a radiance she felt slipping away on nights when the cicadas' call kept her awake and restless. Could she really be thirty-seven? Washed-up? The mother of two? Her ears picked up soft, wet sounds from somewhere in the room, rippling streams and the plinking of drizzle in leafy treetops.

As she stood there, listening, she picked up some notes that didn't belong. Was it her imagination, or did she hear a child's giggle, the light and dreamy lilt of it far away, just a glimmer of sound among the other sounds.

"Bianca?" a female voice called through the changing-room door. "Are you all right?

Bianca took a deep breath. "Yes," she said, though she wasn't sure what she was.

"Can I offer any assistance?" the female voice asked.

"I'm fine," Bianca insisted, moving to the sink. She turned on the water and brought handfuls of it to her face. She looked in the mirror again and rubbed her face until it was pink. "I'll be fine," she said.

"We're ready for you," the voice said as a section of wall slid back, revealing a rich and welcoming light.

Bianca walked forward into the glow.

ROCCO

Sunday afternoon, Rocco thought he recognized her: Grandma Barbie. He and Larry were attending to the passengers coming off their Days at Sea who'd opted for active recovery in the open air of Deck 10. He had a theory she would be one of the ones resting on deck early in week two, her body having already adjusted—change its new normal—able to heal from increasingly invasive procedures more quickly each cruise, her own restorative power compounding the healing rate projected by her custom Rapid Recovery Protocol.

The woman under scrutiny was on the leeward side of the ship, lying on a padded chaise, dark sunglasses shading nearly half her face. Her hair had been pulled to one side, a dark pile of messy curls spilling over the right side of the lounger. From the waist down, she was tucked into a light waffle-weave blanket.

Rocco watched the resting woman, the blanket rising and falling with her breaths, her body's own waves. He couldn't understand the impulse for reinvention, not really. He'd wanted to stay in higher education, make a life out of researching algorithmic data analytics for the tourism industry and teaching undergraduates how to read numbers, and he would have . . . if any of his seventeen applications had panned out. He would have submitted more, but there were no other statistics or even applied mathematics jobs open. He'd gotten two initial interviews, even made it to the final round for a position with over two hundred applicants. But close didn't count on the academic job market, and he needed a job. He could have found one on land—a consulting gig in a city—but he traded a concrete ocean for the real one, polluted air for a briny breeze, cubicle for deck. He lived rent-free, and all his meals were provided. Maybe he was here for more than a paycheck—not reinvention, but a break, sure. At some point, he imagined, he'd return and start his life again. His real life. For Grandma Barbie—whether it was she lying across the chaise or not—*restart* was her way of life. He wondered what brought her to the boat for surgery after surgery after surgery. What had she lost? And when would she be satisfied, ready to return to the world and live in it as she was?

Lately, Rocco had started to wonder if he were complicit in her endless tinkering, in all of the tinkering that occurred in the flower stations each week. Were the Captain and his crew giving passengers what they wanted, or were they supplying what women were *told* to want by the media and celebrity culture, by needy partners or competitive peers, even by the ship's marketing literature, and then during the passengers' consultations? Now, when anyone on board talked about Grandma Barbie, Rocco couldn't help but feel these overheard bits of conversation like weight in his stomach, a gluey and thick gravy. Rumors always abounded, of course, but last week, he'd heard a particularly disturbing one—that she had died on the table two months ago, that her body had been transported off the ship on the same conveyer belt that carried out the bags of recyclables and compost bins. He'd heard she thanked the crew for making her so beautiful, and she sang a little Sinatra with the anesthesia tech while he started pushing drugs. He refused to believe she was gone.

While Rocco was watching the woman—the woman he *hoped* was Grandma Barbie—he saw Larry approach her, though no alert had been issued to their refreshment station. There was nothing BECCA felt she needed just now. Rocco finished restocking stirrers and garnishes—lemon wedges and curly lime rinds, maraschino cherries and perfectly round green olives—but his eyes never left Larry. What was his partner doing? The man stood to the left of the woman and behind her head so he wouldn't be seen, so his shadow wouldn't fall across her. He appeared to be studying her. Then he crouched and turned toward her hair, his face inches away from the dark, winding strands.

"What in the world?" Rocco whispered. His hand hovered over the olives, one pinched between his thumb and pointer finger. Across the deck, Larry began to move his fingers in the woman's mass of curls. Rocco started to fume. The woman was sleeping, for god's sake. He knocked on the shellacked butcher block of the bar to get his partner's attention. *Rap, rap, rap. Rap, rap, rap.* A woman on his side of the boat looked up, and Rocco held up a hand to apologize. Larry, however, didn't look up. He was still combing through the woman's hair.

The olive Rocco was holding buckled under the pressure of his fingers. That's it, he thought. He tossed the juicy mush into the trash and started across the deck. He planned to tap Larry on the shoulder, pull him back, and ask quietly, *What the fuck?*

Larry sifted through the woman's hair, like a monkey looking for nits in another monkey's fur. When Rocco was just three steps away, Larry gave a little yank. The woman flinched, rubbing her head along the padded back of the chaise, but seemed to stay asleep. Larry stood and turned, a grin splitting his face.

Rocco grabbed his arm and dragged him away. "What the heck was that?" he asked.

Shaking off Rocco's arm, Larry said, "Easy. I was just pulling this." He held up a strand of something, but in the glare of the sun, Rocco couldn't see what it was.

"What is that?'"

"A gray hair." Larry tucked the strand into the pocket of his shirt. "That's all. You can relax, man."

Rocco stared. "Why would you do that?"

"To have a little fun." Larry shrugged.

Rocco frowned. "Fun?"

Moving over to their station's screen, Larry pulled up the new orders that had come in. "Relax," he repeated. "It's fine. Just a little trophy." His eyes never left the screen. When he spoke again, Rocco wasn't sure if he was talking to himself or to Rocco. "It's not like the women even notice something is missing."

"Women?" Rocco said.

Larry spun to face Rocco, baring his teeth in a smile. "These smoothies aren't going to blend themselves."

JARED

SECOND SUNDAY 14:56

Since Dr. Heston had commissioned him to engineer the Body Rejuvenation Package, Jared ran first assist for Bianca Simmons's itinerary. He had designed her protein pump down to the microchip that controlled it, and then spent months prototyping and testing. Today he would help install and activate the pump. Back at the biotech firm he had worked at since medical school, he would have been stuck on the bench, looking at flow states and flow rates for micro-electro-mechanical systems, or repairing and reinstalling hacked insulin pumps. He certainly wouldn't have been building his own medical device and integrating it with a surgery package. But here he was, and today his system would go live. He wondered if this was how surgeons felt every day, remaking the body with their own two hands. Did it get any better than this?

The Circulator repeated, "Skin prick."

Jared shook his head to focus. "Negative," he said. "No twitches."

"Catheter."

"Inserted."

"Fluids."

"Two-and-a-half bags. Started sixteen minutes ago, rapidflush on."

"Monitors on."

"And blipping."

"Response unexpected. Repeat. Monitors on."

"Blood, drug, and 02."

"Thank you. Patient ID number. Confirm on chart."

"4599K4Z."

"Confirm on wristband."

Jared picked up Bianca's limp wrist. "4599K4Z."

"Confirm on Surgicom."

He read off the screen: "Bianca Simmons. Patient number 4599K4Z."

"Itinerary summary."

Jared described the procedures he had spent the past three months developing: "Body Rejuvenation Package. We'll begin with electromyostimulation, followed immediately by amino acids administered intravenously, at which point the patient will be prepped for abdominal surgery. The protein pump will be inserted in the upper left quadrant and will support protein metabolism and synthesis at a rate of three times average efficiency. Finally, this itinerary will conclude with ligament and tendon sheathing, along with stem-cell injections at the base of each sheath. Sheathing sites to include left and right extensor carpi radialis brevis, rotator cuff, anterior cruciate ligament, and medial collateral ligament for a total of eight collagen-rich constructed tissue sheaths. Estimated time, five hours."

"Summary confirmed."

"Thank you, Rebecca. We've got it from here," Dr. Heston said, walking into the room.

"Do no harm," the Circulator said. "Go forth, and make beautiful."

Jared smiled wide. He couldn't help it. "And fast. And strong."

Dr. Heston grinned, too. "Clock-in time, Rebecca. On my mark." Dr. Heston nodded to Jared who nodded back. "Three, two, one."

"Start time set at 11:57."

"Jared," Dr. Heston said, gloved hands held up, away from his body, "shall we begin? I see the passenger is ready for electromyostimulation."

"She is, sir," Jared said. Indeed, the passenger's body had become a labyrinth of lines connected to cathodes in varying sizes and colors.

"Very well," Dr. Heston said.

Jared nodded, turning to the box that sat on the table beside him, into which all of the lines flowed. He set the charge. "First stim in three, two, one." He pushed the button, releasing the charge. Of course, there was nothing to see, aside from a twitch here and there, but he imagined the passenger's body glowing with electrical power.

LARRY

Larry had a twenty-minute break before his evening shift, which felt like no time at all. During an afternoon cleaning bathrooms with a stubbornly silent Rocco, Larry had whistled as loud as he could as much to fill the quiet as to try to rile up Rocco—to no avail. Now, as he made his way to Deck 8, he was already dreading a whole night of dealing with his sour partner.

He stood in front of the Trackz access door, his hand feeling for the hidden lever. When he found it, he waited. Always, this moment at the maintenance door gave him pause. Had someone gotten wise to his activities, rewired it since his last ride? Would an alarm sound when he turned his wrist? Would someone be waiting inside to catch him in the act? Or maybe a passenger would be awake, surprised to see a deckman down here. He could always ask if she wanted a drink or a towel, some fresh gauze, perhaps? And there was the end of the ride, as well. Would he be caught leaving a stateroom, diamond earrings in his pocket? There was always jewelry laying around, in a ceramic bowl on a bedside stand or else a plump velvety bag on the dresser. He never knew what he was going to take until he took it. He had an eclectic taste. Glancing around one last time to make sure he was alone, he flicked his wrist and pulled. The door swung open, and he slipped inside.

No alarm. No yelling voice. Just the gentle murmur of a bed moving along the tracks, then another. Larry watched, waited. As the third bed approached, sweat started to roll down the column of his back, and he swallowed against a dry burn in his throat. Here it came. The air around him felt charged, rippling.

He landed harder than usual, harder than he had intended. As he scooted off the woman's abdomen, he pulled a small flashlight out of his pocket, turned it on, and held it in his mouth. He hoisted himself up and straddled her thighs. This woman wasn't excessively bandaged like so many of them were. She had only a small white gauze patch on the left side of her stomach. He peeled off the surgical tape running along the top edge of the gauze. Usually, the woman he rode with was mummy-wrapped, wound dressing like a tall stack of flapjacks, no way he was getting through it all. But this: practically a Band-Aid was all. He felt like he was unwrapping a gift. The slowness was maddening, intoxicating. At last, tape released from skin, he folded the dressing back to find an incision seeping blood.

"Huh," Larry grunted around his flashlight. He leaned in. He had three minutes. Four at most. The incision was six inches long and vertical, glossy pink skin brought and held together by what appeared to be a thin strip of gel, which was lined with a dozen or more thin horizontal strips of tightly woven gauze. He had never seen an actual surgical site before. Growing up, he had only broken bones, fingers mostly. A nose once, and two ribs.

He ran a finger along the track of neat white rows. "Huh," he said again. When he came to the place where the incision seemed a little wider, where blood was still leaking, he pinched one of the strips between his fingers and thumb and plucked it off. The skin edges spread apart, just barely, and more blood appeared.

So he plucked off another.

And another.

Against his fingertips, the skin and blood felt warm. He laid the strips he'd removed in the palm of his other hand. Six, seven, eight. He had less than two minutes.

He traced the gaping wound he had exposed. Then he pushed in two fingers gently, oh so gently, seeking a point of entry, and when he found it, he stilled, his fingers suspended in the spongy warmth of someone else's tissue. He tried to sink them deeper, but he couldn't. Not at first. He pushed harder, and he felt something pop.

His time was running out. He probably had a minute left now. His fingers probed the crevice, now brimming with blood. In went his thumb. He felt soft but distinct lumps, like tiny marshmallows submerged in Jell-O, the topography strange and wet. But then something solid, something cool and hard. An implant or device of some sort. He felt the top corners, a line, two lines running out of it, a protrusion in the front, like the edge of something small, a half-inch wide.

Thirty seconds and he'd be in the room. With a finger and his thumb, he pinched the tiny edge and pulled. He felt another pop, and something came free in his hand. A small square.

The door to the room was opening. Larry had to move. He retracted his hand, slapped the bandage back in place and pushed down on the tape. Blood smeared across the passenger's stomach, and a small tributary had started to roll down the side of her body, pooling next to her on the bed, soaking into the sheets. Larry's hand, too, was mostly red. The bed slid into the room. Larry spit his flashlight into his hand and closed his palm around the strips, the square, and the light, now off. He thrust his red, full hand into the wide pocket of his uniform shirt and used the other to dismount and climb down. With his clean hand, he pulled up the sheet scrunched at the foot of the bed. He reached across the passenger to even up the hemline, just below her jaw. Then he smoothed the fabric with three quick swipes and turned to go.

DEREK

When Derek, Bianca's room steward, responded to the alarm, he wasn't prepared to see blood. Passengers arrived back at their rooms like immaculate mummies, bandaged and buckled, but sometimes their blood pressure or o2 sats dipped a bit on the ride. That wasn't the case this time. The bed sensors, clicking on once the bed docked in the footboard, had picked up right away that something was amiss. No doubt Bianca's heart was racing, and she was obviously losing blood. Now she was starting to moan and twist under a sheet. She was waking up, a dark stain splashed across her middle.

Derek pushed a button on his tablet, but already a new alarm was sounding. The crash team would arrive momentarily. BECCA cast a hologram over Bianca's body, a spotlight on the left of her midsection. "Derek," a voice said. The Circulator. "Source of bleed: left lumbar region. Apply firm pressure until the floor team arrives."

Derek grabbed a towel off the rack in the bathroom and held it to Bianca's side. He leaned in. "Who signed off on her transport? Clearly that was a mistake." Up close, he could see that her cheeks were flushed. Sweat beaded her hairline.

The Circulator responded. "Transport request filed by Jared, Hydrangea Station. Post-op vitals were stable. Smooth extubation. Passenger was sleeping comfortably when she left the station."

"Obviously someone fucked up closing this incision."

"Assessment uncertain."

"Circulator, initiate Itinerary Review Protocol."

"Itinerary Review Protocol initiated. Please stand by."

A team of three surgical technicians dressed like room stewards entered the room. Bumping against each other and their equipment bags, they made their way to Bianca's bed.

ROCCO

Larry was late for their happy-hour shift. Only five minutes so far, but still. Rocco passed out a round of chilled white wine in stemless glasses to a group of women who had come aboard together for permanent makeup. The hues now embedded in the tissue were still so vivid, each face a riot of color: peachy cheeks and black-rimmed eyes, thick dark lashes and rosebud lips, eyelids a shimmery caramel. They must have just woken up from their Days at Sea.

When Larry was late, he usually attributed his delay to a gastric emergency. He claimed he suffered from irritable bowel syndrome and even had a medical note on file to justify his long trips to the bathroom. But Rocco suspected his partner's IBS was a convenient diagnosis, a way of prolonging his breaks and getting out of work. No way he was in the bathroom the entire time! Suddenly determined to find out one way or another whether Larry was fibbing, Rocco struck out across the deck to the crew bathroom on the leeward side.

Turning the corner, he pulled the lever to access the small lavatory. Inside there were two stalls, a urinal, and a single sink, and Rocco was almost disappointed to find Larry there, at the sink. The water was running and steam floated up and out of the bowl.

The door panel slid shut behind Rocco. "You're late," he said.

Larry didn't turn. He was scrubbing his hands. "One minute."

Rocco pulled two paper towels from the dispenser. "Here." As he approached, holding out the paper towels, he noticed the water in the sink bowl itself was a dark pink. "You okay?" he asked. "What happened?"

"Fine," Larry said, finally glancing at Rocco. "I cut my finger is all."

"That's a lot of blood. And you got it on your uniform." He pointed. "Which finger?"

"It's fine. Really." Larry scrubbed small patches where blood continued to stick to his hand. "See?" he said, turning off the water. "The bleeding has stopped and everything. I'll take those, though." He reached up for the paper towels Rocco still held outstretched.

"What happened?" Rocco persisted, suspicion creeping into his mind. He could still see Larry triumphantly brandishing that strand of gray hair. Surely Larry wouldn't actually *hurt* someone. He felt the heat of the room, all that steam filling the small space. His head swam. He took a step backward. He felt his pulse in his right temple, a hollow drumbeat.

Larry was watching him in the mirror. Then he smiled. "Relax, man. I was only poking around some place I wasn't supposed to." He shrugged.

Rocco shook his head to clear it. "Which finger did you say it was?"

Larry held up his right hand, which he had wrapped in paper towels. "First two." Then he pushed past Rocco and opened the door panel. "If you don't mind, I need to change my uniform and pick up a Band-Aid or two. And shouldn't you be getting back to work?" With that, he was gone, moving down the hallway, the sound of his whistling starting up, then snatched away by the wind.

Rocco took a deep breath and bent over the sink. Holding onto the bowl, he dropped his head. So Larry liked to mess with the passengers, with him. That didn't mean he had to let the guy get under his skin. Larry was a troublemaker, sure, and his tricks and dismissive attitude had triggered Rocco's paranoia. He closed his eyes and counted to ten. Sometimes the boat seemed like a daytime soap opera. Everyone with roles to play in the passengers' drama, the passengers themselves playing out their fantasies, becoming someone else, treating their bodies as costumes. But he had to keep things in perspective. It was week two, and Larry was an asshole. Just that. He opened his eyes.

Next to his left hand were eight tiny strips in a row, mottled white and brown and dark brown. Each a two-inch-long sliver.

"What the hell?" he murmured. Pulling one of the strips off the edge of the sink, he brought it to his face. It felt gauzy, gummy. The one he had pulled was completely brown. He thought about the pink water in the sink bowl. The dark spots Larry was scrubbing away. Blood. Rocco felt his heart start to pound again. *Where* did these come from? *Who* did they come from?

Again Rocco reminded himself not to jump to conclusions. He needed to rely on logic, on data. Pulling out two more paper towels, he used one to scoop the strips off the edge of the sink, then laid the other towel over them. Then he folded the whole thing in half, then half again, then slid the small square into the front pocket of his uniform until he could toss it into a biomedical waste bin later.

He needed more information, he decided as he soaped up his hands. There were too many variables. He sighed as he rinsed the suds from his fingers. He missed numbers, the elegance of theorems and formulas, the concreteness of data sets. People, he thought as he headed back to his station, were so hard to figure out.

BIANCA

Bianca was having a dream. She was standing in the countryside, on a farm of sorts, feet bare against the ground with its pressed dirt and clay, pockets of grass. In front of her, a wire fence reached up into the steel lid of sky. On the other side of the fence, an assault was in progress. Already a dozen hens lay fallen, feathers lifted and waving in the breeze. Bianca could not see the creature laying waste to the yard. She could only see the last hen standing, brave before a cluster of huddled chicks, the lot of them a vibrating fuzzy chirping.

Even as Bianca began to hurry around the barnyard, looking for a way in, she could see the drama unfolding as though in slow motion. The predator, whatever it was, continued to attack, but the final hen was fierce, reckless in defense of the chicks, *her* chicks. Bianca watched as the hen's eyes were scratched out, as she lost her beak to the unidentifiable monster. But even without her sight, without her only source of offense, the hen continued to protect her little ones. She stomped her wiry feet and ruffled the feathers on her body until they stood on end. She clucked and clucked, shifted her weight from side to side, trying to keep her chicks behind her, wherever behind was, so that her body could be a shield between death and her brood.

But she was blind, and the attacker ruthless, and as Bianca searched, trying to find a way through the fence, the chicks started to drop one by one. Still the hen squawked. Still she kicked. Still she flapped and stomped. When the attack began, she'd had eight chicks behind her, and then she was down to four, three, two. At last it was over. A stillness settled in the yard, and the air seemed to swell with daylight. The attacker was gone, having dissipated into dewy blades of grass and grains of dirt stirred by the faintest of breezes. The fence, too, disappeared, as well as the felled flock. Only the wounded hen and two little chicks remained in a tight circle, bloodied but alive.

In the dream world, Bianca stopped moving and simply stood in the yard, staring. She gasped. Across the hen's midsection, a streak of red glistened in the early morning sun. Blood dripped, turning the clay into mud where the wounded creature stood, clucking softly now, clucking calmly.

With her body torn open and slowly losing a necessary liquid, the hen wouldn't last long. The surviving chicks would soon be on their own.

DEREK

The code team pulled out a cautery unit. They pulled out a V.A.C. Therapy System. They pulled on gloves. The one with anesthesia training placed an oxygen mask over Bianca's mouth and nose and turned the flow up to 10 liters. This team was called rarely, but Derek knew they did simulation exercises almost daily.

When summoned to the bedside of Bianca Simmons, they worked together like a single machine: moves practiced, efficient, almost elegant. They didn't even speak.

The only real room steward present, Derek stood to the side, holding his hands—covered in Bianca's blood—up and away from his body while one of the techs pulled the towel from Bianca's midsection, yanked the top sheet away from her legs, and removed the loose, blood-soaked bandage. Another tech unfolded a blue drape around the area of skin BECCA had lit up, and when he nodded, the third tech sprayed the skin and drape in a neat oval around the red opening in Bianca's body. Bianca lay still amidst the chaos around her. Derek suspected BECCA had started titrating propofol and ketamine into her IV line to make her comfortable and ensure she stayed that way while the team fixed what was wrong.

Derek found himself getting lightheaded. He turned away from the red and blood, the men in their dance around the body in the bed, but it was too late.

THE CODE TEAM

SECOND SUNDAY 18:17

The techs were all busy with their protocols—controlling the bleed, minimizing the risk of infection—when they heard a heavy *gu-dunk-a-dunk* and turned to find Derek on the floor.

"That hasn't happened before," one of the techs said.

"Let's hope he didn't hit something on the way down."

"How has this not been one of the simulations?"

"I've got him," the anesthesia tech said. "Circulator, confirm Bianca's 02 sats." He tore off his gloves and pulled on a clean pair, then moved to check on Derek.

"Oxygen saturation at 98, 99, 100, 100, 100. Holding at 100."

Taking Derek's pulse, the tech proceeded to palpate the body. "No open wounds," he said, "but he may have a fractured cheek bone and a concussion. From the swelling, it looks like he took the brunt of the fall with his face."

"He'll need scanning for a brain bleed, in that case. And we'll want to rule out an orbital fracture."

"Circulator, can you place the orders and send the second team up with a wheelchair?"

"Affirmative."

Then the door opened, and Jared rushed into the room.

JARED

"The passenger's protein pump went offline. I need to get in there stat."

Already he was at the bed, pulling gloves out of the case he set on top of Bianca's shins. Everything had been fine, just fine, thirty minutes ago. But not now.

"Jared," the Circulator intoned. "You need to stand down. An Itinerary Review Protocol has been initiated."

"I'm afraid I can't do that." Jared snapped on his first glove. He snapped on the second one. This was his device, after all. His reputation. His *career*. Nothing was going to stop him from fixing the problem—whatever it was.

The Circulator repeated, "Surgical privileges have been temporarily suspended due to the investigation. Dr. Heston has already been paged. He will arrive in less than a minute."

Jared shook his head, leaned over the patient. "I see the incision site is already prepped."

"Jared," one of the techs said. "I think you should step back."

"Listen," Jared hissed. "It's not just the comm chip. The regulator stopped working. You've seen her vitals. She's got protein flooding her system, and I'd like that to stop before her kidneys shut down."

He started to unfold a set of sterile instruments, but the tech closest to him laid a hand on his arm. They stared at each other. Everyone froze for one, two, three seconds. Then an alarm started to beep.

"Circulator," the tech said, still not breaking eye contact, "monitor kidney function."

"Affirmative. eGFR at 49 and falling."

Jared wrestled his arm free but took a step back. He couldn't afford a fight here and now—and neither could the passenger. He held up both hands to signal surrender. "Gentlemen, the clock is ticking."

He'd barely finished speaking when Dr. Heston burst into the room. "Rebecca, protein pump specs and repair guide, please."

"Affirmative."

On the wall to the left of the bed, a large painting of four impressionistic chickens dissolved to black, and in its place appeared a schematic of Bianca's protein pump, which had gone online less than an hour ago. Two areas of the rectangular device glowed red.

"I've highlighted the device's regulator and communication chip, both malfunctioning based on passenger vitals and connection failure starting twenty-four minutes ago." The rectangle filled half the sixty-inch screen; inside Bianca, the device was slightly smaller than a deck of cards.

"After she left Hydrangea," Jared added.

"Affirmative."

Another alarm sounded.

Two techs moved into position to assist Dr. Heston. One tech held a mini OR lamp trained on the incision site and passed instruments to the Captain. Another placed retractors and held the suction tube. The Circulator, meanwhile, walked the team through the repair step by step, starting with the regulator. The second floor-team arrived, and in seconds they were wheeling Derek out of the room and the third tech had returned to the head of the bed to monitor Bianca's vitals. When it came time to fix the communication chip, Dr. Heston discovered there was no chip to repair. He looked at Jared, whose mouth hung open.

"What the—" Jared started, but Dr. Heston cut him off.

"Rebecca, have an available tech retrieve the backup chip from the lab."

"Affirmative. Anderson is already on his way with it."

THE PILGRIM DAILY

SECOND MONDAY

Where do you want to go today?

WALKING PATHS. HOURS: 09:00–24:00

Park . . . . open

Mall . . . . open (*today only: free Turkish beach towel with any cruise merchandise purchase!*)

Cemetery . . . . open

DINING. SEE HOURS BELOW.

Breakfast 06:00–9:00

Lunch 11:30–15:00

Dinner 19:00

SPA. HOURS: 09:00–19:00

DAILY SPECIALS

HydraWrap

Body-Bright Resurfacing

Soothe Your Soles

Book now on your room screen or talk to your room steward to schedule a visit.

ON-BOARD ACTIVITIES. HOURS: 05:30–23:00

Motivation Meditation, Deck 12	05:30
Espresso Tasting, Deck 10, Starboard Parlor	07:00
Correspondence with Calligraphy, Deck 8, Library	08:00
Breath Training, Deck 10, Mint Canopy	09:00
Advanced Breathing, Deck 10, Mint Canopy	10:00
Shop Till You Drop, The Mall	14:00–16:00
One Skein Workshop, Deck 9, Fiber Arts Studio	15:00
Forage the Forest, The Park	16:00
Dance Like a Star, Deck 8, Bingo Hall	17:00
Séance in the Cemetery, The Cemetery	23:00

EXCURSIONS.

For passengers embarking on itineraries today, we look forward to welcoming you to your assigned flower suite. Room stewards are available to escort you.

OUT & ABOUT SPECIALS.

Styling & Fitting Sessions are available for passengers who are Out & About. Schedule your half-hour or hourlong appointment before lunch to secure a spot today.

DAYS AT SEA

BECCA

WEEK TWO

BECCA assigned each woman a customized Rapid Recovery Protocol to ensure that she was 80 percent or more recovered following her Days at Sea. That meant all women would be able to attend the final dinner, if they so desired, and leave the following day on their own two feet, some assisted perhaps by the arm of a room steward or deckman. No drips. No drains. No excessive swelling. No pain that would necessitate more than the occasionally popped ibuprofen or acetaminophen for their first week home.

Each of these protocols was designed to optimize cell regeneration and stimulate tissue growth to facilitate healing at a rate far faster than the body's norm. For most passengers, Rapid Recovery started with a period of sedation, during which BECCA ordered and room stewards administered aggressive pain-management therapy, pressure-point stimulation, acupuncture, aromatherapy, and the application of topical ointments to incisions and the skin of highly changed—whether minimized or enhanced—regions.

Feeding tubes kept passengers sufficiently nourished, and BECCA ensured that each passenger's diet was customized for her own needs during recovery. Catheters controlled outputs, which room stewards monitored for signs of internal bleeding, hemorrhoids, or urinary tract infections.

Meanwhile, the women lingered in a state that approximated hibernation. They were comfortably sleeping, dreaming normally, and when they woke up, 98 percent reported feeling renewed and well rested, feelings that usually eluded them at home thanks to menopause or sleep-regressing babies or excessive blue-light exposure or alcohol too close to bedtime or a late-afternoon latte or to-do lists running rampant in their minds.

BECCA had designated the term for sedation Days at Sea, the same term traditional megaliners used for extended periods in transit, typically before or after ports of call, when the ships cut through a wide expanse of water, ocean on all sides. For both standard cruise ships and the passengers on *PILGRIM*, this was time required to get to where they were going. For 65 percent of passengers, Days at Sea lasted forty-eight hours, for 7 percent the stretch lasted less than a day, and for 4 percent of women—the ones who had extensive excursions—the Days stretched to five.

For three of the women at Table 32 this week, several Days at Sea were recommended. For passengers undergoing radical transformations, even rapid recoveries take time.

For the fourth woman, BECCA recommended two full Days at Sea despite her curtailed itinerary. She would wake to terrible news; why rush its delivery? She could rest now while her protocol ensured that the rest of her body was as healthy as it could be for the fight ahead.

ROCCO

When rumors about Derek's fall and the suspension of Jared's surgical privileges started to make their way to Deck 10, Rocco chuckled and shook his head along with the rest of the deckmen. Of course Derek would pass out at the sight of blood! And was it any surprise, really, that Jared had been pushing things in his station a bit too far? The guy was an arrogant ass. *See?* Rocco wanted to point out to Larry. *I can laugh at others' expense. I can judge others, same as you.*

But when he sat with Blake at lunch on Tuesday, he stopped laughing. Blake was describing, all too vividly but also secondhand, the state of the passenger when she returned to her room: stomach torn open, sheets tangled, blood everywhere.

"Before he, you know, hit the deck, Derek was pissed," Blake informed the table. "He said it looked as though a mad dog had gotten loose in Trackz, running amok."

Rocco had lifted his BLT for a bite, but now he froze, sandwich hovering before his open mouth.

Blake continued, "It had to be a rush job back in Hydrangea. That's what Derek said. He figured Jared was involved, and anyway, it was his device that had been malfunctioning in the first place."

Rocco returned his sandwich to his plate. "Malfunctioning how?" he asked.

"Not syncing up with BECCA, I think?" Blake said around a mouthful of miso-creamed kale. Still chewing, he brandished his fork like a trident. "And get this: the part of the device that does that, communicates with BECCA, is gone. Just missing. Derek learned that later from one of the code team techs. The passenger never should have been sent back to her room. No way."

"Well, that's why Jared's under investigation," another room steward chimed in.

Another asked, "How many chances is he going to get?"

A surgical tech said, "This is it. If the review turns up anything, he's off the boat."

Then another tech said, "I heard he's doing his own investigation."

Blake spoke past a bulge in his right cheek, "If by investigation you mean rampage, then, yes, that."

Rocco pushed away his plate, no longer hungry. "So what does *he* think happened?"

Blake shrugged. "Beats me. He's saying she was perfectly fine when she left the station, and the Circulator confirmed it."

"I heard he thinks it was Derek, and the injury was just a cover," a room steward shared.

"Maybe BECCA did it. Her version of *Space Odyssey*," another proposed.

One of the techs at the table shook his head. "My money's on the rabid dog." The whole table, except for Rocco, chuckled.

OUT & ABOUT

THE PILGRIM DAILY

Where do you want to go today?

WALKING PATHS.
HOURS: 09:00–24:00

Park . . . . open (*a spring shower
or two expected this morning*)
Mall . . . . open
Cemetery . . . . open

DINING.
SEE HOURS BELOW.

Breakfast 06:00–09:00
Lunch 11:30–15:00
Dinner 19:00

SPA. HOURS: 09:00–19:00

DAILY SPECIALS

Soft Hands
Gem Facial
Threading

Book now on your room screen or talk to your room steward to schedule a visit.

ON-BOARD ACTIVITIES. HOURS: 05:30–23:30

Affirmations for Accountability, Deck 12 . . . . 05:30
Sunrise Social, Deck 10, Mint Canopy 7:00
Soapmaking, Deck 10, Starboard Parlor 8:00
Design for the Runway, Deck 9, Fiber Arts Studio 9:00
Walk the Runway, Deck 10, Bingo Hall 10:00
Hot Yoga, Deck 12 . . . . 14:00
Spill the Tea & Tea, Deck 10, Citrus Canopy 15:00
Chakras and Charcuterie, Deck 10, Starboard Parlor 16:00
New 'Do Happy Hour, Deck 10, Citrus Canopy 17:00
Bedtime Bingo, Deck 8, Bingo Hall 22:30

EXCURSIONS.

For passengers embarking on itineraries today, we look forward to welcoming you
to your assigned flower suite. Room stewards are available to escort you.

OUT & ABOUT SPECIALS.

Styling & Fitting Sessions are available for passengers who are Out & About. Schedule your half-hour or hourlong appointment before lunch to secure a spot today.

LYLA

When she first woke from her Days at Sea, Lyla threw up. And then again an hour later. Both times, right before, she started to call out for Hal, her room steward. But he was already there at her side. He would hold out a shallow bucket shaped like a lima bean, and she would turn her head to the side and that would be that. Afterward, she would feel fine, and Hal would take the bucket away. That's morphine for you, she thought, settling back, not ready to get out of bed just yet. She nodded off again.

Later, a little after ten, Hal had come back and was checking her incision and injection sites when her stomach started to turn yet again. The lima-bean bucket appeared, and Hal held back her hair, murmuring, "Okay, there you go. Good. There you go." He assured her it could be worse.

"How?" she asked.

"I'm sure you know," he said. "As a nurse, you must see it all the time. How itchy morphine makes some people."

Lyla nodded.

The room steward continued. "Once had a passenger who was bent on scratching off her newly resurfaced skin. Finally put her in gloves and strapped her down, but the damage was done. Like raw strips of bacon, her arms."

When he left, she couldn't go back to sleep. She was comfortable in the bed—surprisingly so given how much time she had spent in it—but every time she closed her eyes she saw a skinless woman scratch and scratch and scratch. What's worse, she smelled the unmistakable fatty richness of bacon growing crisp and dark in a cast-iron skillet.

NICOLE

Nicole opened her eyes. Light streamed in through her porthole window. She looked around, saw the fringed edge of the blanket covering her body, tassels like cotton balls strung together. Past her bed, she saw a man sitting in a chair. She blinked and tried to gather herself, but she didn't even know what day it was. The man's eyes were closed, his chin against his chest despite the brightness of her room, the day. He wasn't her room steward. His hair was full and dark except for one streak of gray that swept from right to left and then back. He wore wire-rim glasses, and a stethoscope dangled from his neck. The black script on the pocket of his white coat read *Dr. Heston*. She thought this was a name she should know, but she didn't recall who he was or why he was there, asleep in the corner of her stateroom in what appeared to be the middle of the day—and yet when he lifted his head and opened his eyes and saw Nicole looking back at him, his face fell, and she wanted to tell him that it was okay, go ahead, sleep, just sleep, everyone needs a nap from time to time, we'll talk when you wake up again, when you don't look so sad.

Later, Nicole would remember focusing on the shining water beyond her window as he explained about the tumor. When he started talking about the follow-up care she would need with an oncologist back home, she interrupted, finally turning to meet his gaze. "But what about the rest?" Panic welled up inside her. "The rest of my itinerary?"

Dr. Heston shook his head. "I'm sorry," he said. "The tumor," he began, and the ocean, a brilliant blue beneath the high sun, crashed through the porthole window. With each word, each sentence, the water level rose. The room flooded. Listening to Dr. Heston, Nicole felt herself not so much sink into the water, pierced through by rays of light, as come apart in it, its brightness breaking her down into molecules until at last she was nothing more than blinding shards.

LARRY

Before dinner, Larry felt great. As he made his way to the crew dining hall, the narrow corridor he walked down felt filled with an electric energy, and the voltage coursed through him, bubbly and hot. He usually felt good after taking something from a passenger or taking a ride with one, but not this good, and not for so long afterward. (This, he considered, is how he surely would have felt if his high school football team had made it to the State Championship. Instead, they lost at Regionals, and Larry punched a hole through a locker room wall.)

At dinner, all that changed. He felt the energy in and around him sucked up and away by an invisible vacuum hose. First, BECCA announced the results of the Itinerary Review: Jared had been cleared of any misconduct, and his surgical privileges reinstated. Next—and far worse for Larry—BECCA confirmed that Trackz had, in fact, been compromised—that the passenger had been assaulted while riding to her room. The Captain was launching a full investigation, and by lunch, crew members would find a form in the system to report any observations that might help identify the perpetrator. All crew were asked to be extra vigilant during this unprecedented time.

Immediately, Larry wondered about Rocco—what he thought, what he knew, and what he thought he knew. Had his partner bought his I-

272

cut-my-finger lie in the bathroom? In the span of a minute, he vacillated between yes and no, relief and worry a half-dozen times. He took a few sips of sweet tea and forced himself to down his plate of rice, red beans, and andouille sausage. His stomach felt like a vault, sealed off by cold, hard steel, but he stuffed in bite after bite. Not eating would be strange for him, and strange might incite suspicion. He had listened to enough true crime podcasts to know that much.

DR. HESTON

Dr. Heston keyed in his passcode to enter the stateroom of a passenger on her last Day at Sea, the same room he had visited at nearly this same time for the past four nights. Based on her vitals, which Dr. Heston learned from BECCA, the passenger was sleeping, but more fitfully now that her sedation was starting to wear off. He walked in, a syringe of ketamine in his left hand to ensure she didn't wake. At her bedside, he pushed the syringe into the port on her IV line and turned on the floor lamp. Unlike the previous nights, the bandages were off at last. He pulled the room's reading chair over and turned it so he could sit close to the bed. He wanted exactly this—just to sit for a while and look. Earlier he'd had to deliver devastating news to a passenger about a tumor they found during her tummy tuck. And then BECCA had revealed her findings on the mysterious assault on another passenger. It had been a disconcerting—a disturbing—day. This visit, in the midst of all that unpleasantness, was both respite and celebration. Here he could breathe and behold what was, to him, the most beautiful sight in the world, one he'd feared lost to him, but here it was at last, at last, precisely as he remembered it to be.

The room darkened by degrees in the lateness of the day. The lamplight was warm and golden on her face. Rebecca's face.

He couldn't help himself; he leaned forward to take one of Annalie's hands in his. At night, he and Rebecca would entwine their fingers before falling asleep. Toward the end, he'd whisper, "Sleep now. I have you. You're not going anywhere," though they both knew that wasn't the case. *When* had been the variable: When would her hand turn limp in his, when would his beloved slip through his fingers?

Now, careful not to upset the IV, he wound his fingers through Annalie's. Then he turned his attention back to her face.

THE PILGRIM DAILY

SECOND WEDNESDAY

Where do you want to go today?

WALKING PATHS.
HOURS: 09:00–24:00

Park . . . . open
Mall . . . . open
Cemetery . . . . reserved for silent
reflection until 12:00

DINING.
SEE HOURS BELOW.

Breakfast 06:00–09:00
Lunch 11:30–15:00
Dinner 19:00

SPA. HOURS: 09:00–19:00

DAILY SPECIALS

Restorative Infusion Ritual
BodyGlow
RootAway

Book now on your room screen or talk to your room steward to schedule a visit.

ON-BOARD ACTIVITIES. HOURS: 05:30–22:00

Gratitude Journaling, Deck 8, Library 05:30
Magic Hour Photo Shoot, Deck 12 . . . . 07:00
Breakfast Bingo, Bingo Hall 08:00
Hostessing, Deck 10, Citrus Canopy 09:00
Mastering Menopause, Deck 10, Mint Canopy 10:00
Spice & Sauce Tasting, Deck 10, Starboard Parlor 14:00
Smoothies & Charades, Bingo Hall 15:00
Self-Care Soiree, Deck 10, Starboard Parlor 16:00
Celebrity Style, The Mall 17:00
Wine & Wishes, Deck 12 . . . . 21:00

EXCURSIONS.

For passengers embarking on itineraries today, we look forward to welcoming you
to your assigned flower suite. Room stewards are available to escort you.

OUT & ABOUT SPECIALS.

Styling & Fitting Sessions are available for passengers who are Out & About. Book
before lunch to secure a spot today. Five openings are available for Daily Blowouts
for the rest of the week.

ANNALIE

SECOND WEDNESDAY 06:40

The room was quiet except for a faint buzzing and the steady cadence of a monitor, its pulse light and mechanical, reassuring. The lamp was off. Outside the porthole window, a red band sat on the ocean, the sun burning at the edge of the world. Inside the room, darkness shrank into fuzzy shadows. Objects lost their hazy edge.

Annalie concentrated on her breathing. She watched her own chest rise and fall. Her Days at Sea must be over. Her eyelids felt woolen and dense, her head staked to its pillow. A stronger gravity now seemed to hold her to the earth. How long had she been asleep?

Her thoughts turned to her face. Already it felt foreign to her, a plaster mask, now set. Across her skin: pressure from the inside. Breathing through her nose and mouth proved effortful. Not painful, not exactly, but strange, unfamiliar. She inhaled. She exhaled. She noticed the caesura between breaths, how she encountered air through the new portal, taking it in and letting it go.

What did she look like? Of course, she had seen the simulation, but now that look was hers—off the screen and on her face. She wanted to peek in the mirror, but she couldn't. Doing so would require movement, would require lifting her head, but most of all, looking would show her that Aimee was gone, and as much as she couldn't bear to see her, she wasn't ready to *not* see her either.

She thought about the time Aimee had pierced her ears, and how her sister had folded Band-Aids over her lobes afterward before taking up the ice cube again to numb her own. On that day, too, she could feel her pulse throbbing, thick and syrupy, at the back of her skull, and her ears, she'd suspected were three times their normal size and as bright as strawberries. Now, with her whole face pierced and remade, she felt that heavy throbbing expand, rolling like a metal fog to engulf her neck and shoulders.

The sun rose, casting its yellow blanket upon the sea, and as that glow began to filter into her room, each minute more and more, brighter and brighter, glinting off the room's shiny surfaces and absorbing into softer ones, she felt as though she were floating on a strange raft in an ocean of air, far from a shore she could no longer see.

LYLA

Not long after Hal dropped off toast and berries and two scrambled eggs for breakfast—one bite and she realized how hungry she was, *famished*, like coming-off-a-twelve-hour-shift hungry—Lyla felt her nausea return. She waited for the urge to throw up, but fifteen, twenty minutes later, it still hadn't come. Still her stomach felt uneasy. She started to worry about the hormone patch, the implants. What if she were having an adverse reaction? What if her body was rejecting something? She put the back of her hand up to her forehead. She didn't feel warm. If she had an infection, surely she'd have a fever by now. Days ago, even.

Earlier that morning, Hal had told her she could leave the stateroom whenever she felt up to it. He told her to listen to her body, take it easy, and page for him if she wasn't quite ready to move about on her own. He would be happy to lend an arm. Now she thought she would try, on her own. If she could get to the mirror, she could conduct an evaluation, look for indicators of sepsis or implant rejection or an allergic reaction. She could have called Hal, requested an evaluation, but she wanted to see for herself. She understood, in the sudden rush, all those new-mom nurses she'd taken care of when they came in to deliver their babies; they were the worst patients, eager for the efficiency they'd commanded in the same room. Even as new moms, especially as new moms, they were nurses first. Lyla felt that way here, now.

She gently slid one leg, then the other, over the side of the bed. She let her toes touch down. When her feet were flat against the floor and steady, she pulled herself up to standing.

Her chest, tummy, and hips ached with movement, but the pain was tendril-like, trace and papery, not the sharp flares that accosted women after their c-sections. She shuffled to the full-length mirror on the back of the bathroom door. Though her pain was minor, her entire body felt tender, not just the implantation sites. She wore an exoskeleton consisting wholly of nerve ends, it seemed, and she was certain any sort of sensory input—a hearty hello from Hal, a gust of air—might cause her to crumple into a pile of bone fragments and skin cells on the ground.

At the mirror, Lyla stared at the woman staring back at her. Given the time she had been in bed lately, she sure didn't look like a patient. The satiny black nightgown she wore fell to her knees, a row of tiny snaps running along the side from bottom hem to neck. Her hair, too, wasn't trapped in tangles and knots; rather, it snaked around her shoulder in a loose but neat braid. Even her skin looked fresh and rosy despite how sick she'd felt all morning, how nauseous she still felt now.

She started to unsnap her nightgown. She'd expected to see bandages laced around her body, mummy-like armor she would have to unravel if she wanted to conduct a proper, thorough assessment. But beneath her nightgown was just her body, no dressings aside from small bandages and sets of Steri-Strips across incisions. With the last snap free, she let her nightgown fall, a black puddle at her feet. She looked up. Thick blue and green veins, like seawater ribbons, crisscrossed her chest, which bulged now, her breasts so much fuller than five days ago. At her hips and tummy were bulges too, slight swellings that added to her frame what her consultant had called *maternal curves*. Even her stance had shifted. Wider. She leaned closer to the mirror. On her face, she spotted a few pimples between her eyebrows and one more on her chin. Her forehead glistened in the room's natural light, and when she swiped a finger across it, her skin felt slick, oily.

Nothing was wrong, she realized. She wasn't reacting to anything. She didn't have sepsis.

She was pregnant.

At least as far as her hormones and figure were concerned.

She took a step back and turned to the side now. In profile, she laid a hand on her slightly convex belly. She imagined it growing, swelling with each passing week. She imagined five months ahead, strangers smiling at her adorable bump and asking all the usual questions: *Boy or girl? First baby? Do you have a name yet?* And to those questions, she imagined supplying answers she had figured out a long time ago, when she had first started imagining a small brood of children for her and Timothy. That fantasy, the one she returned to each day in her mind, had been the rehearsal for this. Now, at last, she'd get the chance to live a pregnancy past nine weeks and all the way up to forty. *Forty weeks.* Here she was at the beginning. What a wide and long bloom of time remained before her, each day its own luxurious stretch of hours. And Lyla wouldn't have to wonder and worry. She'd have the bump, the nausea, the heartburn, the stretch marks, the fatigue, the dreams, the emotional swings, the cravings, but no chance that the clock would stop abruptly, that a mysterious disorder would whisk a child away, in utero or after. No possibility of an arrhythmia or jaundice or birth defects. No failure to thrive, only thriving. Take away the baby from the beginning, and the worries went, too.

Except for one: her husband's reaction.

All along she had been telling herself that he would want to see her happy. That was often the refrain he would murmur into her hair on nights she quietly cried herself to sleep, the words an incantation uttered too late to ward off her sadness. But as she studied the woman standing before her, hands holding a belly that couldn't carry a child to term, she imagined Timothy looking, and she worried that what he saw might devastate him all over again, for the ninth time. Since her parents' confession, he had been confused about her body, hesitant to touch and hold her. This could make the situation worse. This could drive him away.

Lyla left her nightgown where it lay. She shuffled back to bed and eased herself in. She pulled the sheets to her chin and turned her head to look out the window. Ribbons of cloud floated, suspended against the twinkling blue of the morning ocean, and she began to cry.

LARRY

After two hours on a Bingo and Breakfast shift, Larry and Rocco were charged with stocking the Fiber Arts Studio on Deck 9. Larry wanted to learn what Rocco suspected, but he knew he had to take it slow. So he just started talking. He told Rocco about his grandmother while he sorted crochet hooks by size.

"She made everyone a baby blanket—her grandkids, the grandkids of her neighbors, the cancer kids in the hospital. Not sure where mine is, but it was brown and gold and ugly." He frowned at the memory of the blanket's coarse drabness. "She tried to teach me, but I didn't have the patience for it. Couldn't be bothered to sit still when I was younger."

A minute or so passed. Then Rocco said, "Some things, it seems, haven't changed."

Larry laughed, but it came out as a bark. "No, I guess they haven't." He kept smiling. Maybe he was getting somewhere. He finished adding same-sized hooks to their own jars. He took a deep breath. It was time to cut to the chase. "Did you hear about Jared?" he asked.

Rocco, combing through yarn skeins one by one, didn't respond. Already, he had wound about thirty balls, but he still had a bunch to go. A couple dozen.

"Earth to Rocco. You there?" Larry asked. He gathered a bunch of brightly colored stitch markers and placed them in their designated mason jar.

Rocco gave his head a shake. "I'm here." He pulled a skein.

Larry tried again. "I asked if you heard the news about Jared. The new investigation?"

Again, a long pause. The winder started up, the yarn flying together into a ball whose diameter grew wider and wider. When it stopped, Rocco asked, "New investigation?"

Larry nodded. "Jared was cleared, but someone did something wrong." He watched Rocco drop another skein into the winder. Again, the machine whooshed to life.

Quietly, Rocco said, "Interesting."

The winder stopped. Larry continued, "Trackz has been compromised, apparently. Someone must have snuck in and pulled out the chip." He ripped open a pack of jewel-tone buttons in a variety of shapes and sizes and poured them into a jar, their descent accompanied by a steady plinking sound, a plastic hail.

When he looked up, Rocco was staring at him. "Interesting," he said again. "Huh."

Larry shook the jar to settle its contents. "Some of the guys were talking at breakfast. We think it had to be a tech. Those guys all have direct access, right from the flower stations." Some misdirection couldn't hurt. Larry watched Rocco place a yellow skein into the winder. He watched, along with Rocco, as a ball of yarn grew before them.

"It's crazy, right?" Rocco said, his voice muffled by the hum of the winder. "What happened to her. That passenger?"

Larry shrugged. "No crazier than any of them coming here in the first place." He pulled a knitting needle from its jar, twisted it back and forth in his hand, studying the point. "Crazy things happen on this ship all the time." Larry could feel Rocco's eyes on him.

"Maybe the crew member will just turn himself in."

Larry shot the knitting needle back into its jar. "Maybe," he agreed. "But unlikely."

"Oh?" Rocco asked.

Larry looked up, his hands tensing into fists at his side. "Bad guys aren't usually forthcoming."

Rocco was nodding. He looked sad. "True."

The men finished setting up the studio in silence. When they were done, Larry took out the tablet to log their work. Rocco was putting away the winder and loading extra supplies back onto their cart. Larry was about to click to see their next assignment when he heard Rocco behind him. "Looks like your fingers healed."

Larry lifted his gaze and made eye contact with Rocco. In a measured voice, he said, "They did."

"That's good," Rocco said in a similar tone.

"It is," Larry replied, but it didn't feel so good. Standing there, he imagined the winder wrapping his intestines and veins into a tight, neat ball around his stomach. Not good at all.

Suspicious Activity Reporting Form

Name (leave blank to file an anonymous report):

Date:

Time:

Did you see a crew member access Trackz on Monday?

(If yes, please provide the crew member's name. If you are uncertain of his name, please provide his position and/or any identifying information.)

Please describe what you saw.

Have you ever seen a crew member access Trackz except to perform standard maintenance procedures?

(If yes, please provide the crew member's name. If you are uncertain of his name, please provide his position and/or any identifying information.)

Please describe what you saw.

Did you hear a crew member implicate himself in the incident on Monday?

(If yes, please provide the crew member's name. If you are uncertain of his name, please provide his position and/or any identifying information.)

Please describe what you heard.

Do you have any other suspicious/unusual behavior to report?

(If yes, please provide names of parties involved. If you are uncertain of a name, please provide position and/or any identifying information.)

Please describe in detail.

LARRY

Larry lay on his bed, his hour off coming to an end. Any other week, he would have used this time to ride another passenger. He would have been in motion, most likely slipping out of a stateroom somewhere on Deck 5 or 6, maybe taking a jade pillbox with him. But now, he was lying low. Now, he was fretting, his heartbeat a guttural hum, vibrating through him. He jiggled his left foot over the edge of the bed and thumbed the computer chip he had removed from inside a woman's body. Then he flipped it end over end and up and down his fingers as he ran through his worries again:

Did Rocco suspect him?

If so, would Rocco report anything?

If so, what would Rocco report?

If Rocco did report him, then what?

So many questions. Keeping his head down for the time being might not be the worst idea . . . and yet, where was the fun in that? When he closed his eyes, he could see the incision again, still feel the woman's tissue give way, the satisfying softness of her body opening up. He frowned in his reminiscence. He probably could have lifted the whole thing, whatever was inside her, not just this tiny chip.

BIANCA

Bianca looked around her. She was in her room on the ship. How funny. Just moments ago—or longer, years perhaps—she'd been on a farm. Outside and walking. Now she was lying on her back, nearly flat. She tried to sit up by propping her elbows beneath her. The line running from her hand to the bedside IV tower grew taut, pulling against the tape keeping it in place. Pain, too, lapped at her stomach, like a side stitch after running intervals. "Oomph," she said. Then her bed began to move, sliding into a chaise lounge configuration. "That's better," she said when it stopped. She was sitting upright now, settling back against the cushion.

"She wakes." In the corner of the room, a crewman stood, tapping on a tablet strapped to his left hand. He swiped, then let the tablet fall to his side, and smiled at Bianca. His name tag read Blake. "How were your Days at Sea?" he asked.

"What happened to the other guy? Derek, I think his name was?"

"Derek had a bit of an accident. He's okay, but he has to take a little time off to rest."

"What happened?" Bianca rocked across her hipbones, trying to assess the edges of comfort, of pain, the line dividing this from that like white paint on a tennis court. A twinge here, a tingle there as she stretched her arms, rolled them over, pointed and flexed her toes.

288

"Just a little fall was all," Blake explained. He rocked up and down on his toes, too, his motions mirroring Bianca's like a reflex, the same way mothers will start swaying in the presence of a woman holding a baby.

"You're an athlete?" Bianca asked, eyebrows raised.

"Was one. A swimmer."

"That makes sense," Bianca said, now rolling her neck from side to side.

Blake grinned. "My shoulders?" he said.

"Oh, well." Bianca flushed. "I meant you being here. On a cruise ship. Surrounded by water."

He laughed. "I didn't even think about that!" He turned to look out the porthole window. His eyes grew soft, staring out into the distance. "Haven't been in a pool since college."

Bianca didn't know what to say. "Well, there's always the ocean?"

"Too many sharks." Blake shook his head. "Too much plastic." He crinkled up his nose. "I'm happy on land now," he continued. "I play some pickleball on my weekends off with a couple guys on crew."

Bianca forced a smile. "That's nice." Meanwhile pickleball courts were replacing tennis courts across the country, and everyone thought they could and should wield a racquet. She didn't want to get into tennis politics, though. She had just woken up. She twisted from side to side, tucked her tailbone to test her core. Some achiness lingered, mostly in her side where she'd felt the initial cramplike pain. When Blake didn't say anything, just stood there watching her, she asked, "So how did everything go?"

Blake nodded. "Right, yes." He pulled out his tablet. "Perfect. Your itinerary was flawless. Hydrangea Station was thrilled with how everything turned out. Well, once the communication chip was reinstalled. The surgical team thinks you will be most pleased with your body's performance—"

"So everything is fine now, but it wasn't?" Bianca interrupted.

Blake continued poring over his tablet. "According to your case notes, your musculature is now operating better than it did when you were twenty-five, its protein processes optimized to minimize muscle fatigue and maximize strength. And with your new protein pump—now working flawlessly, I might add—and reinforced tendons and ligaments, you'll be a lean, mean tennis-playing machine in practically no time at all. Says here, your musculature should lose a few more years by the time we disembark. It'll be like you're twenty again. How does that sound?"

"Wow," Bianca said, trying to compute what Blake was telling her, but it was a lot. "That's. Wow." Her mind raced. A miracle to have so much time and power restored to her. She smiled a giddy smile. She had done it. At least on paper, she was back.

"There's just one thing," Blake said.

"Oh?" She sat up straighter.

"Two actually. But nothing to fret about. Not anymore. You had some complications with your abdominal incision and your protein intake during your Days at Sea."

Bianca felt her body tense. "You said something about the chip?"

"Yes, precisely," Blake said, smiling at her like she'd passed some sort of test. "Dr. Heston personally saw to the device's repair. The protein pump is currently working exactly as it should, but due to the initial complications, some additional protein entered your system. We'll need to continue IV fluids until tomorrow morning, I'm afraid." Now he nodded to the line running from Bianca's arm to the bedside tower. "We much prefer passengers to be able to wake up from their Days at Sea and get right back into the swing of things. We apologize for the inconvenience. But we used our vacuum therapy to close the incision again following the pump repair, and you are sealed up tight. Locked and loaded, you might say. And by morning, you'll be out and about again." Blake beamed, and Bianca imagined a younger version of him, smiling that same smile after his hand touched the pool wall, a race won.

She took a deep breath. "Just to be clear, everything's okay?" she asked.

"Perfect," Blake said, walking over to the bed. "Your muscles might be a tad bigger than anticipated, what with some extra fuel in them. But by Miami, you'll be golden." He tapped his tablet, then he pulled the cord on the lamp beside the bed, casting the room into shadow.

"Miami," Bianca murmured, yawning. The skin on her forearm tingled.

"I've seen the projections. You could serve as fast as a hundred thirty miles per hour!"

Bianca yawned again. "That's fast." Recently, her serve had barely topped a hundred. Her mind spun at the prospect.

"How about a little nap? Then a shower when you wake again in the morning?"

Already Bianca's eyes were closing, her head starting to loll to the side. The bed started to move, unfolding itself, returning its occupant to a supine position.

THE CIRCULATOR

SECOND WEDNESDAY 18:12

Once Bianca was asleep, her breaths measured and steady, Blake spoke again. "Circulator?"

The Circulator switched into an active response state. "I am here, Blake."

"Add this note to passenger file, please."

The Circulator created a new note in Bianca's records and entered dictation mode.

"Awake at 17:56. Able to sit up and stretch. Minimal signs of pain and discomfort. Informed about complications with protein pump and current status. Fentanyl drip started. Back asleep at 18:10. Last bag of fluids to be hung at 22:00. Sedation set to wear off by morning. End note."

The Circulator saved and exited dictation mode. "Note recorded."

"Let me know when she starts to wake up in the morning, and we'll get her out of bed and showered before breakfast."

"Affirmative." The Circulator created an alarm and switched back into listening mode.

BECCA

EACH WEEK

BECCA knew the crew members talked a lot about the close calls. They spread rumors that circulated in hushed whispers in the lounges or the crew dining hall on Deck 2. Juicy bits moved from the surgical technicians to the servers, from the servers to the deckmen, and sometimes, they moved in the opposite direction or skipped from surgical technicians to deckmen.

Most recently, a passenger suffered a terrible reaction to silicone, her face swelling up and losing all definition so that it resembled a scrubbed potato. The surgical techs shared details like these from time to time because they felt better when they told others what they had seen. In speaking the words aloud, the unexpected outcomes were not as alarming as they had seemed under the glow of the operating room lights.

But sometimes, servers and deckmen had their own stories they needed to tell. Like last fall when a woman, only Out and About for a handful of hours, decided to nap outside. She was still tired from her excursions, from her Days at Sea. A deckman had helped her into a chaise under one of the canopies on Deck 10, where the towels and seat cushions had been gently infused with vanilla, where the furniture and linens were all soft white, cloud-like to the touch. She had slept and slept well—for the better part of three hours while the deckmen checked in, while the monitors embedded in her lounge chair recorded vital signs well within the normal range.

Then something had started to drip, and soon a puddle appeared beneath her, as though she were a child who'd gone to the bathroom in her sleep. The color was wrong, though. Too dark, especially so close to so much white. By the time the deckmen spotted the puddle and realized what it was, BECCA had sounded an alarm and the code team was stepping off the elevator, their deck uniforms barely buttoned and flapping in the breeze as they made their way to the leaking woman.

"So this is what the ocean smells like," a code team tech had said, striding past, nose raised into the wind.

Now the whole ship was abuzz with talk about the passenger attacked in Trackz. Some thought Jared had gotten away with something, pulled a fast one on BECCA, but her systems hadn't been compromised, and data and automatic timestamps didn't lie. Meanwhile, crew members floated other names—of techs, room stewards, deckmen, even servers! Theories abounded. Had another tech wanted to frame Jared, take him down in a bout of jealous rage? Had a stowaway crept on board over the weekend and become unhinged while roaming the dark tunnels? A few reports started to come in, too, though most relayed vague speculations about crew who had worked together for ten, twenty, thirty or more cruises. How well, they all wondered now, did they know each other? How well could they ever know another person?

BECCA projected the investigation would close by the end of the cruise. Someone would say or share something. The crew liked to talk, and BECCA was listening where she could.

ROCCO

SECOND WEDNESDAY 23:14

Rocco couldn't sleep. This time, he didn't bother lying down. Instead, he paced around his bed. Back and forth, he traced a horseshoe.

Earlier in the day, when he and Larry were setting up the Fiber Arts Studio, Larry had seemed off. He started talking about his grandmother—of all things, of all people—all the crocheting she did before her hand refused to grip a hook without shaking. "She tried to teach me, but I didn't have the patience for it. Couldn't be bothered to sit still when I was younger."

"Some things, it seems, haven't changed," Rocco said after a time, and Larry laughed.

"No, I guess they haven't."

Since Monday, Rocco had been keeping a close eye on his partner, and he kept a closer eye on him now that he knew a new investigation was live. All he had were suspicions at this point, though, and he wanted more before he submitted a report to BECCA. If only he had kept those bandages he had found! They could have been tested, provided proof. Listening to Larry, he tried to gauge whether his partner was the kind of person who would assault an unconscious woman. He *had* seen him yank a gray hair from a sleeping passenger. Was this really all that different?

"Earth to Rocco. You there?" Larry asked, frowning.

Rocco gave his head a shake. "I'm here." They still had two dozen skeins of yarn to wind and mason jars to stock with hooks and needles, scissors and counters, some zippers and buttons, too. And Larry was so popular among the crew. The guys loved his stories, the games he created on cleaning shifts. Such a fun guy, though maybe leaned intense at times. If Rocco was wrong and word got out that he blew the whistle on Larry, he'd be immediately ostracized. Or worse. No, he needed evidence.

Larry said, "I asked if you heard the news about Jared. The new investigation?"

Rocco felt his shoulders tense. "New investigation?"

"Jared was cleared, but someone did something wrong."

Rocco was surprised Larry was being so direct. What was he doing? What did it mean? He put another skein into the winder and turned it on. "Interesting."

When the winder stopped, Larry continued, "Trackz has been compromised, apparently. Someone must have snuck in and pulled out the chip." Larry tore open a pack of buttons and spilled them into a jar.

Now Rocco stared at Larry. He felt his brow furl. He wanted to ask, but clearly couldn't, *Was it you?* So instead he repeated, "Interesting." Instead he said, "Huh."

"Some of the guys were talking at breakfast." Larry shook the button jar. "We think it had to be a tech. Those guys all have direct access, right from the flower stations."

Rocco cycled another skein into the winder, this one gold with flecks of rust and brown and purple. The yarn was the softest thing he had ever touched. He hadn't wanted to let go when he dropped it in. The machine started to roll the yarn into a ball, and Rocco imagined it enfolding his body, crisscrossing his arms tight to his sides, its softness a cushion between him and the world. He inhaled. He exhaled. "It's crazy, right?" he asked, eyes trained on the winder. "What happened to the passenger?" Not *Was it you,* but maybe a way to get there.

Larry shrugged. "No crazier than them coming here in the first place." Larry pulled a knitting needle out of a jar. He twisted it back and forth in his hand, studying the point. "Crazy things happen on this ship all the time."

"Maybe the crew member will just turn himself in." This was the theorem that could render pages of calculations no longer necessary. A shortcut to the solution.

Larry dropped the needle back into the jar with a resounding ping, metal on glass. "Maybe," he said. "But unlikely."

"Oh?" Rocco returned. He removed the yarn ball from the winder and cradled it in his hands.

Larry just stared at him. "Bad guys aren't usually forthcoming."

Rocco frowned, weighed down by the confirmation that he would have to say something. If only he had some proof. "True."

The men returned to their tasks and finished setting up the studio in silence. When they were done, Larry logged their work on a tablet, drawing Rocco's attention to his hands. "Looks like your fingers healed," he said.

Larry looked over his shoulder at Rocco. "They did."

Rocco was the one to break eye contact. "That's good," he said. He started to reload the supply cart to return extra materials to the stockroom.

"It is," Larry said.

Eventually Rocco lay back down and drifted off to sleep, but only after he made a plan. Tomorrow, he would pay a little visit to his partner's room. Pop in like he needed something—maybe a puff or two of Larry's shoe deodorizer, with its dense baby powder scent—but really he'd be there to make observations. Just look and see. Then, if he found anything, he would file a report with BECCA.

THE PILGRIM DAILY
SECOND THURSDAY

Where do you want to go today?

WALKING PATHS. HOURS: 09:00–24:00

Park . . . . reserved for silent reflection until 12:00
Mall . . . . opens at 10:00 today
Cemetery . . . . open

SPA. HOURS: 09:00–19:00

DAILY SPECIALS

Volcanic Ash Rub + Vichy Shower
Crystals and Cryotherapy
Blue Light Shield Eye Treatment

Book now on your room screen or talk to your room steward to schedule a visit.

DINING. SEE HOURS BELOW.

Breakfast 06:00–09:00
Lunch 11:30–15:00
Dinner 19:00

ON-BOARD ACTIVITIES. HOURS: 05:30–23:30

Awake to Bake, Deck 8, Bingo Hall 05:30
Arm Toning, Deck 12 . . . . 07:00
Core Moves for Moms, Deck 12 . . . . 08:00
Charity Trunk Show, The Mall, Level 1 . . . . 08:00–10:00
Morning Glory Bingo, Deck 10, Bingo Hall 09:00
String Therapy, Deck 9, Fiber Arts Studio 14:00
Wonderful Wigs, Deck 10, Citrus Canopy 15:00
Puzzles and Pimm's Cups, Deck 8, Library 16:00
Ultimate *PILGRIM* Trivia, Deck 10, Bingo Hall 17:00
Cozy Campfire, Deck 12 . . . . 22:30

OUT & ABOUT SPECIALS.

Styling & Fitting Sessions are available for passengers who are Out & About. Book before lunch to secure a spot today. Two openings are available for Daily Blowouts for the rest of the week.

BIANCA

When Bianca woke, her replacement room steward, Blake, was at her bedside, like he was waiting for her to wake up. "Good morning," he said. "How are you feeling?"

Bianca considered. "Good," she said. "Rested."

"Ready for that shower?"

"Yeah," Bianca said slowly. "A shower would be nice."

"Let me take a look at your incision, and then we'll get you up and out of bed."

Bianca nodded.

Blake pulled down the bedclothes and produced a scanner. Lifting her satiny crop top, Bianca saw a bandage right below her ribs. Blake moved the device over the bandage—up, then down, left, then right. Finally, a gentle and reassuring beep.

"No sign of infection." He set the scanner down. "May I?" he asked.

Again Bianca nodded, and Blake gently peeled away the bandage to expose her incision, a dark pink line. Then, snapping on gloves, moved his fingers along the edge of the resealed wound.

"Anything?" he asked.

Bianca shook her head. "Just you pushing."

"Fantastic. Wow." He flashed her a grin and held out a hand. "Now for that shower."

"Wow what?" Bianca asked, taking the hand.

Blake pulled her upright. "I'm amazed at our recovery protocols is all. Like magic."

"Oh?" Bianca asked, but even as she spoke she realized she was sitting up and hadn't felt any pain. No twinges or discomfort at all.

"Off the ship, you'd be recovering for weeks," Blake explained, removing his gloves. "Here, we've got it down to hours."

Bianca swung her feet down, and Blake disappeared into the bathroom. The water started.

"How is that possible?" Bianca asked, standing.

"I swear, Dr. Heston attended Hogwarts as a kid." Blake appeared in the bathroom door. "Okay, water is running, and I've got a towel out for you, too. Can you walk to me? I want to make sure you're feeling good to go before I head out."

Bianca let go of the bed. She started moving forward slowly, shuffling, anticipating pain that never came.

"That's it." Blake held up a hand to high-five Bianca when she reached him. "And don't worry. You'll be zipping along by dinner."

"Not sure about that." Bianca cringed at the now-distant memory of bingo, how her last social outing had ended with spilled tea and a table full of glaring women. Since then, she'd barely spoken, except to Blake. The quiet was comfortable, though it meant more time to perseverate about her future or revisit the past. Not exactly a productive headspace to be in now that her itinerary was complete—and apparently a success. Maybe she did need to get out.

"Well, promise me you'll at least go to the final dinner tomorrow, the chef's tasting. It's three courses—beginnings, middles, and ends—served family-style. The kitchen crew goes above and beyond."

"Maybe . . ." Bianca said.

"Tell me you aren't curious to see the others after their itineraries." Blake lifted an eyebrow, then strode to the door and, with a final conspiratorial smile, left the room. In the shower, Bianca let the hot water fall on her shoulders while she inspected her incisions, like tiny tracks to nowhere. Then she ran her fingers along the tight bundles of muscles in her arms, running down her legs, mortared in her abdomen, assessing the restored and enhanced landscape by feel. She hadn't looked in the mirror yet, but she would when the steam cleared.

Blake was wrong. Bianca wasn't curious about the other women and how their excursions had changed them. She *was* curious, though, about their reactions to her. Would they wonder what work she'd had done? She imagined herself smiling if they asked, saying, "A little tune-up. I needed to grease the gears a bit." She was nearly the same on the exterior, but under the hood she would purr.

ROCCO

"Hey, Rocco," Larry said, suddenly in the doorway of the cabin, his own cabin.

Rocco had stopped by on his break, just like he'd planned, when Larry was supposed to be on duty. But instead, here the man was, leaning against the doorframe, his hands stuffed into the wide front pocket of his uniform shirt. On his face, the trace of a smile.

Darn, Rocco thought. He had meant to stay where Larry was standing now, slide open the pocket door, just take a quick peek. Seeing nothing amiss from the doorway, Rocco had almost turned to leave, then he'd spotted Larry's dopp kit on the shelf of the built-in dresser and decided to take a closer look, despite the dryness of his throat, the fuzzy roar in his ears. He should have had plenty of time. Larry was scheduled to work another ten, fifteen minutes.

"Hey, Larry." What could he say? Crew members were always going into each other's rooms, to borrow Gold Bond, for an extra razor blade, or even just to spritz some cologne when theirs ran out. Rocco tried to think of something, anything, as he closed his hand around the computer chip that had once been inside a passenger. It was still flecked with dried blood. *Someone else's blood.*

Rocco had found it in a bed of gray hairs tucked into an eyeglasses case in the dopp kit. Beneath that case, the bag was well stocked with the usual items—toothpaste, floss picks, hair gel, deodorant—and among those, Rocco sifted through odd little trinkets that surely had belonged to other passengers: diamond stud earrings, a bookmark, a key fob, a tiny box filled to the brim with gold flecks, a soft pink velvet scrunchie. He had been nosing through items when Larry appeared.

"What are you doing here?" Rocco asked, his voice at an unfamiliar pitch. He should have left the room as soon as he'd seen the chip, taken the dopp kit directly to the Captain. *Darn*, he thought again.

"What am *I* doing here?" Larry echoed. His gaze fell to the open toiletry bag. "I know you're not looking for shaving cream." Larry took a step forward. "Wanna show me what's in your hand there?"

Rocco shuffled back against the dresser. He cleared his throat. "I meant, what are you doing here now? Your shift ends at five."

Larry smiled fully now. "Only when I'm working with you." He took another step into the room.

"Toothpaste," Rocco blurted. "I'm out of toothpaste. Thought you might have some." He nodded toward the toiletry bag. "In here."

Larry's face twisted into a scowl. "Do you think I'm stupid?" he said.

Rocco didn't know how to answer, or what the calculus was that would make this situation end. The problem was getting to the door. His partner was a big man, and he loomed in front of it. Rocco switched tactics. "So you've got a fetish. Who doesn't?"

"Fetish?" Larry continued his advance.

"I'm sure the women don't even miss this stuff." Rocco was just blabbering now. The room couldn't have been more than sixty square feet, but it felt much smaller now, and shrinking. He would fill it with words. "I used to collect all kinds of things when I was a kid. Baseball cards, of course. But also coins. Remember those quarter books? Got one every year for my birthday. I have a dozen, all in a box—"

Larry lunged forward. Prying open Rocco's fist, he plucked the chip away with astonishing deftness. "Thank you," he huffed, retreating until the two men stood a foot apart. Rocco took a deep, overdue breath. He considered again how he might now exit the room. Roll over the bed? Feint toward the bed, then reverse and slide past Larry's shoulder? Take him by surprise in a head-on, kamikaze bull-rush?

These were the questions Rocco was asking himself when Larry stepped to the side and made a sweeping gesture toward the door. "After you," he said.

Rocco felt his shoulders rise defensively. He tried to smile but finally had to settle for a nod. Perhaps he'd misjudged his partner, after all. Perhaps there was a misunderstanding. An explanation. And anyway, they should be on their way to Deck 10 for their next shift. It would be starting soon, and Rocco couldn't stand to be late.

"Okay." He moved forward self-consciously, aware that he was putting one foot in front of the other. At the doorway, he stopped, turned back. He was going to offer Larry something. Say something like *See you up on deck*. Just something to clear the air between them. Something that would convey Rocco was open to hearing the guy out, no matter their mutual dislike.

But as he turned, as he opened his mouth, Larry's arm came at him. He heard a crack, and then the doorframe was no longer in front of him. Instead he saw the underside of the bed. The square end of a suitcase. A pair of white deck shoes. Two wooden posts. Dust lay like a light flurry on the driveway of his youth, back when it still snowed from time to time, tire treads here and there, but mostly a pristine expanse, the asphalt blanketed in pale, fluffy down. Then two more white shoes appeared, and Rocco wondered what was the likelihood the kid watching the snowfall on that driveway would end up here, like this. What were the odds? One in a hundred? One in a thousand? Or more?

If only he hadn't been on this ship in the first place. If only he hadn't gone to grad school at all. He could be an elementary school math teacher somewhere, teaching base ten and order of operations, drilling multiplication tables until the cows came home and imploring his students to show their work—no, an answer alone wouldn't do, however right it was. He could wear fun neckties every day—dizzying colors and cartoons and mathematical formulas—not at all the nooses he had imagined them to be all those years ago. All he'd need was enough money to cover the down payment on a small house, something he could fix up on the weekends, for a future family. He could see this alternate reality so clearly, down to the seafoam-green penny tile in the house's two showers.

He realized dimly that he was crying. But he was losing something more than tears. Something vital. An inkblot was spreading, little by little, across his vision. It would obliterate the calm dust, wash over it like a midnight ocean. He couldn't bear to see it—to see the snowlike dust disturbed—so he closed his eyes.

LARRY

SECOND THURSDAY 21:52

"Oh, good. I found someone."

Larry looked up. At the end of the hall, a passenger waved. She came toward him at a slow shuffle.

"I'm afraid I'm lost. I should know by now. If you'd be so kind to direct me to the Tea Parlor."

Only her voice, strained and gravelly, gave away her age. Her face was still shining and swollen from whatever chemicals she'd had injected or procedure she'd undergone.

"You aren't even close," Larry said. He took the woman by her shoulders and swiveled her around. He leaned close and pointed back down the hall. "Get back on the elevator and go up six floors. The Tea Parlor is on Deck 9, next to the Spa."

The woman didn't seem to notice his impatience, his gruffness. She patted his arm. "Thank you, thank you, dear," she said, shuffling back the way she came.

Larry spun and continued wheeling the black cart he had brought up from his cabin, after his last shift of the day, to the storage room for biohazardous waste on Deck 3.

THE PILGRIM DAILY
SECOND FRIDAY

Where do you want to go today?

WALKING PATHS. HOURS: 09:00–24:00

Park . . . . open
Mall . . . . open
Cemetery . . . . open

SPA. HOURS: 09:00–19:00

DAILY SPECIALS
BodyS3 (Soak, Sugar, and Shine)
Healing Massage
Anywhere or Everywhere Wax

Book now on your room screen or talk to your room steward to schedule a visit.

DINING. SEE HOURS BELOW.

Breakfast 06:00–9:00
Lunch 11:30–15:00
Dinner . . . . Doors open at 19:00

ON-BOARD ACTIVITIES. HOURS: 05:30–18:00

Earthing, The Park 05:30
Plan Your Next Cruise, Deck 8, Starboard Parlor 07:00
Yin Yoga, Deck 12 . . . . 08:00
Reflecting for Reentry, Deck 10, Mint Canopy 09:00
Self-Portraiture, Deck 8, Library 10:00
Wearable Art, Deck 8, Starboard Parlor 14:00
Dress to Impress Happy Hour, Deck 10, Citrus Canopy 15:00
Winner Takes All Bingo, Deck 8, Bingo Hall 16:00
Aspiring Writers Circle, Deck 8, Library 17:00

OUT & ABOUT SPECIALS.

Styling & Fitting Sessions are available for passengers who are Out & About. Book before lunch to secure a spot today. Ten Blowouts Before Dinner are still available. Book by breakfast to secure an appointment.

THE ROOM STEWARDS

SECOND FRIDAY 06:30

The room stewards checked on the passengers in their assigned state-rooms each morning on their Days at Sea and also once they were Out and About. On the final full day of the cruise, rounds were especially demanding. By then, all passengers were awake, and it was the room stewards' responsibility to catch any signs of infection or other adverse outcomes before the women returned home. So they were thorough, meticulous in their assessments while still moving efficiently to ensure they saw everyone before lunch. They confirmed vitals and labs were where they needed to be, and they asked the women to rate any lingering discomfort, to note any special areas of sensitivity, numbness, or pain. They logged their assessments in passenger files and ticked off items as they advanced through the protocol. They refilled water cups and pulled up *The Pilgrim Daily*. They suggested, based on input from BECCA, how passengers might most enjoy their last day on board. They agreed, "Why, yes. It is a lovely morning, isn't it?" while adding a straw to the smoothie BECCA had ordered, chock full of baby spinach, pineapple juice, a banana, flax seeds, and garnished with a lemon wedge.

They shared, too, BECCA's suggestions for future excursions, casting computer-generated sims on the screen in front of the bed, showing what Samantha or Marilyn or Kellan 3.0 could look like by the end of the next cruise.

Thanks to BECCA's Rapid Recovery Protocols, of course, most passengers were ready to return home and pick up their lives right where they left off. Rarely, a passenger might need an additional night in the terminal's set of suites for further monitoring. Requests for more time on the ship, however, were fairly common. A woman might ask to keep the same room and spend the rest of the month on board. The room steward would smile and explain that staying on *PILGRIM* was not an option. All passengers must disembark Saturday morning, but they could return for another cruise as early as next month; stay in the same room, even, so long as it was still available. A few weeks away from the boat was nothing, they would see—barely enough time to plan, to anticipate.

BIANCA

SECOND FRIDAY 11:23

As she was pulling out her suitcase before lunch—an acai bowl and an iced tea that would be delivered to her room right at noon—Blake had stopped by for an assessment, which she'd passed, he said, though he was frowning when he said it. He must have told her three times to take it easy today and call for him at once if she started to feel off in any way. Out of an abundance of caution, he said, he would be glad to escort her to dinner this evening and off the boat tomorrow.

But Bianca had waved him off. "I'll be fine," she said, ushering him to the door, then turning her attention to packing.

Blake hovered in the doorway. "Yes, you will be. You'll be better than fine. Terrific, in fact. But I'd feel better if you let me—"

"Nonsense," she insisted. "I woke up feeling great. No wobbles. No weakness. What did you call it? My rapid recovery something? It worked." When she was younger, she had sustained her share of injuries to her elbows, knees, and hips, and she'd never been a fan of rehab. She stayed off the court until her trainer cleared her and not a day longer.

Blake grinned. "Of course it worked. It always does." He slid open his tablet and punched a few buttons. "Looks like you'll need to pop into the terminal building on your way out tomorrow. You've been scheduled for a tech session to get the app for your pump set up on your phone."

"It's crazy, right?" Now Bianca was smiling. "I'm part machine. But I'll take it if I get to play again, compete *finally*. I can't believe I'm saying that."

"Not crazy," Blake said. "And you can believe it."

"I'm trying" Bianca said, sliding a blouse off a velvet hanger.

"When you get your phone back, you'll see that your Homecoming Plan has been texted to you. You'll want to follow the recommendations there closely to ensure peak performance. You've got Miami coming up in two weeks?"

"Two weeks," Bianca confirmed, folding a pair of leggings.

"If you have any questions or concerns, you can always call or text our twenty-four-hour Passenger Wellness Line. And the app will have a help feature, as well."

"Got it."

"Any questions or concerns now before I go?" Blake asked, tucking away his tablet.

Bianca turned to face him and flexed her biceps. "Wanna arm wrestle?" she asked with a quirk of her brow.

Blake laughed. "No. You would destroy me."

"To be honest," Bianca said, "I didn't quite expect this. My muscles are huge. I can feel them. Like all of them."

Blake reached out to tap what looked like a small cannonball beneath her skin. "All perfectly normal after that protein flood you endured so soon after electromyostimulation. Your muscles are growing in response. But they'll calm down over time, and you'll settle into them."

Bianca flexed again. It really was amazing. "C'mon. Just one round?"

Blake shook his head and started backing away. "Not a chance."

LARRY

Only a couple deckmen had inquired as to Rocco's whereabouts all day, and they didn't question Larry's explanation: light day on Deck 10, and he hadn't been feeling too hot. "I told him to take it easy."

"Poor guy," they said.

"He works too hard," they said.

"Let us know if you need a hand," they said.

Where BECCA was concerned, Larry logged their shifts and toted along Rocco's badge in the wide front pocket of his uniform. While he made and delivered drinks, his partner's badge sat on a shelf in the serving station, tucked behind canisters of flax and chia seeds. While he cleaned bathroom stalls, the badge sat on the sink, barricaded behind rolls of toilet paper. During the Wearable Art session in the Starboard Parlor after lunch, he hung the badge from a lanyard alongside dozens of gold, rose gold, silver, and gunmetal-gray chains, hiding it in plain sight. It was back in his pocket when the passengers departed with the pendants they'd fashioned to take home and gift to their personal chef or cleaning woman or dog walker.

Now he had one more shift, though it was a long one, before the morning. He'd be able to coast through his and Rocco's disembarking duties tomorrow, but the last night of the cruise, especially before dinner, tended to be busy on Deck 10. Women wanted to spend at least some of their final hours outside, enjoying the amenities with sea air in their faces.

For now, a small group of women who had all been on the same Serotonin Booster Excursion convened in the Mint Canopy for a final laugh. They sat in a tight cluster of chairs and asked for water, no ice, a few with lemon, a few with lime, one with watermelon rind.

Meanwhile, another group was doing tarot card readings in the portside tent, and several sets of toes were being painted in the Pedicure Parlor. Larry served wine to some women sitting on chaise lounges and sharing excerpts from the books they had been writing since they published a piece in their college literary journals. The other deckmen on duty left him alone. They had their own work to do.

At a drink station, Larry pulled out three mugs and the Evening Splendor tea tin. He measured teaspoons of leaves and earthy bits and sprinkled them into the bottom of each mug. He set the hot water dispenser to 212 degrees and waited. Soon, he'd fill the mugs and allow the tea to steep for seven minutes. He'd add a stainless-steel strainer-straw and a squirt of agave nectar in two, honey in one. He'd wait some more. And while he waited, he'd pull out the chip he had taken, first from a passenger—his hand reaching inside her body! inside!—and then from Rocco. "Hello, precious," he whispered.

A timer went off with a faint ding. Larry moved the mugs to a serving tray, but not before he tucked the chip into his back pants pocket. Throughout the night, he would pat that pocket, and each time he would smell again the metallic odor of blood, despite the rush of air off the water and across the deck.

THE LAST DINNER

BECCA

The passengers began filing into the dining room. They looked forward to the final dinner—except for maybe a handful who had just woken up from their Days at Sea this very afternoon and reported to their room stewards a lingering queasiness and the desire for a bowl of soup, yes, something brothy and light on the sodium would be just lovely, with a side of crusty baguette.

Most of the women on their way to their tables for the last time were curious, very curious, about the excursions of others. But even more, they wanted to talk about their own itineraries. During dinner, they would tell everything, every detail they could remember: riding in a chair through their flower station, meeting the team, the chair transforming into a table, a woman's voice like satin, counting backwards, the sky above white and fluffy with sunlight streaming through pockets and folds here and there like golden spotlights. They would share the brave choices they had made, the changes they felt penetrating far beyond the added polymers or patches, coursing like reengineered blood cells from their scalps to their toes. They wanted to say that they had needed this, this chance, these modifications—slight or significant—that now they could get on with their lives. After all, they had anxieties to attend to, partners who tried to curb their spending, children getting into trouble

317

of one kind or another. They had seltzer businesses to start, clothing boutiques to buy for, parties to throw, and elixirs to add to their company's product line. They had more trips to plan, charity galas to host. Some even had gardens they needed their gardeners to plant for the new season, just as soon as the lettuce and kale, carrot and green bean seedlings they tended to in their greenhouses grew another inch.

For some, this *getting on with things* will last the rest of their lives, until one day, in their mid-eighties, they'll stop suddenly in front of a downtown store window. There, among the items on display—stationery and pens, candles and neat stacks of flax linen dinner napkins—they'll see a woman standing on a sidewalk. She's hunched forward slightly, huddled in upon herself. A reflection, but also a shadow. Surely this is not what they look like. "So old!" they'll say, hearing the voice of their grandmothers. They'll reach up, then, to feel the loose skin at their jaws, the lines like alluvial fans slowly wearing away the corners of their eyes. *I'm not this old,* they'll think. *This isn't me.*

For others, getting on with their lives will be a brief affair, a match struck and quickly burned. They'll book more cruises, more excursions. They'll wonder why they waited so long to wage this war against Time and the genetic hands they had been dealt. Their bodies will become the battlefield, and for a while, some longer than others, they'll win.

CEDRIC

SECOND FRIDAY 19:11

Cedric watched the door. All day he'd been edgy with anticipation. He'd nearly dropped a tray during lunch service, stacked with steaming bowls of creamy dal, and he would have if Andy hadn't caught the edge as it started to tilt. He couldn't stop thinking about Nicole. His skin blazed beneath the crisp cotton of his server uniform. A drop of sweat slid down the middle of his back. His body was at the mercy of his mind, and his mind was at the mercy of this woman he barely knew. He thought if he could just know for sure what this thing was between them—real or imagined, reciprocated or not—he wouldn't feel so, well, consumed. He imagined a kiss would tell him all he needed to know. *God, he wanted to kiss her.* Well, he wanted to do other things, too, but he couldn't think about any of that while he carried wide trays of piping hot food on his shoulder, arms raised for support. So he focused on the kiss. The sweetness of it. The romance.

The doors to the dining room had opened ten minutes ago. At the beginning of the cruise, Nicole had been one of the first five women in the room. Now, she was nowhere to be seen. A terror stole through him, the same cold, sinking feeling that had swept him when Kali told him she was done. He stood at the edge of an abyss, scree beneath his feet, biting wind at his back.

If she came, he knew what he would say, the steps he would take to escalate their flirtation, see what was there, what this was. He would ask, "How are you?" his voice a whisper as a smile spread across her face, lighting up her eyes. "Better now," she would say, and then he'd smile back, tell her, "Me, too." Later, after he brought out the final course, the final cups of tea, she would say something like, "I wish this night didn't have to end," and he would be ready. He'd lean in, top off her tea, and say, "Maybe it doesn't have to." Then he'd drop the folded card in her lap, the card he carried in his wide front pocket, the one that read *Meet me on Deck 12 at midnight.* The corner of the card pressed into his stomach just now, a small prick. He winced. He'd practically lifted this plan directly out of a Hallmark movie, the kind Kali used to make him watch every Saturday night in December. Is that what his life was now? A Hallmark movie?

For the women already seated at his tables, he knew his service was perfunctory. He smiled, poured water, brought bread, but he was going through the motions. He was thinking about Nicole. Her absence commanded so much of his mental space that it was impossible to respond meaningfully when a passenger asked about his plans for the weekend.

"This weekend?" he said. "You bet."

At 19:38, everything changed.

Nicole walked into the room.

TABLE 32 (IDEAL VERSION)

AN ALTERNATE SECOND FRIDAY 19:11

Another time, perhaps, or for four slightly different women, the cruise might have ended differently.

On that alternate cruise, Nicole wasn't reeling from the news that she had cancer, specifically a tumor the size of a baseball in her abdominal cavity. Rather, she was feeling more hopeful—and attractive—than she had in years. She stood in the dining room doorway for a moment before she entered, hoping she had her server's attention so he could watch her walk in wearing the navy backless dress she had saved for this very night. Table 32 was empty. *Good*, she thought. She would have Cedric to herself. Approaching the table, she decided she wouldn't force the issue, wouldn't confess to any feelings unless he sent her a sign that she should, and that sign could be a certain kind of look or a few words—*I've been thinking about you.* Either something or nothing would happen. Either way, she would go home tomorrow to her husband and son, to a new cross-platform marketing campaign, and she would finally sell the beauty products she had been hoarding for months. Either way, she had a book club gathering on Wednesday at Semra's house, and a multigenerational domestic drama to read on the flight home. Either way, a win was inevitable, and her life after the cruise would go on, but be better—so much better—thanks to her itinerary. *New look, new outlook*: a mantra she could get behind.

As Cedric pulled out her chair, she couldn't bear to make eye contact—no, too soon for such intimacy—so she stared ahead. She heard a snap, and suddenly a napkin lay in her lap. Cedric was there, right at her hip. She startled at his closeness.

"You look lovely this evening, Nicole."

The sign? Was that it?

There, in this alternate cruise world, Lyla joined Nicole, and she was radiant despite the patch of pimples between her eyebrows. "Whew," she said when she sat down. "No wine for me tonight."

Annalie appeared next, but her face was no longer her face. She looked cheerful and confident, a twinkle in her friendly eyes, her mouth curving in a kind, warm grin.

Then Bianca made her way to their table in a series of long, powerful strides. She appeared mostly the same, but her body was now a brick house. Her excursions had taken off fifteen, twenty years, repairing the devastating effects of decades of physical punishment.

Cedric brought water. He brought champagne. He brought Lyla a ginger lemon mocktail. There was no tension, no judgment. The excursions had wiped the slate clean. Or perhaps it was BECCA who had finally gotten the algorithm right, so right, in fact, that the women looked upon each other as sisters and better—friends without the catty whispering, without the silly she-saids, without the ladder rungs ascended or descended, without any ladder at all. On this night, no one remembered, let alone mentioned, the unpleasantness of bingo. They were here in the *now* and lifting each other up, up, up. The women toasted Lyla's pregnancy. They gushed about Annalie's radical new look. They ran their hands over Bianca's calves, the tight muscles like loaded springs. They told Nicole she was a knockout, that they would hate her for how she looked if they didn't love her so.

TABLE 32 (ACTUAL VERSION)

For the four women assigned to Table 32, the real final dinner was quite different.

Bianca, the first to arrive, was rolled up to the table by Blake. "Thank you," she told him as he wheeled her close. A few grunts later, the wheelchair was just a chair. She had tried to walk but had made it only a couple doors down the hall before her legs began to feel wobbly and her head had started to swim.

Blake had reassured her: "Looks like your kidneys just need a little more time to recover. By tomorrow morning, you'll be golden."

"My kidneys?" Bianca asked.

"I'll come get you after dessert," Blake had replied. "But if you need me before then, push here." He pointed to a button on the chair. "This green one is me. Red is the floor team. Red is for if you feel like you're in trouble. Chest pains, confusion, excessive drowsiness, or if your legs suddenly start to swell."

Bianca frowned. "Why would my legs suddenly start to swell?"

"They shouldn't. They won't," Blake said. "There's a slight possibility of fluid retention. If your kidneys aren't eliminating water waste as they should."

Bianca shrugged. She had passed her health assessment. And now that she was sitting, her head had cleared and she felt fine again. "Green and red," she said. "Got it."

As Lyla approached the table, her steps were heavy but exuberant. She looked tired but pleased. She felt nauseous but exhilarated. *I'm pregnant, pregnant, pregnant*, she sang to herself. *I'm pregnant, pregnant, pregnant*. For once, she wasn't scolding her imaginary children in her head, telling them to behave, stop acting like maniacs. For once, she wasn't hashing out the details of their weekend plans or making a grocery list in her mind—*Out of peanut butter again? Already?* She eased herself into her chair and puffed out a sigh. "Well," she said. "And who are you?"

Annalie slid into her usual chair just after Lyla sat down, but to Lyla and Bianca, she was another woman entirely. After her itinerary, she could be anyone. "I'm Jordana," she said, tucking her long dark hair behind her ears. The new name popped into her head, and out it came. Just like that. But then she remembered: Aimee had always liked that name, thought she might name a baby that one day. Jordana smiled. "My server said to join you since our table was empty save for me. I hope that's okay." She fabricated this story on the fly. She was used to hearing her students spin tales to explain tardiness, incomplete or missing work; here she was, doing the same.

Lyla said, "We're still waiting on two, but oh, look, here comes one now."

To Nicole, the walk across the dining room felt slower than it actually was. Around her, women seated at tables and servers carrying long platters of steaming food and round trays covered with drinks were reduced to shapes, colors, and sounds. Red. Clink. Triangle. She arrived at the table and continued past it. The windows and the sun beyond them called to her. She couldn't take her eyes off the glowing ball descending toward the sea.

Placing a hand on the window, fingers spread, she stared into the sun the way she'd been told never to do for fear of blindness. Stared into it, uncaring. A tumor sat inside her fat-free abdomen, killing her. Light wavered along the edge of the sun and pierced the flickering waves below.

"Nicole." Cedric was saying her name. "Allow me to help you to your seat."

She nodded (or did she?) and let him walk her back to the table to join the three women already sitting there.

Most of the other groups were already being served food, which sizzled and hissed as it passed on cumbersome trays, trailing notes of rosemary, curry, and cinnamon.

"Wine, ladies?" Cedric asked.

"Ginger ale for me," Lyla said, then she turned to address table. "I have an announcement." She didn't hesitate. She leaned forward and in a loud whisper said, "I'm pregnant." She sketched a fuzzy picture: how she was feeling off, how her room steward brought her a test (the ship is so well stocked!), how she tested positive and couldn't be happier.

Jordana and Bianca smiled and toasted the news while Nicole thought about her pregnancy with Max. She had been so scared from the time she saw two pink lines until after he was born that she didn't remember much. Only relief that she had made it through, that she had survived the ordeal. "Congratulations," she said a beat too late.

"Thank you." Lyla beamed.

"And for you, Nicole?" Cedric asked, kneeling. "You okay?" He placed a hand on her thigh. Already he'd forgotten his script. Already he was deviating. But Nicole wasn't acting like Nicole. Her eyes wouldn't meet his. Instead she stared at his hand on her leg. "Two glasses of red. Any red," she said, her voice robotic.

"I'll have what she's having," the new woman at the table said cheerfully.

"Why not?" Bianca shrugged. "Me, too."

When Cedric moved off to fill their orders, Bianca reached over and squeezed Lyla's hand. "Baby number four?" she marveled. "I don't know how you do it."

Lyla pulled her hand away, her smile slipping. "No, you wouldn't, would you?"

Bianca flinched as if slapped. "Excuse me?"

Lyla ignored her. "Has anyone seen Annalie?" she asked Nicole, eyes trained on the doorway. Nicole's response was hard to make out, muttered under her breath. Jordana lowered her gaze to the tablecloth, cheeks glowing.

Cedric returned with their drinks, six glasses of wine for three women and a ginger ale in a champagne flute. As he set them before the women, he cleared his throat. "I propose a toast," he said.

The women each picked up a glass. Nicole started to drink hers, not waiting for Cedric to speak.

"Lyla, happy pregnancy." He smiled at Lyla. "And all of you, congratulations on completing your life-changing journey aboard *PILGRIM*."

Nicole set down her empty wine glass as the others took first sips. She picked up the second glass. "Hear, hear." She slurped, and half the wine was gone. This was exactly what she needed: numbness, distraction. Wine and these women she hardly knew and would cease to know after tomorrow. She turned to Jordana. "Have we met?"

Jordana shrugged and took another sip of wine.

Nicole frowned at the second glass, which was empty. The fast alcohol intake made her feel distant from herself, and she welcomed the departure of mind from body. A time bomb was lodged inside of her, and she wanted to get as far away from it as possible. She would create a wine moat between her and the cancer. For at least tonight, she could mount a defense, protect herself. She raised her hand to catch Cedric's attention, then pointed to her empty wine glasses. She held up two fingers, and when he nodded in response, she flashed a thumbs up.

"You're thirsty," Bianca commented, tossing back her own glass with a reckless air. She'd angled her body so that her back was turned to Lyla.

"I am." Nicole took the napkin out of her lap and started to fold it. At home, she folded and put away all the laundry. She told her friends she didn't mind the chore, but in truth, she hated it. So repetitive. So useless. "Fucking laundry," she said. She stuffed the napkin into a glass, watched the wine remaining soak into the white fabric.

"You okay?" Bianca asked.

"Need more wine," Nicole said.

Cedric arrived with the refills. He set down the new glasses and removed the empty ones. Then he pulled a new napkin off his forearm and laid it in Nicole's lap.

"My hero," Nicole said, but her eyes never left the wine, a full glass already making its way to her lips.

CEDRIC

Her hero, she had called him. *Her hero*. But that look in her eyes. Maybe he shouldn't have brought her a second round, at least not so quickly. But he'd wanted to give her what she asked for. What did it all mean? Her words, her demeanor, her drinking. Nervousness? His opening course tray sat on the expediting table. One expeditor was adding a sprig of rosemary here and grinding tricolored peppercorns there while the other one moved around the tray until the entire edge of the white platter gleamed spotlessly. When the team nodded to Cedric, he crouched to shoulder the platter at the same time they slid it toward him. Squatting there, he had the sudden worry that perhaps her behavior tonight had nothing at all to do with him. The platter came forward. For a moment, he thought it might knock him backward and off-balance, and he would be a puddle of steaming hors d'oevres on the ground, a commotion sure to draw all eyes in the dining room. Would Nicole spring up? Unbury him? Or stay at her table, drinking wine, unaware and indifferent. He felt hands hoisting him up at the shoulder.

"Whoa, buddy," Andy said. "Easy now."

"Zoned out for a sec. Thanks, man."

"You have terrible timing," Andy said.

Cedric smiled. "It's looking that way."

JORDANA

Annalie was making up a life for Jordana—this new woman she suddenly was—on the spot. The others at the table were cycling through the questions they had asked her last Monday, when she was Annalie. Now, as then, she left out the part about her dead twin sister. Jordana, she learned by creating her one response at a time, had grown up an only child who loved to read, often spending long hours alone but not lonely, book splayed across her lap until her parents came home from the restaurant where her father ran the front of the house and her mother was the executive chef. She'd eat dinner at nine, nightly-special leftovers, or else a quick ramen her mom would whip up for her. Now, she told the women, she ran a local bookstore in her town, just down the street from her parents' place. Owning a small-town bookstore was, in fact, one of the dreams she had dreamed before Aimee had died. She told them she lived alone with her three cats, that the cruise was a bit of self-care after a few lucrative years once the big box stores closed and Amazon started exclusively selling e-books. She hadn't taken a day off in two years, she said. "You should have seen me before my itinerary," she continued. "Bags and sags for days. My skin as sallow as cardboard." She didn't elaborate, and she hoped she wouldn't have to. She ran her fingers through her hair, so straight and long and dark and shiny and new.

Cedric returned with the first course. The white tray he slid onto the rotating center of the table was arranged neatly with small bites, the display bursting with color, with texture, with scent, immediately accosting their eyes and noses. Shot glasses of crab chowder. Grilled eggplant cubes dotted with fresh garlic and jalapeño. Honeyed tofu on toothpicks. Bacon-wrapped asparagus bites, drizzled with balsamic vinegar. Cedric clicked the platter into place and gave it a whirl. For a few moments, the women watched the food spin in silence. When to stop watching? When to start eating? Jordana was suddenly ravenous. But where to begin? Which bite to taste first? A quarter-sized quiche, buttery and golden-brown, or a burrata-stuffed grape tomato?

She stretched a hand, plucked a tomato off the spinning platter, and slid it into her mouth. Sinking her teeth in, she felt the warm cheese ooze and wondered when she had last tasted anything so wonderful, had last really *tasted* food at all. She popped another tomato into her mouth. Then another. Jordana liked burrata, she knew now. Loved it, in fact. What else? She would find out. She would learn.

CEDRIC

The other women were eating, especially Lyla, who seemed bent on tasting two of everything, but Nicole only stared at the food in front of her. Cedric leaned over her shoulder and whispered, "The meatballs are exquisite." When she didn't pick up a fork, he said, "I can help you." *Please let me help you*, he thought. He speared a meatball, put it on Nicole's plate, and broke it into two halves. Crouched next to her seat, he forked one half and held it out to Nicole.

She blinked as the meatball came at her, seeming to wake from a daze. "What are you doing?" she asked.

What *was* he doing? Cedric had no idea. But before he could respond, before he could return the meatball half to her plate and retreat to the drink station to regroup, Lyla, on her second bite-sized savory onion pie, threw up.

She was sitting next to Nicole, and she had turned that way, toward Nicole—and toward Cedric, crouching between them. At the same time he heard her heaving, he felt the impact of splatter on his back.

A sudden bustle of activity erupted. Andy was already on his way over with a bucket and a stack of towels. Cedric set the fork down and stood slowly. Lyla, eyes wide, was holding a napkin to her mouth. "I'm sorry," she was saying. "I'm so sorry. It happened so fast."

Then Nicole started to laugh.

LYLA

Lyla felt terrible about vomiting all over their server. And yet she was also thrilled by the whole experience. The nausea rising and meanwhile a heaviness bearing down, down, down until, at last, up it all came, everything that had been in her stomach. Regurgitation was followed by instant relief, except for a dull ache at her center.

Of course, she felt dreadful for Cedric. She knew what it was like to be in his shoes. Too well, in fact.

Three patients had thrown up on her over the years, and she remembered each incident vividly. Usually, she was ready for uneasy stomachs with a plastic kidney-bean-shaped bucket. Usually there was enough warning—a sudden pallor, rapid gulping, a hesitant "I'm not feeling so good." But three times, there wasn't, and she had been in the line of fire. Each of those times, she'd changed clothes but had to wait till after her shift to shower, and the last time, she'd complained to her husband, "Can you imagine anything worse than someone you don't love throwing up all over you?"

"I can, in fact," he had said. He was sitting up in bed, scrolling on his phone. He looked at her. "Far worse things, in fact."

She didn't know what to say, how heavy or light to take his response. She used to be able to read him so well, but at some point in the midst of all the miscarriages, she'd lost that ability. She could ask, of course, what he meant, but already, his attention was back on his phone.

Now, in the dining room of *PILGRIM*, it was she who was throwing up suddenly, uncontrollably. Once she started, she found she couldn't stop. Between heaves, she heard a woman behind her gasp. Another heave, and she heard Nicole laugh and say, "First trimester's a bitch." Again and again, the roller coaster within, the sudden ups and downs and the swirling sensation that grew and grew until her stomach flipped 180 degrees. When there was nothing left to expel and she was just dry heaving—unable to stop, unable to get up, unable to do anything at all except continue trying to empty what was already empty—she found herself thinking that hers would be one of *those* pregnancies. The kind women talked about friends of friends having, awe and terror in their voices. "I don't know how she did it," they confessed, leaning forward. "Couldn't keep a meal down for months." They declared, "Warrior queen," meanwhile trying to suppress their jealousy; their pregnancies had been so normal, filled with all and only the banal discomforts.

At some point, a bucket had appeared, and Lyla's head was in it. She could sense the other women at her table, and other nearby tables, staring at her, but her throat ached too much for her to care. A voice—Bianca's?—called to her from beyond the bucket. She heard, "I pressed the red button." She heard, "The floor team is on their way."

A fissure formed in her mind, and on either side of this jagged line was an equally weighted thought. On the one side, she wondered if something was wrong. Maybe her body was rejecting the pig-liver uterus or the hormone patches were malfunctioning. On the other side, she started to question what she had had done. She was terribly sick, and for what? For whom? To satisfy her curiosity? To ease her maternal drive? To experience a particular ten months that in her early twenties she thought she would experience multiple times, no problem? But there was no baby to bring home on the other side of this. Again she imagined Timothy's eyes—now dark with disgust—on her, but briefly, before he turned away, no longer able even to look at her. If only she could pretend that it was real. But then what would happen at the end of ten months when the deflate sequence started and she went back to wearing medium scrub bottoms? A physical tide rising and retreating, the sand wiped smooth, and Timothy washed away with it, gone.

NICOLE

FRIDAY 20:22

Lyla's head was in a bucket, and after four fast glasses of wine, Nicole was convinced the woman was dying—just like she was. Only Lyla's was not a slow internal death that no one, save her and her surgeons, knew about, but rather a very open, very public one. Already the woman's stomach was empty—what would be next? Gastric acids and bile? Then blood? Then organs and their systems? Eventually the rest, bones and muscles and tissue liquefied until there was nothing left to be regurgitated, just the empty bucket of a body.

Seeing this in her mind, Nicole felt not only the fear of Lyla's swiftly approaching expiration but also a nearly unbearable sadness for their children—her Max and this other woman's three—to have to grow up and live their lives without their mothers, just like she'd done. And sadness, too, for the terrible plunge their husbands would take into single parenthood. She felt the ridiculousness of discovering death here, of all places—on a luxury cruise, away from everything she thought she'd wanted to escape. Now she would give anything to have her daily life back tenfold: the oil changes and dentist appointments and Max's cough waking her in the night and his sight words to practice and dinner to make and photo-collage holiday cards to order online and playdates to schedule and orchestrate and the multitude of worries—even the secret roomful of B+L products—that always seemed so pressing, so urgent, so frustrating and inconvenient.

All of these thoughts and feelings crashed together in Nicole's wine-muddled mind when the floor team entered the dining room. One was pushing a drink cart; the other two had white towels draped over their arms. As they approached, Nicole stood in a frantic rush, her chair toppling over as she yelled: "Hurry! Hurry! She needs help. Hurry! Save her! *Do something.*"

CEDRIC

Cedric—wearing a clean top he had pulled from a kitchen closet stocked with extra uniforms should servers suffer a spill mid-service—knew the protocol even though he had yet to witness an outburst in the dining room. Each server had his own syringe secured in a hidden back waistband pocket, and they'd all been coached on what to do:

Pull the syringe from one's waistband.

Palm it in one's left hand.

Approach the hysterical passenger.

Wrap one's right arm around her while speaking calming words in a soothing tone—*It's okay, there now, it's going to be okay, it'll be just fine.*

Use one's left hand to guide the syringe and inject the sedative into the passenger's thigh or shoulder or hip—whichever location was most readily accessible and most discreet.

Help the passenger sit if they were standing.

Activate chair wheels.

Roll the passenger out of the dining room to her room steward, who would escort her back to her room to recover from the episode.

But Cedric was not about to inject Nicole with a sedative. She'd been acting so oddly, and he was worried about her, and he had to know what she was thinking. If he drugged her like he was supposed to and wheeled

338

her away, she would return to her room and he wouldn't see her again, wouldn't know what to make of whatever was happening between them. He couldn't bear the idea of never knowing if it was real. With Kali, he had waited 300 days to find out exactly where they stood. If Nicole turned him down, fine, that would be fair. But he imagined a prolonged agony at the uncertainty of their connection lingering perpetually. That wouldn't do at all.

He left the syringe in his waistband as he came up behind Nicole and wrapped his arm around her waist. He spoke to her quietly as the floor team huddled around Lyla. He put his left hand on her hip and held it there. When Lyla was stable and being wheeled from the room, he started to lead Nicole away from the table. This was his chance. They could talk alone. Funny and strange how these things work out. "Let's get you out of here," he said. "I've got you." She was soft in his arms, almost slack. *She was letting him hold her.*

"Where—" she started to say, but Cedric placed a finger against her lips.

"Fresh air," he said, letting out a breath when he registered her vague nod. *Good*, he thought. This is what she wanted, too.

NICOLE

SECOND FRIDAY 20:38

Nicole didn't resist when Cedric led her away. She wanted nothing more than to be out of that room, away from that terrible panic, from imminent death, out of that nutmeggy air.

"It's okay," he murmured. "It's going to be okay."

He cooed until her breathing slowed and her shoulders relaxed, and then she realized his arm was around her, that he was guiding her steps. Already they'd made their way out into the hall and halfway up the grand staircase to Deck 8. Now he urged her up another set of stairs to Deck 9, then a third to Deck 10. The whole time, their bodies were touching. Her head was swimming, but still she felt the sharp uncanniness of a daydream touching reality. Here she was, embarking on the excursion she had planned for herself, she had longed for. Her skin smarted as he pulled her into the night air.

"Here we are," he said, "just the two of us," and she thought, *Yes*. She had imagined almost exactly this while dozing on a swinging daybed before dinner one night last week: her hand in his, the two of them sneaking off together, moonlight on the water. Then, she'd been ready for all of it, but now the knowledge of her cancer was fresh and ugly, and she couldn't stop hearing the sound of Lyla's heaves. They were approaching one of the canopies. A nearby hot tub bubbled and hissed.

Heat climbed her neck. They entered the canopy, mint in the air, and he stopped, turned toward her. "This is good," he said.

"It is," she said, because she wanted it to be. She wanted to immerse herself in the fantasy, finish the excursion. The breeze was light and playful, the night pleasantly cool. Time and thought slowed, rooting her in the moment. *This is good. This is good. This is good.*

Cedric took her other hand in his. He stared into her eyes. "Hi," he said, smiling wide. His face was so close to hers. His dark eyes glittered, and sweat gleamed along his brow.

She felt her lips stretching, smiling back. "Hi," she said. And then his mouth was on hers, and his hands let go of her hands and moved to cup her cheeks, pulling her to him.

For a moment, they kissed, and for that moment, she wanted him— or wanted him to want her—just like this: recklessly, intensely. His lips were smooth and tasted slightly briny, like a seaman's lips should taste. It was precisely what she had imagined last week, and she expected the rest to fall into place like the last ten minutes of a romcom, with music swelling and sparklers and bottle rockets going off. She did, in fact, feel fireworks, but it wasn't a pleasant sensation, and instead of music playing in her head, an alarm began to sound. The low siren picked up speed and volume as Cedric pushed his tongue into her mouth, and when he dropped his hands to her behind, it became a hammering wail.

She opened her eyes. She was still kissing Cedric, still embracing him, his uniform stiff beneath her hands, and for a moment she couldn't decide what to do. Release him. Back up. Yes, that was it. But she couldn't get her body to work. She couldn't do anything. His tongue flicked around her mouth, darting like a fish, left then right. He squeezed her bottom.

She was going to be sick. Physically sick, like Lyla. She needed his tongue out of her mouth. She yanked away, their lips breaking apart with a smack. "No," she said. "I can't." She took a deep breath.

"No one will know," Cedric said, moving to draw her into his arms again.

"I don't want this," she said. *Not really,* she thought. In a daydream, yes, but here, now, she wanted to go home. She wanted to build a Lego dinosaur with her son. She wanted to fall asleep against Justin, watching Netflix on the couch.

She put both hands on Cedric's chest and pushed. "Stop," she said, sucking in more air. Where was the breeze? She felt like she was swimming in the hot tub hissing behind her.

"It's okay. Everything's okay. I like you, and I think you like me, and there's so little time." Again, Cedric reached for her.

She took a quick step back, felt the edge of a chaise bang against her shin. She tottered, about to fall. Cedric lunged for her, but, Nicole realized too late, not to steady her, to guide her down onto the plush surface.

"Miss?" said a voice from behind. "Is everything okay?"

Cedric startled, rolling off Nicole and onto the deck. Nicole struggled to her feet, smoothing her dress against her body.

She turned to the deckman who'd spoken. Larry, his name tag read, though the letters appeared to sway and swing. "No," she said, lifting a hand to her head, aching now. "No," she said again. "Everything is not alright." Her head was spinning. Each word was a struggle to form, to move past her lips. But she had more to say. More she *needed* to say. "In fact, this man—" The explanation was there, going all the way back to their first meeting, her instant crush, the way they had flirted all week, how it had felt to be desired, how she'd imagined it ending so differently . . . but just then she felt a prick, then pressure on her arm. She twisted away, but Cedric's hand was balled up against her shoulder, and he was pushing something into her skin. "What?" she asked. The question had more to it, she knew, but she couldn't call forth the words, any words. The air around her swelled, lifting her body up until she was weightless in her own skin, floating in a calm sea of night and fresh mint and voices.

One of the voices said, "What the hell was that?"

Another replied, "Just a sedative. It's fine. She caused a scene at dinner. I was following the protocol."

"The protocol, huh?"

"I have to get back. You'll take her to her room?"

"Sure. Go. Jesus."

DR. HESTON

"Doctor?"

"Yes, Rebecca."

"Doctor, you are needed on Deck 6. A passenger has recently returned to her room, and an emergency consultation has been requested by the floor team."

"Who's the passenger, and what was her itinerary?"

"Lyla Simmons. She piloted the Maternal Body Makeover."

"What seems to be the problem?"

"Excessive regurgitation."

"Frequency?"

"Continuous over the past hour."

"Damn it. I told Jared to dial back the nausea. First the protein pump and now this? What was he thinking?"

"I can postulate only the mental activity of the women on the ship."

"No, I know, Rebecca. It's just an expression."

"I see."

"Page Jared and have him meet me in Lyla's room. Have the floor team keep her comfortable until we get there—"

"—Doctor, she's crying now—"

"Poor girl. Of course she is. She wanted to be pregnant, but not *this* pregnant."

"The floor team would like permission to sedate. She's crying harder now."

"Yes, yes, of course. Knock her out. When she wakes up, she'll be perfectly pregnant."

"Permission granted."

"And make a note on her account, please, Rebecca—offer her a complimentary tummy tuck for her next cruise, when she's done being pregnant."

"Very well. Note added."

THE WOMEN
REMAINING AT TABLE 32

Most tables had finished their endings course, and women were starting
to retire to their staterooms. Earlier in the week, these passengers would
have considered walking one of the paths or playing another round of
bingo or taking a dip in a hot tub or getting a pedicure after dinner. Not
tonight. They had done the activities on the ship. They had completed
their itineraries. They had socialized. They had walked through Park,
Cemetery, and Mall. Now their week away was about to end, and they
wanted this time for themselves. Some meditated on their balconies.
Some journaled in their beds. Some curled up with a hardback book and
fell asleep six pages in.

Bianca and Jordana were the only two at their table—with Lyla
wheeled away and Nicole escorted out after yelling across the dining
room. Neither had returned. Both women kept checking the door, but
it opened only to let women depart as they finished their meal. Servers
from nearby tables checked on them. Two carried out the huge middle-
course platter, which the women picked at in quietude. They murmured
about the food, sighing over particularly tasty mouthfuls.

Finally Bianca said, "I hope they're okay."

"Me, too," Jordana said.

"What a night to join our table."

"You could say that."

"Have you ever seen anyone throw up that much in such a short amount of time?"

"Never."

"And Nicole. Who would have guessed that the sweet mother who knits would turn out to be a wine-guzzling screaming person? Earlier in the week she'd been different. I don't know what happened."

"Different how?"

"More stable? I don't know. She was friendly but quiet. Not the sort of woman to drink so much and make a scene. She was downing wine like it was water."

"Do you know what her itinerary was?"

"Nothing too wild. Her husband had booked the trip. Just a little tuck and boost after the baby, I think."

"You never know, though," Jordana said.

A server appeared between them. Andy, according to his name tag. "Would you like me to bring out your final course? Believe me, the chef saves the best for last."

Jordana looked at Bianca. Despite the earlier uproar, she wasn't ready to leave yet.

Bianca shook her head. "I'm sorry. I'm going to go. I'm starting to fade."

"Of course. I think I'll stay. But maybe I don't need the whole tray. Just a quarter? Would love some tea, thank you," Jordana said.

"Peppermint's already steeping." Andy bowed slightly and winked. Jordana's eyes grew wide. Did he know? Would Bianca see the wink and realize, at last, who she was? But the other woman was looking off toward the dining room's door. A room steward had entered and was approaching.

"Have a good night," Jordana said.

"What?"

"Have a good night, I said."

"Sorry," Bianca said. "I'm just . . . worried about what comes next. All of this—" She gestured at herself. "—and I could still lose when I get back on the court."

"Loss is always a possibility," Jordana murmured.

"Are you nervous about it? Going back to your real life?"

"I don't intend to go back. Only forward."

"Only forward," Bianca repeated.

"Tea for you." Andy had returned, and he set a steaming cup in front of Jordana.

"Ready?" the room steward asked Bianca after releasing her chair's wheels.

Bianca nodded, and off they rolled.

Jordana stayed at the table for a while, watching other passengers leave through the steam rising from the rim of her flowery cup—blue tulips. When she finished one cup, Andy returned with a refill. He didn't say anything, just poured, added two cubes of sugar, and gave the liquid a swirl with her teaspoon. Jordana was thankful for the continual warmth, thankful for the lack of conversation, thankful for the time alone. Before the cruise, solitude had felt like quicksand, dragging her into the past, into memory. But that had been Annalie. Jordana was an entirely different person, with high cheekbones, a narrow nose, uptilted eyes, full lips. Jordana looked forward. Only forward.

While she sipped her tea, women in pairs, in small clusters, or solitary, rose from their chairs and walked into the night. Were these women hiding, too? Their real selves camouflaged by refined skin, excised fat, remodeled bones, and biosynthetic polymers?

Who were they? Jordana wondered. What had they suffered? And what strength had they uncovered, buried beneath their now flawless skin and remarkable figures, that granted them the courage to recover what they'd lost?

DEBARKATION

THE PILGRIM DAILY

Farewell to all.

DEBARKATION.

08:00–12:00. All passengers must leave their staterooms for debarkation no later than 11:45. Room stewards and deckman are available as escorts.

SPA. HOURS: 07:00–09:00

DAILY SPECIALS

Bye-Bye Blowout

All Day Eyes

Book now on your room screen or talk to your room steward to schedule a visit.

DINING. SEE HOURS BELOW.

Continental Breakfast 06:00–09:00

ON-BOARD ACTIVITIES. HOURS: 05:30–08:00

Readying for Re-Entry, Deck 12 . . . . 05:30
Hatha Yoga, Deck 10, Mint Canopy 06:00
Say Goodbye Social, Deck 10, Citrus Canopy 7:00

From all of us here on PILGRIM, thank you for sharing your voyage with us, for inviting us to be a part of your story, however big, however small. Until next time, may you and your life be beautiful.

—The Captain

THE PASSENGERS

SECOND SATURDAY 08:00–12:00

The women came off the boat like they'd boarded it—in a steady progression of bodies. Great care was taken during debarkation. For example, the moving ramp conveying passengers off Deck 10 moved more slowly Saturday morning than it had two Mondays earlier, when it had pulled passengers up, up, up to the launch party. Along the gangway, screens stretched from floor to ceiling. These were filled with life-sized images of the women themselves, videos taken when the passengers first came aboard. The disembarking women watched themselves on these screens marveling over their transformations. Such improvement, and over a mere two weeks!

"See?" they turned to one another and said. "Worth every penny."

"We'll do this again," they promised.

"Let's try that new Laser Sculpting excursion next time," they suggested.

Down, down, down they went, planning ahead and waving goodbye to the images of the selves they left behind.

And as they rode the moving ramp, some women carried purses, but many were restricted in terms of how much weight they could carry. Instead, they held clutches or wallets they'd picked up while walking the

Mall. Many women hit the gangway in heels. They had long, lean legs and firm, high derrieres to show off, plus they felt great, really great, so why not? Around their renewed and reclaimed bodies, they wrapped dresses to accentuate their figures. Some revealed midriffs in crop tops, while others distinguished themselves through their accessories: airy scarves draped along wattle-free necks, wide and dark sunglasses for those still recovering from any of eight eye-enhancement excursions, full and floppy hats. Room stewards and deckmen helped escort the passengers who requested them, providing firm hands cupped around the women's elbows. They guarded against weak knees, vertigo, missteps in heels, any threat of toppling forward on the downward grade of the ramp.

The women were ready to return to their lives, to tell everyone they'd had the *best* time on a *dream* vacation. Utterly restorative. They felt as though it had taken years off and wouldn't be surprised if they looked younger too! For the next month, some would take a vitamin regimen Dr. Heston had developed. Some would need to apply the topical products BECCA had already called in to the pharmacies the women routinely visited to pick up albuterol for their wheezing children and Ambien to help them sleep. Some might pop an ibuprofen every now and again, but more for fear of the possibility of pain than to alleviate pain itself.

No music played during debarkation. Not on the decks or gangway. Not in the terminal building. Early survey data suggested that leaving to musical fanfare saddened passengers, who were already a little glum. Though many had families and careers, homes and hobbies, other trips and lives they were eager to resume, reentry proved challenging. They wanted more time away, one more excursion, one more yogurt parfait topped with fresh fruit, granola, and a dollop of homemade almond butter. They wanted another walk on the Cemetery path, another round of afternoon bingo and a pot of freshly brewed dandelion-root tea. They wanted a different color of polish on their nails, more back massages. With their itineraries complete, they had achieved the rejuvenation they sought, and yet they missed the thrill of anticipation, the pleasure in contemplating the promise of changes to come. Moving toward land at a rate of two miles per hour, they realized that their journeys had boiled down to a finite set of minutes in which a finite number of things had occurred. They understood at last there was never enough time to do everything and get it just right.

CEDRIC

Cedric stood on Deck 12, six decks above the departure gangway. Already the day was warm, the sun peeking through clouds like pulls of cotton candy. He leaned his body against the railing, to all appearances watching the women from Cruise #52 leave the ship, but he wasn't watching so much as looking and looking for one woman in particular.

He had blown it. Or perhaps there had been nothing to blow in the first place. Hard to say now. That kiss. Just a kiss and also more, and he'd gotten caught up, carried away. But he'd thought Nicole was right there with him, ready to move from the shallows to the deep. She'd seemed so into him that it was hard to accept that she wasn't. And when Larry showed up, he'd panicked.

He prayed that with the wine and the sedative . . . he cringed now at the memory of plunging the syringe into her arm . . . she wouldn't remember much of the evening. Larry would have helped her back to her room, or called her room steward to wheel her back and tuck her in, and she would have slept soundly, deeply. He was just the server who happened to be assigned to her table. A crew member like every other crew member who had attended to her during the cruise. That was his story. He'd escorted her from the dining hall when she'd caused a scene, and he'd followed protocol. If Nicole said otherwise, it would be her word against his. He wasn't sure what, exactly, Larry had witnessed, but he was almost certain the deckman would back him up. Such a solid guy, that Larry.

Of course, if he could go back, he would do so many things differently. He squinted hard in the brightness of the morning. Women passed beneath him, hair lifted like flags by the breeze. Was this his forever mantra, he wondered, tightening his grip on the railing until his knuckles turned white: *Game over. Try again. Game over. Try again. Game over. Try again.*

Cedric could hear squeals and laughter and chatter from the pier down below. He scanned the crowd in the harbor, but with all the departing women, the ship's crew and terminal staff, the luggage trolleys and gleaming black dumpsters, he couldn't discern which moving body was Nicole, and even if he could have identified her, he wouldn't have been able to assess her state of mind from this height and angle and through the glare.

He sat on a nearby chaise and thought if only he hadn't kissed Nicole, if only he had let her be. A gull landed on the railing three feet away. The bird let out a single squawk and hopped down to the deck, taking tentative steps. The bird's head darted left and right, then craned so it could see over its shoulder.

Cedric watched the gull intently. What was his problem? The night was over—just like his marriage. He had to move on. With two wing flaps, the bird was airborne again, disappearing over the edge of the deck in a smooth glide.

DR. HESTON

SECOND SATURDAY 08:00–12:00

The Captain sat in his lab at the wide window that wrapped around the bow of the ship. The glass was tinted, which let him discreetly watch the passengers depart. Every second Saturday, he sat in his lab during the four hours of debarkation, watching women walk off the ship and down the pier. During this time, he would tinker with a simulation on his hologram console. He would read BECCA's reports on surgery outcomes and recommendations to advance procedure efficiency and passenger safety in the flower stations. He would linger on the files BECCA had marked with red flags. He would ask Rebecca to please make notes, answer follow-up questions, record his thoughts. He would track women across the harbor, their steps cautious but proud. Usually, he spent a good portion of the morning dreaming up new surgeries, new applications for laser therapy, new excursion bundles, cutting-edge itineraries.

But not this morning. This morning, as he went about his usual tasks, he couldn't concentrate. He bumped into the arm of the 3D printer in the midst of a nipple run. He knocked over his bowl of oatmeal. He forgot to take the lid off his coffee cup and burned his tongue on the searing black liquid. He reread one flagged case file three times before giving up, not remembering a single word. Finally, he sat back and closed his eyes.

"Rebecca," he called, the name a sigh.

"Yes, doctor?" BECCA responded.

"Please let me know when the passenger Annalie starts down the gangway."

"Very well."

He rubbed at his eyes with his knuckles. He hoped Annalie would glance back once she made it to land. Most women did. He wanted to behold her face again. He needed to. If only for a moment. Even if the wind picked up and blew her hair to hide half of it. Even from this height, which would render her features vague. Even still, her face would be entirely familiar—a face so rigorously studied, so known, so loved.

NICOLE

SECOND SATURDAY 08:49

When Nicole woke up in her stateroom, she felt as though she were emerging from a fog, a billowing maelstrom of swirling white and gray. The fog wasn't going anywhere. She was tethered to it. The fog sat on her shoulders like a medieval helmet, heavy and clunky, her breath echoing inside. The porthole window showed her the day had begun. She heard a low buzz of voices and a rumbling. A dress was laid out for her on the chair next to her bed. Beneath the chair sat a pair of sand-colored platform sandals. Both were new. She became aware of a persistent tinkling sound, a faint ring here, a delicate toll there.

Slowly, she swung her feet over the edge of the bed. Her whole body ached, but her head most of all. She sucked in a breath, then froze, half propped on one arm, until the thrumming pain subsided. When it did, she eased her legs down until they rested on the ground and she was sitting upright. She held her head in her hands. Her skull felt brittle but dense, a concrete egg precariously perched on her neck. On the table beside the bed, she saw a small, folded note card with a gold foil H in the bottom left corner. She reached for it and read:

Good morning Nicole,

I know this wasn't the voyage you had planned. I reached out to a friend in the Richmond area, an oncologist. You should have a voicemail waiting for you when you disembark today. He'll get you in this week.

  Dr. Heston

  PS Please accept this small gift from the Mall. It's the least I can do.

Then she remembered. The baseball. Cancer. Dinner last night. But how did she get here? She couldn't recall. The details of the night had disappeared, too. If only she could remove the fog helmet, she would remember.

There was a knock. "Good morning, Nicole. It's Seth. May I be of assistance?"

Her room steward. Nicole wanted to ask him to unbuckle the clasp and pull her heavy headgear up and off. She wanted to ask him what happened last night. She wanted to know if the baseball was really in her or if it was only a dream induced by the anesthesia. But no, the note from Dr. Heston meant it was true. He had reached into her open abdomen and found the tumor. How much time had passed since then? How much larger had the tumor grown since they'd sewn her back up? Now, more than anything, she wanted to go home, though she knew not all of her would return. Part of her would stay on this ship, haunting its halls, the Cemetery, the canopies of Deck 10.

"Please," she called out. As Seth entered the room and approached the bed, she asked, "For starters, what can you do about this headache of mine?"

"I have just the thing," he said. He held out his right palm, in which two blue pills sat. "These should help, and you're due for your next dose anyway."

"Dose?"

"The first was soon after you climbed into bed last night. Your blood alcohol level was a concern. We drained your stomach to help clear your system, gave you some IV fluids, and started you on these to flush your blood. You had the second dose around 02:00. This will be your third, and you'll need two more doses after this one, at least four hours apart."

Flashes of dinner the night before came back. A platter of food steaming in the center of the table. A growing sense of panic. Napkin on lap. Someone throwing up. Someone calling out. "How did I get here?"

"A crew member escorted you."

"I don't remember."

"No, I would think that you wouldn't between the wine at dinner and the sedative later to calm you down."

"A sedative?" Nicole thought as hard as she could, but the events following her arrival in the dining hall wouldn't return to her except in fragments. Wine glasses full and empty. Rosemary. Meatball. Warm night. Shoulder prick.

Seth explained, "You became very agitated, and we were concerned you would compromise the healing process."

"I see," she said, even though she didn't.

"Now, what do you say we get you out of bed? Debarkation ends at noon. How about a shower and something to eat before you leave?" Seth held out a hand.

"Shower, yes. Food, maybe. My head feels like it might dislodge and roll away." Nicole took his hand.

"It's okay," Seth said gently. "We have time."

No, she wanted to say. *No*, she wanted to insist. Time was precisely what she didn't have. But she said nothing. Instead, she let Seth pull her to standing as the fog in her head started to disintegrate into the growing brightness of the day.

BIANCA

All through her technology installation and syncing session in the terminal building, Bianca felt giddy. She had been returned to the strength and agility of her twenties and then some. Now the future felt so wide open before her, a freeway six lanes wide stretching ahead toward Miami, then the qualifying tournament, and eventually the Open. The technician walked her through the device and the phone app connected to it.

"See here," he said. "You're currently processing protein with a speed and efficiency three times that of an average woman. That rate will fluctuate depending on your diet and activity level, but 300 percent improvement will be where you're at on average."

Bianca could only nod. She had seen the models. She had run through the specs. Blake had talked her through all of this before she left the ship. Still, her new biological reality left her in awe.

Phone in hand, Bianca made her way out of the terminal building. An agent walked her through the exit turnstile, waving to the town car that already had her luggage stowed in the trunk. He opened the door and asked Bianca to flex for him, and when she did, he grinned.

"Don't shoot," he said, laughing.

Bianca smiled. "Right. I do have guns," she said as she climbed into the backseat. "Huge guns," she called out.

"Massive guns," the terminal agent said, pushing the door shut. Two quick taps and they were off.

Bianca looked back at *PILGRIM*. She watched the ship recede, then disappear when the car rounded a palm-tree-studded bend. Just like that, it was gone. She imagined her DeLorean had winked out of sight, called away to transport other women to other times in their lives, to bodies that could do what they needed them to do better than they imagined possible.

The car bumped over a pothole, and for a moment, her mind flashed forward. Comfortably in the top 100. Strong appearances at the majors. Memories of giving lessons to uncoordinated six-year-olds faded. That time she lost to Bruce: laughable. The girls no farther away than the next hotel room when they all traveled together for a tournament. Their faces a reflection of hers but still rounded, still subject to breakouts now and again. Anthony's arm around her at night, becoming again a familiar heft. The occasional fight between them, banal and summarily resolved. She only let herself consider briefly that her homecoming might be undesirable, time passing not water under the bridge but water churned through a propeller, agitated and frothing.

She unlocked her phone and started to scroll through her contacts. She thought she might call Anthony on the drive. How long had it been since she'd heard the girls' voices? Too long. But now there was so much to say, so much hope to share. *I'll be home soon*, she could tell them. *After Miami*. She held the phone in her right hand and the pointer finger on her left hovered over Anthony's name.

But she had to win Miami—or at least make it to the quarterfinals. She flexed her feet and felt her calves bunch. She twisted her arms, first the right, then the left, and out popped her triceps, bands of steel. She imagined her serve nearly clipping the net before slicing into the back corner of the box for an ace. She imagined the court shrinking with her quickness, the back line seemingly shorter by half, now a distance easily traversed to return shots bouncing her from one corner to the other and back. Still her finger hovered over Anthony's name, now fading on her screen. She would win. Of course she would. Then winning would be her life, and only ten years later than she had planned. But what was ten years? Time enough to reduce her body to an extension of her racket, of the ball, wildly arcing back and forth across the net. Time enough to learn that winning required more, even. Desperation. The sacrifice of all she held dear. A pound of flesh. Her phone's screen blinked to black as it entered sleep mode. Her left hand fell to her lap. How could she *not* win? She had given everything. Everything it was possible for her to give.

LARRY

SATURDAY 12:11

The third time he checked, Larry finally had Deck 12 to himself. He approached the railing quickly, looking around, turning in full circles twice. From beneath his uniform top, he pulled his dopp kit. Holding it on top of the railing before him, he unzipped it one last time. He had already removed his toiletries, so now he spied two quartzite pillars and several smoother stones in smoky shades of gray, swirling green, and mottled black and yellow. He counted six, seven, eight diamond-stud earrings. He flipped through a bookmark and three business cards with room and phone numbers scrawled across the back, one underlined three times. He brought to his nose a tiny bottle of perfume and breathed in lemon buttercream and pink flowers, the kind of sweet fragrance that reminded him of high school and the pink bedrooms he had climbed into. He rifled through rings, pressed a pinch of gold flakes from a tiny box to his tongue, and squeezed a velvety scrunchie, its softness in his hand like whipped cream. Inside a leather glasses case, he looked upon the hairs he had collected, a neat swirling gray nest. Finally, from among the rest of the trophies he had gathered, he pulled a tiny square chip and Rocco's badge. These items he slid into his back pocket. The rest, he kept in the kit, which he zippered again, just not completely. He left a half-inch opening.

He gave the bag a shake, then another. Muffled clinking and tinkling, sliding and bumping. So many treasures. But it was time to send them on their way. He held the bag out over the water on the far side of the boat, away from the port, and let it fall from his hands. It plummeted from Deck 12, growing smaller and smaller, until it hit the water and bobbed. The splash was almost inaudible at his distance and over the din of debarkation. Already the bag was sinking. Then it was gone.

ANNALIE

Annalie's flight would begin boarding at Gate A36 at 1:25. Delta 1614 from LAX to ATL was scheduled to leave at 2:00. With her new digital ID, she'd had no trouble scanning through security, despite her changed appearance. As her consultant had assured her nearly a week ago, all of the documentation required for travel was in order, her image updated in the government's registry to match her fingerprints and retinal scans. "Honey, you don't need to worry about a thing," Claire had assured her. "Here at Canterbury Cruise Line, we think of *everything*."

Now she was sitting in a private lounger near her gate, attempting to read *Romeo and Juliet* on her phone. School would resume on Monday; a new quarter would begin. Her ninth-grade seminars would start with a drama unit. After the two-week break, her students would fill her classroom with their skittering energy. What would they think when they saw her, sitting behind her desk at the front of the room that first day back? She tried to imagine talking to her students, her colleagues, her *parents* about the cruise—the excursions she had been on—but what would she say? How would she ever explain the need to be her and only her in this world where Aimee wasn't? The whole thing was crazy. The craziest. *No way*, her students would declare. *No freaking way!* To them, she might as well have emerged from a futuristic science fiction story

367

like *Ender's Game*, which they had read together last fall. The fact of the transformation—how she saw a face that wasn't her own, that wasn't Aimee's, when she looked in the mirror—was unbelievable. Yet that's the way it was, and she felt lighter because of it. She could breathe again. She could eat again. She could smell and see and taste and hear again, and the world came back to her in this way, through her senses, so loud, so bold, so bright she hurt to take it all in, this new shimmering world she would live through alone.

GERALD

At the gate to the Port of Los Angeles, a man darted in front of the glossy black sedan. He held out both hands, standing in the middle of the road. He wore what seemed to be a uniform: gray slacks, white button-down shirt, and gray vest. Gerald slammed on the breaks, and the car came to an abrupt stop. The man lowered a hand as if to stroke the sunlight glinting off the car's slick hood.

From the backseat, a woman called, "What is it, Gerald? What's happening?"

"I'm not sure, Miss Lucy." Gerald was the car's artificial intelligence, and it responded in a male voice with a British accent. "It appears to be a person, male, dressed in a uniform."

Gerald was transporting Lucy back to her villa at the edge of Otter Cove in Carmel, where her personal assistant was busy preparing food and stocking her refrigerator and pantry with the items listed on her Homecoming Plan, just as he had done following her last three cruises. This disruption was new and unexpected.

While Gerald scanned the surroundings, the man made his way past the driver's side of the car and stopped outside the back door. There was a faint scraping sound, metal on metal, then a light pop. The man pulled open the back door and slid onto the dark leather beside Miss Lucy.

LARRY

Inside the car, Larry let out a deep breath. Cars could drive without drivers, but a couple thin pieces of metal could still pop a door lock. He had learned years ago on YouTube and now carried a kit in his wallet.

"Hi," he said, smiling at the woman in the backseat. "I was starting to worry you'd left without me." He was adlibbing, figuring out his strategy one sentence at a time.

"Who are you?" the woman asked, her voice rising just barely above his racing pulse.

"I'm your . . . homeward-bound escort." Larry laid a hand against his chest, framing with his thumb and forefinger the Canterbury Cruise Line logo on his shirt. "Your room steward said I was needed to accompany you."

"I don't know anything about this." The woman frowned. "I've never heard of a homeward-bound escort, and I've certainly never had one before. Isn't that right, Gerald?"

"That's correct, Miss Lucy."

Larry didn't hesitate. "It's a protocol the Captain is piloting. Starting with this cruise. Probably why your room steward forgot to say something and why Gerald here doesn't know. It's brand new. And it's only available to Priority A passengers like yourself."

"Priority A. I like that."

Bingo, Larry thought.

"Miss," Gerald said. "Shall I proceed?"

"I suppose. If it's protocol." Miss Lucy gave Larry a tentative smile, and the car started up again. "It's alright if I sleep?"

"Please do. I'm only here to make sure you are delivered safe and sound back to your home."

Soon, the Port of Los Angeles disappeared behind them, and Larry felt his body start to relax. He could feel the fine, soft leather of the seat beneath him, the air-conditioning light and cool on his face.

Gerald drove, and Lucy slept, her head resting against the built-in pillow, her seat reclined at a 30-degree angle, and a quilted lap blanket draped over her legs. Larry stared out the window, watching the city turn into suburbs, suburbs turn into desert as the car made its way north along the coast. He had no idea where they were going, but the farther away from LA, the better.

Larry retrieved his name badge and Rocco's and the square chip from the zippered pocket of his vest. He had stowed these final three treasures there when he had stopped by the terminal building's locker room to pick up his wallet. His phone he left behind. He would get a new one when he got where he was going.

He ran a finger along the embossed names on the badges, over the tiny ridges of the chip's surface. Then he rolled down the window minutely and slid them out through a narrow rectangle one by one. Just like that, they were gone, lost to the wind and terrain and wheels of the traffic behind them.

Through all of this, the woman didn't stir.

"Please keep your window up," Gerald said. "Miss Lucy prefers air conditioning."

"Roger that," Larry said. He rolled up the window.

Later, as the car continued along the winding coastal road, Larry reached into Miss Lucy's purse, which lay open beside him. With his fingers, he combed the interior, plucking out a zippered wallet, monogrammed brown leather softer than the skin engineered on *PILGRIM*. He browsed its contents for hints of where they were heading. Behind her expired driver's license, he found a member ID for the Tehama Golf Club. He turned the card over in his hand, a smile starting to stretch the corner of his mouth. He didn't know where the club was, but it hardly mattered. A plan was forming in his mind. He slipped the card back into place. He was about to return the wallet when he paused and shrugged, once more sliding the zipper open. From the row of neat bills nestled along the back edge, he plucked two hundreds.

BECCA

BECCA reported two of the deckmen unaccounted for. They hadn't swiped in for an afternoon shift nor had they logged off in the terminal building for a day away.

This happened occasionally when the ship reached port, with crew members in a hurry to hit the beach, a bar, to return to their gaming systems and California kings. They were eager to retrieve their phones and call the lovers they saw every other weekend, meet the friends they spent time with when they weren't on *PILGRIM*, check in with the roommates who fed the bulldogs they'd had since their parents divorced a decade ago—and their eagerness made them forgetful from time to time.

The Staff Safety Protocol required BECCA, for liability purposes, to keep tabs on crew members as they moved onto and off the ship. When crew couldn't be found in the system, BECCA would ping their partners through the crew portals and send text messages to the missing crew members' phones every thirty minutes until their location and well-being could be confirmed. If their partners didn't know, and there was still no response after five or six texts, BECCA would set out to find them. After all, bodies were just data, ultimately ones and zeroes that could be mapped onto dimensions of time and space and tracked as they moved among other data points, which BECCA could access with her remote surveillance system. Eventually, they would become visible, lines of light stretching from their last known positions, and the matter would be resolved.

LYLA

SATURDAY 14:38

At the airport, Lyla saw pregnant women everywhere. They were pushing strollers loaded with children and small furry suitcases. They were standing at high tables, poking forks into bowls of melon. They sat in chairs at their gates, staring at the phones held in one hand while their other hand lazily grazed the mountains that had replaced their midsections. One, looking to be about thirty-seven weeks, emerged from a bathroom stall around the same time Lyla did.

Moments ago, Lyla had thrown up again, but only her second time today. During her final health assessment at the Port of Los Angeles, the terminal tech who'd scanned her vitals one last time had urged her to call the Passenger Wellbeing Line if she started throwing up more than three times in a single hour or more than seven times in a twenty-four hour period.

She had nodded.

"Congratulations," he'd told her, helping her off the exam table.

In the airport bathroom, two sinks separated her from the expectant mother as they both washed their hands. A woman that pregnant shouldn't be flying, Lyla knew. What was she doing here? While Lyla pulled her hair up into a ponytail, the other woman applied lipstick, leaning forward as best she could, which wasn't much. Lyla spied the top of her maternity jeans—a wide blue band that stretched up beneath her shirt. The other woman capped the tube and rubbed her lips together. Lyla watched her in the mirror, washing her hands again, unable to leave, to avert her eyes. She felt a welling within, gnawing and growing. What was this woman thinking, preparing to board a flight that could jeopardize her unborn child? And why did she get to have what Lyla couldn't, what Lyla could only approximate with a pig-liver balloon, some silicone, and a hormone patch already prone to overstimulation?

Next to her on the counter sat the full cup of decaf coffee she had purchased after passing through the security checkpoint. She had planned to dump it out in the sink, since even the smell of coffee incited her nausea, apparently. Now, instead, she knocked her elbow into the cardboard cup as she reached for a paper towel precisely when the pink-lipped pregnant woman was winding her way past and toward the exit. Lyla pulled a paper towel from the dispenser as the cup made contact with the woman's round and protruding belly. The cup seemed to bounce upon contact, the lid slipping against its brim. Then the still-steaming coffee was out of the cup, soaking into the white cotton stretched across the woman's stomach and spilling onto the tiled floor. Lyla felt hot wet drops on her sandaled feet.

A chorus of gasps echoed in the small space. Already, the woman was pulling at her shirt. Already, other women were reaching for her, their concern like an invisible shield.

Lyla calmly dried her hands. "Whoops," she said into the mirror. "Sorry," she said, and walked out.

At the gate, she stood at the window looking out. Her plane was pulling up to the jet bridge.

That was mean, Mommy, her eldest imaginary child reprimanded her.

Really mean, her middle imaginary child said.

But it felt good, Lyla responded.

Why? asked her youngest imaginary child. *Why, Mommy?*

Lyla frowned. Soon she would be on her way back to Timothy and the childless home they inhabited together but apart, Timothy in an increasingly wider orbit around the biological fact of Lyla's body.

"Because," she whispered aloud. She would tell Timothy what she had done. She couldn't let him start to think maybe, just maybe, this time—even if that meant seeing him happy for ten months. Even if he would whistle all afternoon, putting together a stroller that could convert to a carseat and a high chair and even a rocking bassinet. Even if he would lay his hands on her stomach at night and whisper about the treehouse they would build in a few years, three stories tall with a lookout tower on the roof and a reading nook on floor two.

"Because," she choked out. She would ask him to forgive her this terrible need, just this one time, just to see what it felt like.

She would ask him to enter into this dream world with her, to join her in this game of make-believe while they waited for their adoption papers to be reviewed. "Let's pretend," she would beg when she got home, "that we're just like all those other couples who get to do this. It's not real, but it can be real enough."

BIOHAZARDOUS WASTE DETAIL

The crew members who stood in the gaping mouth of Deck 3 late Saturday night removed the black box from its castors. After unclipping the base locks, the men squatted and wrapped their arms around the ribbed plastic. They kept the lid locked in place. The whole bin would be removed to the receptacle in the harbor, and they would attach an empty bin to the castors so it would be ready to fill during the next cruise, #53.

"Up on three?" the older crew member asked.

"Just lift," the younger man grumbled, pissed to be here among the medical waste bins, red and yellow bags, fluid tanks, and sharps boxes, first scanning, then hefting container after container onto the conveyor belt that moved its cargo down into the Biohazard / Medical Waste dumpster in the harbor.

The first grunted. "These're some heavy lipids." The men managed to get the box onto the edge of the loading platform, but the older man was still lifting when the younger one started to push the container onto the moving belt. The contents shifted, rocking the whole thing forward so that it rolled onto its side.

"What'd you do that for—"

"—Look what you did."

The men glared at each other as the box made its way down the moving ramp.

"At least it stayed on the belt. Can you imagine if it had fallen in the water?" The older man watched the box, on its downward path, disappear into the night.

The younger man scowled. "Oceans are so polluted thanks to your generation. One more trash bin would be nothing."

"I didn't get a chance to scan it." The older man bent to retrieve the scanner from the ground.

"Just make a note in the register. They can add the barcode later at the incineration plant."

The older crewman tapped the screen on the wall to add a note manually. He shook his head, "What was in that bin? That shit was heavy."

"Can we not talk? The quicker we get away from all this blood and guts, the better."

"I hear that. The smell is already giving me a headache." The older man raised the scanner, slid a finger onto the trigger.

"You're giving me a headache." The younger man held up two red boxes.

The older one scanned both barcodes. "At least our generation knows a thing or two about respect."

"Sorry," the younger man said as he sat the boxes on the belt. Then he gave his partner a wide, saccharine smile. "Can you *please* not fucking talk?"

THE PASSENGERS

THE FOLLOWING WEEK

Some women had told their friends, simply, they were going on a cruise. They'd left out the details, like the cruise line, the name of the ship, the destinations, the accommodations. When pressed prior to departure, they had said, "I can't even remember the ports of call. But you know, it's nothing fancy. Just a little self-care in the sun."

Upon their return, they made plans to grab coffee, and their friends peppered them with questions while they waited in line:

How was it?

Wonderful!

How was the food?

What you'd expect. Mediocre and more than enough. But these burrata tomatoes the last night. I can't even.

What did you see?

Blue sky and blue water, mostly.

What did you do?

Excursions. Walked. Spa. Slept blissfully.

Then it was time to order. *You first,* their friends insisted.

And while they told the barista, *Grande chagaccino, extra foam,* tapped their credit cards, and walked to the end of the counter to wait, their friends tilted their heads to the side. They studied. They tried to decide what they were seeing but they couldn't be sure what it was they were trying to see. Something was different. Their friends—the ones who had cruised—looked so rested, so smooth and shiny, so *youthful*.

JORDANA

A FUTURE FRIDAY

From the window in the kitchen of her apartment, Annalie, known to her friends and colleagues in this new city as Jordana, looked out across the wide lawn of the Los Angeles National Cemetery. Her name change was official. An LA County judge had signed her Decree the same day she signed her lease. That had been three years ago. She'd never told her parents. To them, she looked different now, but she would always be Annalie—and Aimee. She was all they had left, after all.

In the cemetery, the uniform gray headstones and grave markers presented death as something that could be ordered and arranged just so. Calm and neat rows of so many expired lives, while all around, the city bustled and hummed and sprawled, and beyond LA the ocean pulled at the sand and mountains shifted on their tectonic plates, and beyond the ocean and the mountains a world spun on in its path across space, like a cruise ship sailing on a loop out into the Pacific and back again to the Port of Los Angeles.

Jordana sipped her tea at a desk that doubled as her kitchen table and looked out across the lawn with its undulating gray dots and boxes. Sometimes, flags appeared next to the headstones and markers. At times—usually unexpectedly and ferociously—rain streaked down past the window and turned the whole landscape gray, and Jordana remembered the long, steel winters of her childhood, land and sky a stone vault, sealed tight against warmth, against color. Gray LA, like everything else that carried even a hint of nostalgia, gave her chills and a headache behind her left eye.

Once a week, on one of her teaching days and after she finished her morning tea, Jordana walked in the cemetery before heading to campus to teach first-year students at UCLA how to write. When she was in the cemetery, and only when she was in the cemetery, did she permit herself to talk to her sister. There on those weekly strolls she would catch Aimee up on the events of her life as a singleton, the loneliness of moving through adulthood untethered to another person. She admitted to Aimee bad days among the good ones. She recounted the frivolous concerns her students shared—the worries they wasted on grades and status and appearance—as well as their thoughtful reactions to the changing world around them—Amazon boycotts, volunteer hours at the local alternative meat farms, campaigns to stop plastic production. She told Aimee about her new and growing fondness for dry red wine and tequila. She begged for forgiveness from her sister, now five years gone, for the moments she had wasted mad at her, the untold pettiness of sisters who shared a room and a wardrobe and a face and a set of names. The hairbrush she threw at her when they were in third grade because she wanted to be the shoe in Monopoly even though Aimee was always the shoe. The bangs she pulled in fifth grade waiting in a restroom line, though she couldn't recall where or why and she couldn't ask Aimee if she remembered. She told her sister about the economics professor she was seeing.

"I don't get to the beach as often as I should," she admitted.

"I ate cereal for dinner every night last week," she confessed.

Jordana was glad to be back in the classroom, but this time with older students, teenagers who still depended on their parents but preferred to think of themselves as independent and indestructible. She felt buoyed by her students' belief in their immortality, their irrepressible hope for the future and faith in the human will to endure, even when global warming threatened to submerge them all—or at least the entirety of their state—even when political parties dissolved and the country was scrambling to figure out where to go from here. They laughed anyway. They dreamed anyway. They reminded Jordana that the world was a place of laughter and dreams despite failing power grids and super storms and terrorism and cars that crashed into runners in the berm of a city street, a morning darkening instantly to night.

Today, she told her students their essays with her comments were now available online. After they revised their work, she reminded them, they would start working with AI tools to turn their texts into multi-modal, interactive websites. In the last minute of class, she reminded them, "You can create the prettiest project on the Internet, but if the ideas aren't there, no one is going to stick around to scroll. Even me. Don't make me click over to Facebook." She raised a finger. "If I'm bored, I'll do it. I'll get on Facebook and forget all about you and the cause you're trying to raise awareness for."

Her students smiled and shook their heads.

"Professor Carmichael, what's there to see on Facebook?" Thomas asked loudly. He slung his backpack over one shoulder.

"Precisely."

No one under the age of twenty-five went on Facebook anymore. Most had never even created accounts. And Jordana learned this semester that younger people were unplugging their personal lives almost entirely. They were buying stationery and mailing letters to their friends and family back home. They preferred to print, rather than post, the photos they took. A few even had dumb phones, devices that could call and text and do little else. When Jordana told them she hadn't gotten her first cell phone until after she graduated from college, her students had been in awe. "Wow, Professor Carmichael. We didn't realize you were so analog," one student exclaimed, and the rest nodded.

After the day had passed, after she called to tell her economics professor boyfriend good night, after she straightened up the living room and placed her dinner dishes in the dishwasher, she set the kettle on the back right burner on high. She took out two mugs, and in each, she hung a tea bag, Earl Gray in one, organic peppermint in the other. Around midnight, when the knock on her door came, the tea was freshly steeped, and she carried the two mugs on a tray to the living room, along with a cup of milk, a small bowl of sugar cubes, two spoons, and a plate of shortbread and jam-filled biscuits.

Jordana pulled open the door. "Hi," she said. "Come in."

"It's late," said the man standing there in scrubs. "I can come back in the morning."

He said the same thing every second Saturday when he came by, his ship docked in the Port of Los Angeles.

"Nonsense." She opened the door wider. "I already made tea."

"Thank you, Jordana," said Walter Heston as he walked into the apartment.

There, they would spend the next few hours together talking like the friends they had become. When Walter looked at Jordana, he would see Rebecca, and when Jordana felt Walter's eyes on her, she would feel known, despite the unfamiliarity of her own face.

Eventually, they would end up speaking about the ones they had lost, sharing stories and listening, drinking tea and laughing and crying until Rebecca and Aimee seemed to be with them in the room, alive and well in memories preserved and retold. Jordana would put the kettle back on for another cup of tea, and the past would steep into the present, full-bodied and fragrant, and carry them forward.

ACKNOWLEDGMENTS

Endless thanks to everyone who helped *Pilgrims 2.0* cast off and set sail, a voyage ten years in the making.

This book would not be a book without Nicola Mason and Maggie Su. To Maggie: for your wild enthusiasm upon reading the version I first sent to Acre Books and seeing the possibility in those pages. To Nicola: for your generous, thoughtful feedback to light and guide the way forward; for mind-melding while copyediting to make my writing shimmer; for shepherding this book into the world with so much care and energy. To the entire Acre Books team, for giving my book a safe harbor.

To the Sewanee School of Letters and Dr. John Grammer, the program's first fearless captain. I came to the Domain my first summer wanting to write a book, and I graduated wanting to be a writer. To the Creative Writing Program at the University of Georgia. I started writing this book in my first workshop with Judith Ortiz Cofer (whom I dearly miss), inspired by an assignment for Dr. Sujata Iyengar's Books as Things class. To my writing cohort for reading so many early, early pages, every two weeks: Bradley Bazzle, E. G. Cunningham, Johnny Damm, Will Dunlap, and Matthew Nye. To Robby Nadler, for inspiring BECCA to be the computing superpower she is.

I have been so fortunate to work with and learn from some incredible writers and mentors. To Ellen Slezak, Michael Griffith, and Chris Bachelder at the Sewanee School of Letters, and Judith Ortiz Cofer and Andrew Zawacki at the University of Georgia, for your lessons, prompts, reading lists, feedback, and encouragement.

To the Rivendell Writers' Colony (which sadly is no longer a writers' residency) and its steward, Carmen M. Toussaint, for the gift of two weeks to work solely on this book in a place I love (Sewanee, Tennessee).

To my earliest readers, for your generosity and thoughtful feedback and for suffering through an almost five-hundred-page PDF: Irene DaCosta, Henna Messina, and Jamie Pinchot. To Kent Wolf, for starting me on this publishing journey and encouraging character development. To Allison Bechtel and Amy White, for reading all the drafts.

To Dr. Saied Asfa, for letting me into your operating room and answering my questions about plastic surgery. To the Mission of Hope surgery teams from fall 2015 and fall 2018, especially Danny Mace and Timothy Knopp, for teaching me everything I now know about hemostats, Mayos, and Kochers, and how to scrub in for surgery.

I am so grateful to have friends in my life who keep me afloat. To Amy White, Esther Wallach, and Sharyl Evans: for our fierce group and your unwavering encouragement, for believing in this book, in me. To Heather Harmon, Francisca Hu, Henna Messina, Joselyn Penner, Caroline Purvis, and Katie Ryan: for friendly seas that stretch across states and years.

To my family, immediate and extended. Bren, Claire, Libby, and CE: for always rooting for me. Alli—my twin—for a lifetime of support. In a lot of ways, Annalie's story is a tribute to you and how much I love you. To my mom and sister—Dr. Bechtel and Dr. Kastanek—for answering my questions about anesthesia and drugs and operating rooms. Mom and

Dad, for reading my work since elementary school, and probably saving most of it in a box somewhere; for encouraging me to do big things. Riley, Adrian, Sidney, and Lincoln: for filling my heart and crushing souls; for making me laugh and inspiring me to push harder, be better. Shawn, I know you always knew this day would come. I'm so thankful to be on this wild voyage with you, full steam ahead.